STRICTLY FOR NOW

CARRIE ELKS

CHAPTER
ONE

ELI

"Damn it!" Our center forward throws his helmet at the wall. We lost our first game. And yeah, it's only a pre-season match but that doesn't matter.

The atmosphere in the locker room is pretty much at rock bottom right now. The loss wasn't Carter's fault but he's taking it personally. He's a demon in front of the goal but nobody was feeding him the puck.

And I'm pissed because we've been practicing those set moves daily. They should know better.

"Sit down," I say, looking around the room at the youthful faces screwed up in disappointment and anger. I like that they're annoyed. They should be. They played like a bunch of amateurs out there.

And they're not amateurs. They might be in the American Hockey League and not the NHL but they get paid for what they do.

Now and then, that's supposed to include winning.

Everybody ignores my instruction. Which pisses me off even more.

"SIT THE FUCK DOWN!" I don't like shouting but I'll do it when I have to.

And it works. They all slump on the benches in front of their lockers, their expressions' murderous.

"And shut the hell up," I add for good measure, even though none of them are talking anymore. I take a deep breath and pinch my nose, trying to calm myself down.

This isn't their fault. They're still getting to know each other. Some of them have come straight from high school. I can't expect NHL standards, even if that's what I want. What I'm used to.

"Thank you," I say when the last of them is seated. They're all staring at me as though I'm about to deliver a sermon. Give them some insight that will make it all better.

Last season that was me sitting in front of my locker. It feels like a lifetime ago.

My eyes scan the locker room. It's a nice set up, especially for the AHL. The room is lined with mahogany cabinets, each one with a team player's name etched into it and a hook for their uniform below. Above them our team motto is painted along the space between the lockers and the ceiling.

HARD WORK BEATS TALENT.

Every one of these kids wants to make it to the NHL. They didn't get drafted but they still have a chance. We're a development team for the Boston Razors – the team I used to play for until one final knee injury pushed me out of the top leagues for good.

The development team system means that the Boston Razors can draft any of our players into the NHL at any time. And they can also trade down any of their players to Morgantown. We're like a reserve squad, but hundreds of miles away. Somehow it works.

"Okay," I exhale heavily. "Let's get this over with because

I'm pretty sure none of you will listen to what I have to say. But luckily for you I'm going to say it all again tomorrow when you arrive at the rink at six-thirty a.m., fresh and ready to practice."

"But we don't have six-thirty practices the day after a game," Goran Olssen, our center half complains.

"We do tomorrow." I fix my gaze on him. "And every morning after a loss."

"Ah fuck."

"Tonight I want you all to take a bath. And when you're in that bath – alone," I say for the benefit of Max, our goalie who's known for using his large, sunken bath, for group activities, "I want you to think about every wrong move you made tonight. Tomorrow you're going to recite them to me because we're going to replay that match in the morning with all the right moves. Because this was just a practice run, gentlemen. The next time you lose it's going to count. The season starts in two weeks. You need to be ready."

Somebody groans. I don't respond because if they want to make it they need me to be harsh. To be the asshole. To call them out for playing like they don't care about the result.

Nice doesn't win games. That doesn't mean I'm not kind. When everybody else leaves I'll be here another two hours watching each move myself, then working out how I can improve every member of the team's game.

But for now they need nasty. They need to feel the pain. They need to want to win like they want to breathe.

I talk for another two minutes. I call them out by name, the way I was called out as a rookie all those years ago. My job is to pull them apart then put them together again and that's what I'll do.

And maybe one day they'll thank me for it.

Once they've all left, I let the janitorial staff know that the room is ready to clean. There are no jerseys on the floor or skates hanging around because the team knows I demand a tidy locker room. It's not the cleaning staff's job to pick up after them. Then I close the door and let out a long, frustrated breath because I'm just as pissed as the rest of them about the loss.

"Oh, ah, Eli?"

I look up to see Brian standing in the hallway, a clipboard clutched to his chest. He's the stand in office manager after the old one got fired. Since his temporary promotion he's been found frozen in the hallways like a deer staring at head-lamps more than once.

"Hey, Brian."

"Can I have a word?" he asks, his eyes shifting but not reaching mine. He's in his twenties, but he dresses like he's in his fifties. Or in the nineteen-fifties. I like his shirt and sleeve-less sweater combination, but some of the team used to rip into him about it.

They don't since I ripped them a new one. We don't treat the backroom staff badly. If they weren't here to make every-thing run smoothly, we wouldn't be able to play hockey.

"Sure," I say. "Here or in your office?"

"Here is fine." He looks down at his clipboard as though he's trying to remember what he wants to talk about. "I got a message from Greg."

"Gauthier?" I ask.

"Yep. Wayne's son."

Wayne owns the Mavericks. He's one of the main reasons I came here once I busted my knee for good. When he heard I was out of action, he flew to Boston to talk with the Razors owner before offering me the coaching job.

I thought about it for a long time before saying yes. It took me a while to get my head around the fact that I'd never play in the NHL again. My doctor cleared me to play up to one period per game in the AHL, but my principal job is to coach these rookies into some kind of order.

To make them good enough for the big time.

Wayne's been injured for the past few weeks. His hip has finally given out and he needs a replacement. He's also fired most of the staff, which leaves poor Brian in charge until there's a replacement hired.

"What did Greg want?" I ask him.

"He wanted to let me know about the management consultant they've engaged."

"A consultant?" Why do I need to know this? I manage the players, I don't run the business. "When are they coming?"

Brian looks at his clipboard again and frowns. "Um, I don't know. They're called Mackenzie or Power or something. Anyway, when I hear more, I'll let you know."

"You do that." And it'll change precisely nothing. I'm just here to make sure the team wins and that's it. "Did Greg say how Wayne is doing?"

"His surgery is next week. Hopefully things will get better after that. For all of us."

"That's good." I nod. I have a lot of respect for Wayne Gauthier. And now we have something else in common. I had surgery a few months ago for my career ending knee injury and was just as annoyed as he was, but for different reasons.

"Was there anything else you needed?" I ask Brian, because he's still looking at me as though I'm supposed to do something.

Do a dance. Win a game. I'm not sure what.

"Ah, I just…" He frowns. "What will they do?" he asks.

"The consultants?"

"Yeah. I Googled it and I still have no idea."

I start to laugh, because I need to tell this to Myles and Liam. My older brothers run a consultancy and investment business out of Charleston, about an hour down the road.

"I think they boss everybody about, change everything, then waltz off into the night while we pick up the pieces," I tell him. "But don't quote me on that." I shrug. "I'm just going to keep doing what I'm doing and so should you."

"Okay." Brian presses his lips together. "I think I might have some shredding to do."

"Shredding?" I ask.

"And I need to tidy Wayne's office. It's a mess. We don't want them to find something…"

I put my hand on his shoulder. "It'll be fine. Try not to worry. Greg's probably worried about that bill Wayne hasn't paid." I can't help but feel sorry for Brian. Since most of the management got fired, he's been trying to run the place with a skeleton staff. But this really isn't my problem. Not unless they interfere with the team.

And Wayne wouldn't let that happen.

"Go home, Brian," I tell him, because like me he's been here all day getting ready for the first game. "Nothing bad is going to happen."

Finally, he smiles. "You're right. Thank you. I'll do that."

———

The mood on the rink the next morning is intense. Everybody's pissy because I made them arrive at the center at six-thirty sharp and not one of them is a morning person.

Two of the players are in the rehab room getting therapy for injuries they got from the game last night. But as for the rest, I put them through the usual drills, letting them warm up their muscles and joints by skating around the rink, followed by long rushes – skating from end to end as fast as possible, before I break them into three groups and have them doing short rushes.

They get competitive, trying to beat each other with each rush, and I start to relax. When I sense they're getting bored, I tell them to grab their sticks and we go through some set plays.

"What was that?" Carter asks.

"What?" I say, slamming my stick into the puck to show the impact I want them to use.

"That scream."

I blink. "Nobody's screaming."

"Yes, they are." We both go silent. And then I hear it. The scream is so high pitched it makes me wince. I frown because all but two of us are out here on the ice, so it has to be Goran or Max coming back from rehabilitation.

Please God, don't let the therapist have made their injuries worse. I can't afford to have either of them out for months.

"Keep playing," I tell the team. "I'll see what's going on."

I take less than thirty seconds to make it through the tunnel and into the locker room. The first thing I see is Max, naked as the day he was born, one hand holding his shorts, the other shielding his genitals.

His eyes are wide and staring at the locker room door. I follow their direction and get a ringside view of Goran's bare ass, his legs straddled as he stands over...

Is that a woman?

She's on the floor, flat on her back, her legs splayed out as she stares up at Goran. He's saying something to her that I can't hear, but then she groans and touches her cheek.

"What the hell is happening?" I ask Max, who's trying to put his shorts on while still covering himself. He has to hop on one leg to do it.

"She walked through the door and then stopped dead when she saw us," he tells me, finally decent. "The door swung back on her and hit her in the face. She kind of fell. It's not our fault."

"Who is she?" Everybody knows not to come into the locker room without knocking. "Somebody's girlfriend?"

The woman groans and sits up, her hand still cupping her cheek. I get a closer look at her. Her dark hair falls over her shoulders. Her silk blouse is unbuttoned far enough for me to see the swell of her breasts.

Not that I'm looking.

She's also wearing a skirt and the kind of shoes that everybody knows not to wear near an ice rink. The kind that make your legs look good but are bound to cause some kind of accident.

And yeah, her legs do look good. I drag my eyes away and grunt, because this isn't what I need right now.

Somebody sneaked their girlfriend in and they're gonna get it from me.

"What? Oh!" She blinks when she sees Goran's genitalia right in front of her face.

"Are you okay?" he asks her. "Can I get you something?"

"Get a fucking towel, Goran," I growl at him. Because seriously? Her eyes are wide as she stares at his balls perilously close to her face.

He shrugs and gestures at Max who grabs a fresh one from the pile and throws it over. Goran catches it easily, but the movement makes him... ah... swing in this woman's direction.

She lets out another scream.

I put my hand on my face and groan internally. "Goran, move. Go take a shower or something."

"I just did."

"Then get dressed." I widen my eyes at him. He takes the hint and moves away.

I walk over to the woman who's trying to stand up and gently put my hand on her shoulder. "Is anything broken?" I ask.

She shakes her head.

"Did you bang your head when you fell?" I ask. I've lost count of how many times I've had a concussion, but it's no laughing matter.

"No. Just my cheek." Her voice is soft. "I'm sorry. I

thought this room would be empty." She runs her tongue along her bottom lip. "I was just looking around."

"Okay, whose are you?" I ask her.

She blinks. She has really long eyelashes. "Whose?" she repeats.

"Whose girlfriend?" Or one night stand. We've seen them all. I've chased more than my fair share of women out of the locker room.

"Nobody's." She frowns. "I'm single."

Well okay then. I look at her face again. She looks familiar but I can't place it. "An ex?" I ask because that's even more trouble than a current partner.

She pulls her hand away from her cheek. It's bright red. I'm pretty sure there'll be a sweet bruise there by morning. If she's an ex that could be an issue, because the local press will take that kind of shit and run with it.

And here's the thing about AHL teams. We don't have a PR rep like the NHL teams do. Wayne is it. He deals with the press. They love him.

But he's not here.

She finally stands. I reach out to steady her arm, but she pulls it away from me. Whatever. I'm not going to fight her.

"Is she a stalker?" Max calls out. "We should check her phone."

"I'm not a stalker," she mutters. "And I'm not giving you my phone." Her eyes catch mine. They're hazel with green flecks and for a moment I'm kind of taken with them.

Until she talks again.

"I'm a management consultant," she says, her unusually pretty eyes not quite focused. "And I'm here to turn this team around."

CHAPTER
TWO

MACKENZIE

One week earlier...

My phone won't stop vibrating. It's getting stupid now, buzzing every few seconds. There are ten missed calls – thanks, Mom and Dad – plus a hundred messages on the family group chat. I slide it under my behind on the chair to stop the alerts from filling the air because my boss is giving a speech and the last thing I need is to bring attention to myself.

Or the wrong kind of attention, anyway.

"Three years of hard work," Mark says, a grin splitting his lips. And so it should. My boss' closing bonus for actually finishing this project and handing over a profitable business to our corporate clients will probably pay for a private jet or two. "Three years of sacrificing family life, of missing school plays and parent evenings, of telling our friends that, no, we can't attend their wedding to the love of their lives. And here we are, older and wiser, and we can say one thing to ourselves." He takes a pause, lifts his glass to his lips and looks out at us.

We hang on his words. Possibly because we have no idea what to do next. Sure, we'll be assigned to other projects. Some of us will get promotions, others might take a break, actually go to those school shows.

As for me, I just want to sleep for the next hundred years.

Just as Mark opens his mouth to tell us exactly what we're all desperate to hear, the door to the boardroom swings open. Every head turns to see Alice, Mark's personal assistant holding a phone in her hand.

Mark frowns because he hates being interrupted mid flow. His speeches are legendary, and this speech is three years in the making. I wouldn't want to be in Alice's place right now.

"What?" he asks her. He doesn't bark because Mark just isn't that kind of boss. But the twitch in his eyebrow tells us he's not impressed.

"I'm so sorry," Alice says, her eyes wide and flustered. "There's an emergency phone call."

"For me?" His brows dip this time. Mark's a man who communicates with his eyebrows. You could probably draw a chart for every emotion.

"Oh no, Mr. Simons. Not for you."

A chill shoots down my spine. *They wouldn't.*

But they would. I know they would.

When my family wants to talk, they make sure it happens right then. It's not entitlement, exactly. More like a learned behavior.

And now I'm sitting here on my phone – which has stopped buzzing for obvious reasons – waiting for the inevitable.

"Who is it for, then?" Mark asks her. His right eyebrow is twitching like he can't stop it if he tried.

That's the angry sign.

Alice's eyes scan the twenty of us sitting in the boardroom. Her gaze feels like a searchlight seeking its prey. When it locks on me I take a ragged breath in, accepting the inevitable. I slide down onto my chair, wishing I could disappear.

"Mackenzie Hunter," she says.

I stifle the groan that's been brewing in my throat ever since my cellphone started buzzing.

"Well go on then," Mark says, turning to me. "Take the call before I forget what I'm supposed to say next."

I stand, which is easier said than done in these heels. I rarely wear three inches, but we're heading straight out to a club after this to celebrate and the dress code is *impress or die trying.*

Well it's not, but close enough. We're going to the Colosseum, the achingly hip club that nobody in New York can get into right now. Apart from us, that is. But now I'm regretting my choice of high heels and super tight skirt because I can only shuffle sideways between the row of chairs, muttering apologies to everybody who gets an eyeline view of my ass as I move.

"I'm so sorry," I breathe as I finally reach Alice.

She gives me a sympathetic smile. "It's your mom," she mouths.

Of course it is. I turn to Mark to tell him I'll be right back, but I think his eyebrows are about to fly off his face and stab me. He makes a shooing movement with his hands and I totter my way out of the room.

When the door closes, I let out a low sigh.

"Here you go, dear," Alice says, passing me the phone. "Just hit number one."

"Thank you."

Luckily, there's an empty room next door, so I slide myself in there, bracing myself for the whirlwind that's my mom. My heart is already pounding before I press the button on the phone.

I take a deep breath and give into the inevitable.

"Mom?"

"I've been trying to get a hold of you." She has a soft voice but it still feels like knives stabbing at my head. Or maybe that's just the oncoming migraine I know I'm going to get because phone calls like this never turn out well.

Like the time I got the call to fly to Montreal to bail my brothers out of jail.

Or the time I had to drive to Boston to pick my sister up from her ex's apartment which she'd redecorated – and I use that term loosely – with a can of vermillion paint.

We don't really talk anymore, but that has nothing to do with her impressive knowledge of dirty words.

"I'm in a meeting," I tell her. "Can I call you back?"

"We need to talk about Gramps."

I sit down heavily in a beautifully molded leather chair. Nothing less than the best for employees of Warner Power, voted the best New York Management Consultancy firm three times in the last four years.

"What's up with Gramps? Is he ill?" I ask. I'm not close to him, but I have a heart. And he's in his late eighties.

He's also scary as hell. And shouts louder than anybody I've ever met.

Somebody says something in the background. My mom replies with her sweet voice. "Honey, I have to go to rehearsals now. We'll talk later."

"What?"

"Tonight?" she suggests, ignoring the outraged tone in my voice. Did she really call me out of one of the most important meetings in my life for *this*?

"I'm busy tonight." *Much like I was busy right now.*

"Let's say ten o'clock then," she says. "Bye, darling. Love you."

Before I can open my mouth to tell her I won't be around at ten, there's a dial tone filling my ear. I grit my teeth and put the phone on the table in front of me, before dropping my head into my hands.

And then I let out a long, pained, and very silent scream.

Because that's the effect my family has on me.

————

Somebody has ordered another three bottles of champagne. It's flowing like water and everybody is happy and laughing. I can't remember the last time the whole team socialized together. Our Christmas party was canceled when we came up against a software issue on the twenty-first of December last year. We spent Christmas Day mainlining coffee in the office.

And yeah, maybe I was kind of glad that I had to work because otherwise I wouldn't have had an excuse not to fly to L.A. to spend time with my family. But I did, and that was that.

"So, did Mark catch you after the meeting?" Rachel asks me.

I shake my head at my favorite co-worker. Once the urge to throw myself into a fire had gone, I'd snuck back into the boardroom, but by then Mark had finished his speech and everybody was getting ready to leave.

"I'll apologize tomorrow," I tell her. He's here tonight but he's in the corner booth with our clients and there's no way I want to interrupt them.

"Okay, ladies, I have the perfect thing for you." Allison, our intern, slides into the booth next to us, a glass of champagne in one hand, her phone in the other. She's been working for us for the last two years since she graduated from business school. She also makes me and Rachel feel really old.

"There are ladies around here?" Rachel jokes, looking around.

I snigger.

"I'm serious. My boyfriend's working on this app and I think it'll solve all your problems."

Allison's boyfriend is some kind of digital wunderkind. He's also permanently broke and mooches off Allison, but whatever.

"Does it give you multiple orgasms and then empty the dishwasher?" I ask.

Allison blinks. "No." And I immediately feel bad. She looks so earnest and I don't want to rain on her parade.

Rachel doesn't look like she feels bad at all. "Okay, so will it go for my pap smear for me, and then give me a full body massage while telling me I'm beautiful?" she asks, trying not to grin.

"It's not that kind of app." Allison says patiently. "But honestly, you're going to love it. It's made for older women like you."

Ouch.

Rachel's eyes meet mine. She's been as unlucky in relationships as I have, but for entirely different reasons. She believes in happy ever afters and no man can meet up to her daydreams of Prince Charming sweeping her off her feet.

Whereas, I... just don't believe in that at all.

"Older women like us," Rachel repeats.

Allison doesn't notice the warning in her voice. She just nods like an excited puppy. "For women over forty who haven't found love yet."

"We're not over forty," Rachel points out.

"I know, but you almost are."

I wince again. We're not even close. Or at least, it doesn't feel like it. And any reminder that I'm over halfway through my thirties is distinctly unwelcome.

"By your age a lot of women will take any guy that has his teeth left, right?" Allison smiles, revealing her own too-white set of teeth. I'm slightly concerned that Rachel might smash them out.

She doesn't like being called old. She wore black for a year when she turned thirty.

"Tell us all about it," I say, shooting Rachel a warning glance. I'm pretty sure smashing an intern's pretty smile is a disciplinary offence.

"So, when you reach a certain age, your requirements change," Allison says, her eyes darting from Rachel to me. "You're going to have to spread your net wider. Maybe settle for less than you would have when you were in your prime."

I'm pretty sure Rachel let out a growl.

"So, this app does it for you." Allison continues. "It pre-vets the guys to make sure they understand the ladies they'll be matching with are of a certain age. But also of a certain quality."

"Sure." I nod, absolutely not interested. "That sounds great."

"Fabulous." Allison claps her hands together. "So I can put you on the Golden Mates beta team?"

Rachel turns to look at her, and Allison visibly cringes. "I only go for alphas," she tells her. "So no."

"The alpha testing phase has already finished," Allison whispers. And now I'm feeling sorry for her, because she's worked really hard this year. She's a whizz on spreadsheets and works as late as we need her to. So I nudge Rachel in the chest and she grimaces in response.

"I'll do it," I tell Allison, because I feel bad about teasing her. "Just send me the link."

"Thank you. Ryan's going to be so pleased. He doesn't know many women in the older demographic so it's this or he has to grab random people on the street."

I swallow down a laugh.

"I'm going to call him now," she says, happily, standing and grabbing her glass. "You won't regret this, Mackenzie."

I'm almost certain I will. But at least I've done one good deed today. That should help me feel better when I say no to my family later tonight.

And yes, I don't know what they're going to ask. But this isn't my first rodeo. You have to be firm with my family. They always play to win.

CHAPTER
THREE

.

MACKENZIE

My apartment is small but perfectly formed and I feel lucky every time I walk inside. Finding somewhere to live in New York that's not a rat-infested closet and is actually affordable is harder than finding a date after the age of thirty.

Maybe Allison's boyfriend should develop an app for *that*.

My phone is ringing before I can even take off my stupidly high shoes. I kick them into the air and drop onto my gorgeous sofa that cost me more than three months' wages but is so worth it. It's cream and velvet, and sitting on it feels like a warm hug after a long day. Then I swipe across my phone to accept the video call and try to push my annoyance down because it's not my mom's fault that I have such a strong reaction to her.

Okay, maybe it's a little bit her fault. But a lot of it is just down to circumstances.

My screen flickers into life and four boxes appear and it's then I realize it's a family group chat. In the top corner are my parents. They're still both wearing make up which means they've only just stopped filming for the night. My dad looks like he's wearing a kaftan. My mom is still wearing her skating outfit.

And of course she looks fabulous the way she always does, even though she's almost sixty.

Nobody at work knows my parents are Nancy and Greg Gauthier. If I said those names I'd be treated differently. My mom was America's skating sweetheart in the 1980s, winning the Ladies' Figure Skating gold at the Olympics twice in a row. And then she fell for my dad, the captain of the US hockey team, and the rest was history.

The country swooned when she gave up competing to follow my dad around, getting married and pregnant with my sister, Isabella, within a year. I came next, followed five years later by Brad and Johnny – my twin brothers.

Or as hockey fans know them, *the Danger Twins*.

"It was a bad hook," my dad is saying as I join the call. "But you gotta avoid those confrontations."

"He was asking for it," Brad says, looking angry.

"Doesn't mean you have to give it to him," Dad says.

"Anyway," my mom cuts in, smiling widely. "How is the training going, Isabella?"

"You know I can't tell you that." My sister rolls her eyes.

Like my mom and dad, Isabella appears on *Ice Stars*, the latest reality show to rock the nation. But unlike my parents – who are judges – Issy is an ice dance partner to one of the celebrities who takes part. This year she's skating with Justin Royle, an ex-boyband star from the early 2000s. I haven't caught the show at all, but from what I hear he's got two left feet and spends more time on his butt than his skates.

And I know exactly how that must feel.

Growing up in a third-generation skating family isn't the best if you freeze – literally and metaphorically – as soon as you're near ice.

They're still talking among themselves, and I'm seriously

considering quietly leaving the video call when I hear my name being said.

"Sorry?" I blink. I don't even know which one of them said it. I'm so tired.

"Did you watch the game last night? What did you think?" my dad asks.

"The hockey game?"

My dad looks exasperated. "Yes. Was it a foul?"

I look from him to Brad, whose jaw is tight. He's always been the more vocal of the twins.

"I had to work last night," I say. "Sorry."

"Well it was a foul," Dad says to Brad. "End of."

"Is that all you wanted to talk about?" I ask hopefully. "Because I need to go to bed."

"Oh no, honey." My mom shakes her head. "I told you it was about Gramps."

I know she did, but I was really hoping whatever it was that Wayne Gauthier – my dad's dad – had done, wasn't going to affect my night.

"He needs surgery," my mom says.

"Okay." I nod. "That's a shame. I'll send him some flowers."

Mom and Dad exchange a glance. "And he's got a little trouble at work."

Gramps is eighty-eight-years-old and is still working. He bought a hockey team in West Virginia twenty years ago, when everybody else his age was starting to enjoy retirement and taking cruises.

But hockey has always been Gramps' life. The same way it's everything to my dad and my brothers.

After years of being the most famous hockey player in Northern America he can't bear to let go.

"What kind of trouble?" I ask.

"The IRS kind."

I let out a low breath. "What does his accountant say?"

My dad shrugs. "He fired him. Says it's his fault."

"His office manager then?"

Mom wrinkles her nose. "He fired her, too."

"And he's about to have surgery? How long will he be out for?"

"At least three months. He'll need to go into a nursing facility to recover."

"Oh, that sucks. I'm sorry," I say. "What's he going to do about the IRS?"

There's a little shift in everybody's posture on screen. Like they've suddenly relaxed. It takes me a minute to figure out why.

Because I'm asking questions. They think I want to help.

Oh hell no. "Listen, I think there's somebody at my door. I need to go…"

"You'll help him, right?" Isabella asks. "It's Gramps."

I blink because Isabella and I so rarely interact. It takes me a moment to realize she's talking to me.

"Of course she will," Brad agrees. "She knows we can't do it."

"We can't," Isabella says. "Not with our filming schedule and your game schedule."

"And let's face it, even if we were available we'd be terrible at it." That's Johnny. Okay, so he's not my favorite anymore. "None of us know how to run a business."

"But Mackenzie does," Brad says.

I swallow hard. "I also have a job," I say. One I'm hoping to get a promotion in as early as next week if all goes well.

"You could take leave," Isabella says hopefully.

"I don't have three months leave."

"Pretend you're having a baby. Or women trouble," Brad says.

I roll my eyes at him.

"Honey, please." My mom looks at me in that way only moms can. And yes, I'm thirty-six-years-old and a successful consultant in a dog-eat-dog industry, but it still works.

And I feel guilty.

"I can't," I tell her. "I'm sorry."

Five sets of eyes are trained on me, looking at me as though I just killed their favorite puppy.

"I'm sorry," I say again. But I'm not giving in this time.

My dad breathes in sharply. "Okay," he says. "We'll regroup on this."

It's only when we end the call that I think about the expression that was on his face.

He looked exactly the same way he did when the US hockey team was down three-two against the USSR in the Olympic finals.

And then came back to win four-three and take the gold medal.

———

Every time I walk into Warner Power's beautifully maintained lobby I feel like I should pinch myself. My shoes – not three inchers this time – make a beautiful clacking sound on the marble floors as I head for the bank of elevators, past the twenty-foot long reception desk manned with five assistants who all wave at me, and the thirty foot palm trees – real by the way – which are planted in huge terracotta pots a New Yorker could comfortably live in.

I hear my name being called out and I turn to see Rachel running toward me, her dark hair streaming out behind her.

"Wait up," she says, leaning on me to catch her breath. Rachel and I met on our orientation day back when we first joined Warner Power as fresh faced graduates. We shared an apartment for a while, before she moved into an apartment with her first – but not last – asshole boyfriend. Not that I can tease her about them because I've had a few of them myself.

She's the only employee at Warner Power who knows about my family. Mostly because Brad and Johnny knocked at my door drunkenly at three a.m. one night, and I had to explain why two six feet underage lookalikes were stumbling around our living room.

I was twenty-four then, and they were in their freshman year at college. Both with scholarships, and were celebrating a win against Cornell. When I'd finally persuaded them to sleep in my bed, I'd sat down with Rachel and admitted that I'd changed my name from Gauthier to Hunter.

And yeah, she knew the name. Everybody does. But she didn't change her attitude toward me one bit the way people usually do.

Years later she admitted she Googled my old name. And found out about the incident that shall never be spoken about. And true to her word, she hasn't mentioned it since.

Did I tell you that I love her?

"So how did the call with your mom go?" she asks when she finally catches her breath. She's still leaning on me as I press the button to call the elevator.

"My whole family was there," I tell her and she grimaces. "They want me to drop everything and go help my gramps in West Virginia."

Rachel frowns. "Seriously?"

"Yep. He's having surgery and the IRS is breathing down his neck. So they want me to make everything better."

The elevator pings and we walk inside. "You said no, right?" There's disbelief in her voice. I'd like to think it's because she can't believe they even asked but deep inside I know she doesn't believe I'd turn down my family.

"Yes I did." There. Take that. I feel powerful.

Her frown melts away. "Seriously?"

She knows I struggle with not being able to say no to my family. One of the reasons I avoid talking to them whenever possible. "I'm absolutely serious," I tell her. "It was hard but I did it."

She throws her arms around me. "I'm so proud of you."

I wrinkle my nose but hug her back anyway. "Shaddup."

We stop at the second floor and two guys walk in, blinking when they see we're in the middle of an embrace.

Rachel lets me go. "Just making sure she's warm enough," she tells them, then pats my arm. "Yep, perfect body temperature."

They give her a weird look then start a conversation between themselves about Bitcoin.

"Sorry," she mouths at me.

"It's okay. You give good hugs."

She grins because she knows I'm right.

When we walk out onto the first of Warner Power's three floors we're faced with Carmine, our receptionist and security guard. He tips his head at us and then holds up his hand.

"Miss Hunter?"

"It's Mackenzie," I tell him for what must be the hundredth time.

He nods. "Mr. Power left a message. He'd like to see you at nine."

"Oh. Of course."

Rachel lets out a low whistle as I glance at my watch. It's a quarter to nine right now. We usually get in at seven-thirty, but they gave us a late start after last night's party.

"It's gotta be your promotion," Rachel says as we walk down the hallway to our offices. "The only reason Power sees people is for firing and promotions."

"Who says he isn't going to fire me?" He could have heard about yesterday's debacle with the phone call. Maybe Mark even went to complain to him about me getting called out of the room during the biggest speech of his life.

"Of course he isn't. You've been the biggest biller of the

team for the last three years. You're his cash cow. It's a promotion for sure."

"I hope you're right." I sling my purse onto my desk and shrug off my jacket. It's not that I think I'm going to get fired. I just don't like things out of the ordinary. Especially things that involve my boss' boss. Kenneth Power doesn't get involved in everyday things. He doesn't spend much time with the staff that works for his company. As the outward facing owner, he schmoozes CEOs to win more clients. He's been known to fly in spaceships with eccentric billionaires – yes, he was on *that* flight.

What he doesn't do is make small talk with employees who aren't even partners.

Even though every cell in my body is crying out for a caffeine hit, I don't have time to grab a coffee. I head to the bathroom instead and grimace at my reflection, wishing I'd taken the time to do more than put a dab of concealer on the shadows beneath my eyes and slick on some lipstick.

Which thankfully hasn't transferred to my teeth.

Small mercies, right?

Mr. Power's office is at the far end of the building. It's in the corner, which gives him two views of the city, both equally stunning. As soon as I arrive at the outer office where his three assistants sit, I'm ushered inside, and am absolutely relieved to see that he's smiling at me.

People don't smile before they fire you, do they?

Well maybe sadists do, but I don't think he's one of those. Oh god, now I'm imagining him in a leather suit holding a whip and I think I'm going to be sick.

"Take a seat, Mackenzie." He nods at the leather chair on the other side of his desk. As soon as my behind hits the butter soft upholstery, it gives in an expensive way.

It's not too hard, not too soft. Now I know why Goldilocks put up with the three bears.

"I expect you're wondering why you're here," he says,

steepling his fingers. He has these milky blue eyes that seem to bore right through you.

I don't know how to answer this question. If I say yes, he's going to know I'm anxious. If I say no, I'm going to look like I don't care about my job.

"Well I—"

"You've been holding out on us," he says, a smile still playing around his lips.

I shift on the chair. "I have?" Rachel wasn't lying when she said I was the top biller of the entire team. What more does he want me to do, chop my fingers off and offer them as sacrifice?

"Yes you have, Miss... Gauthier."

Oh. OH! How does he know my old last name?

His eyes haven't left my face.

"I can explain..." I stutter.

"No need. Your father told me all about it last night," he continues, tapping the tips of his fingers together at the top of his spired hands. "I have to say it's admirable that you don't want to succeed because of your family name. So many people today expect to get a leg up on the corporate ladder just because their parents are rich or famous." He smiles benevolently. "Of course you could have confided in me. I would have kept your secret. I've been a big fan of your grandfather and your father for years."

Of course he has.

"My father called you?" I say, my voice thin.

"It was funny, actually. We were just getting ready for bed. He was lucky we weren't already asleep. My wife likes us to retire early."

My mind does a quick calculation. Our family call ended at ten-thirty last night, and I'm almost certain my dad didn't have Kenneth Power's direct phone number in his little black book or Rolodex or whatever the heck he stores numbers in.

Which means he probably phoned my boss' boss after eleven last night.

Oh the mortification of it.

"I'm so sorry he called you so late," I say. I can't wait to tell Rachel about this. The anticipation of her appalled expression is the only thing that's keeping me going right now. I'm thirty-six years old, why is my dad calling my boss?

Except deep inside I know. And that makes me even more embarrassed.

"Oh don't be sorry. It's not every evening that you get a phone call from the amazing Greg Gauthier." Mr. Power is beaming. It's scary. "He promised to send me a signed photograph from your grandfather, too." His voice lowers. "By the way, I'm so very sorry to hear about your grandfather's health. I grew up watching him play. Every boy in my school wanted to be Wayne Gauthier when we were playing hockey."

I'm smiling but it hurts.

"Anyway, enough fan boying." His cheeks are bright red. "Your father told me about your predicament."

"My what?" I ask, my voice strangled.

He doesn't seem to notice. "He explained all about your family problems. That your grandfather desperately needs you."

I open my mouth to reply but no words come out.

"And that you said you couldn't because you were worried about your job."

A sense of doom is pushing down on me. Of course my dad called my boss. Nobody says no to Greg Gauthier.

Or rather he just chooses not to hear when they do.

"So we came to an arrangement that I think will make you happy." Mr. Power smiles.

That's when the fight goes out of me. They've made a deal. Dad's probably offered him an executive box at his favorite team, or something like that. He's the best at giving out favors when he needs something from somebody.

When I graduated college he kept wanting to find me a job with one of his 'friends'. And no, that's not a backhanded way of saying he's pimping me out. He genuinely loves being the one that connects people. Add that to the fact that he's a man who always gets what he wants and my fate is sealed.

"You'll still be a Warner Power employee, of course," Mr. Power is saying. I can barely hear him over the rushing of blood through my ears. "And when you've finished the project, we'll definitely be looking at a promotion. It's great publicity for the company. We're lending one of our top consultants to help save Wayne Gauthier's team. Pro bono. I'll talk to the PR department to see what we can do to leverage this."

"Oh God. Please, no publicity," I say.

His smile finally wavers. "What?"

"I don't want people knowing who I am," I tell him. This is my hard limit. "I worked hard to get to where I am today. I don't want anybody knowing that I'm part of the Gauthier family."

He looks like a wounded puppy. "But it would be so good for the firm." He runs his fingers along his jaw then looks up at me. "How about we don't tell them who you are but still get the publicity? We're still lending our best consultant to a team in need. I'm sure the PR team can make that work."

But that's not how publicity works. I know that all too well. Journalists don't stop sniffing around, not when they sense a story.

And I don't want to be anybody's cheap enjoyment over a coffee. Not again.

"I don't think that would be possible."

"We'll see," he says, and I know that this is already a done deal. I'm going to West Virginia whether I like it or not.

And I don't. I hate it. I'm furious at my father, and at my

mom for not stopping him. Hell, I'm also angry with Isabella, Brad, and Johnny because they have jobs that mean they can't easily be moved to help Gramps.

I'm the odd one out. The anomaly. And this is really, really bad.

Note to self. Get horribly drunk tonight. Because next week everything changes.

CHAPTER
FOUR

MACKENZIE

My cheek throbs as I stare into the eyes of the only fully dressed man in the locker room. And yes, I'm going to have to work very, *very* hard to block out the memories of those naked balls swinging dangerously close to my face.

This was *not* how I was planning to introduce myself to the team.

I'd read the roster as soon as I came in. Pre-season practice is supposed to start at ten. It's seven-thirty. Nobody should be here to witness my self-guided tour of the arena.

And nobody should be here to swing their undercarriages in my face.

"It's funny," Mr. Fully-Dressed says, running his thumb along his darkly bearded jaw. "Because turning the team around is my job."

"And who are you?" I ask him, ignoring the pain in my cheek. My eyes hurt, too, especially when I try to narrow them.

The naked player sniggers. I'd forgotten just how sculpted

hockey players were. I look at the man in front of me, wondering if beneath his sweats and black t-shirt he has the same kind of physique.

And then I look away because hello! Who cares? Not me.

Not one bit. Nope, not even when I can see every ridge of his chest through the fabric of his t-shirt.

"Eli Salinger," Fully-dressed says. "Head coach."

"Great." I force a smile. "I'd like to talk to you later. Say four o'clock in my office?"

"Where is your office, exactly?" he murmurs.

"In the administration block." Or at least I think that's where it is. I only dropped my things off before I came down here to explore the arena. "If you come up at four I'll be there to meet you."

"I'm not available at four."

So it's going to be like this. I expected resistance. It happens with every project. But usually I'm more resilient. Kinder, maybe.

This time I'm feeling annoyed. And it's not this guy's fault. He didn't ask for me to come here the same way I don't want to be here. But we're going to have to work together, anyway.

"Three?" I suggest.

"Six," he counters, like we're bidding in an auction. "I'll be back at the rink by then."

I'm going to be dead on my feet by six. But I don't want to finish my first day without speaking to everybody on the staff. And if he's doing a power play here, I'm going to win.

"That's fine." I nod.

"Okay then. And can I ask a favor of you?" he says, his voice laid back and easy now that he's taken control. He has that same casual confidence my brothers have. Maybe all hockey players have it. Wherever it comes from, it makes me bristle.

"Go ahead."

"Don't come into the locker room without knocking. No matter what time it is. It's bad for the team."

I swallow hard because he's got me there. "I won't."

He winks and I feel the effects somewhere near the base of my stomach.

Okay, lower down than that.

Deciding now might be a good time to leave, I give him a nod then force my eyes over to the two team members I've kind of bonded with in the most ghoulish way. They wave at me as I leave. Or at least attempt to leave. The stupid door won't move at all now.

I think it hates me.

I go to tug at it again but then I feel the warmth of a body behind me. Eli reaches around my waist, his arm brushing mine and I feel the steel of his bicep as he curls his fingers around mine on the handle.

"It's a little temperamental," he says softly, his breath warm against my ear. Then he pulls and it opens with ease. He's steps to the side, and I have to remind myself to move.

"Thank you," I tell him.

"No problem." There's a smile in his voice. I don't look back as I walk through. I'm halfway up the corridor when I hear sudden laughter followed by a sharp reprimand.

When I get to my new office, which is actually Gramps' office and is absolutely covered with papers, trophies, and even some takeout cartons that give me no clue as to how long they've been here, I slump in his comfortable leather chair and let my head fall into my hands.

I can't believe I walked in on two naked players. I have to work with these people. I have to make them believe in me, in the changes I want to make. I have to look them in the eye without remembering how their dicks wobble when they're leaning over me.

I give myself one minute to internally scream, then I take a deep breath and stand up again, determined to get this room tidy so that I can actually think about how we can find the money to pay the IRS.

Because the sooner I do that, the sooner I'll be back in New York, working in shiny lovely offices and not a hellhole like this.

And right now that's the only thing that's keeping me going.

―――――

ELI

"She's kind of hot, that management woman," Goran says as we walk across the blacktop to my car. We've just spent two hours teaching kids with disabilities how to play para hockey. The school contacted us through the foundation Wayne set up when he first created the Mavericks, and we've been coming every week for the last month.

It's been pretty cool watching the students go from barely being able to move their sleds to actually racing around the school gym on them, hitting balls into the goals. We're trying to coordinate a time to change the wheels into blades so they can come to the arena to play on the ice instead of in the gym.

I click my key fob to unlock my car. "I guess she is."

"For an old chick," he adds and I lift a brow at him. I don't know how old Mackenzie is but she looked younger than me.

"Don't call women chicks."

"Okay, for an old woman."

"Also, don't call them old." I climb into the driver's seat.

"Why not?"

"Because it's not nice." Goran's picked this up from the rest of the team. Sometimes it feels like I'm raising these kids as well as trying to shape them into a team. The reality is they've lived, breathed, and slept hockey ever since they were kids. A lot of them haven't had the time to mature into fully grown adults.

"How long do you think she's here for?" Goran asks as I pull out of the parking lot and onto the highway.

"No idea."

"She said she was single though, right?"

I blink. "Don't even think about it," I warn him.

From the corner of my eye I see him pouting. He has these full lips that make it look particularly effective. "Rule one of being a hockey player. Don't shit on your own doorstep."

"I haven't heard that one before." He grimaces. His English is exceptional for being his second language, but he occasionally gets blindsided by idioms.

"It means that you keep work separate from your personal life. You're twenty years old. Go out to clubs, get on Tinder, whatever. Just don't get involved with people you work with. It always ends poorly." I lift a brow. "Believe me."

"You sound like you've had some experience with that," Goran says perceptively.

"Yeah, well I've been around."

I take a left toward the sprawling apartment building where most of the team lives. Goran shares a three bed apartment with Carter and Max. I've been in there once. It's a pigsty. It reminds me of growing up with my brothers.

And makes me glad I don't have to share my place with anybody anymore. I like my own space. I like my house not smelling of sweat and three-day-old takeout.

I pull up outside the door and Goran grabs the handle.

"Thanks for coming today," I tell him.

"Thanks for asking me. It was fun. We'll do it again next week, yes?"

"Yep." After that, it's going to take a little more scheduling because the hockey season can be blocked full and unpredictable. But we'll make it work. "Try to get some rest," I tell him as he climbs out of the car. "See you tomorrow at ten."

"I got rehab," he tells me. "I'll be in at nine."

"Sure thing." He closes the door and I start the engine up, heading back to the arena, and park in the head coach spot. I climb out of the car in a good mood and put my pass against the reader to unlock the door.

It's almost six, so I grab a bottle of water from the cooler in the kitchen and head up the stairs to the offices. I've heard through the grapevine that Mackenzie has taken over Wayne's office, so that's the one I head to.

Hers is the only light still on. Everybody else has gone home. The office staff try to work condensed hours during preseason, because once the season begins everybody is constantly busy.

I knock on the door and a moment later she calls out for me to come in. Pushing the door open I'm surprised by two things.

The first is that she's already made some headway into Wayne's mess. The desk is empty. So is the cabinet beside it. There are still piles on the other cabinets and shelves, but damn, it makes a difference.

It also smells good. As in not like old food and dust and whatever the hell else Wayne gets up to in here.

The second thing that surprises me is that Mackenzie's bruise has already come out. And it's a humdinger, red and black and gray staining her right cheek, all the way up to her eye which is swollen.

"Damn. You should get that x-rayed," I tell her. "Are you sure you didn't break anything?"

She touches her cheek gingerly. I notice her manicure. Pale pink nails. No chips. Nice.

"I went down to the medic's office," she tells me. "She did a scan and everything's fine."

"She tell you how to treat it?" I ask her.

"Yep. Gave me some arnica and told me to ice it every hour."

"And have you?" I scan her face for any signs of lumps. Hematomas aren't funny, but all I see is smooth bruised skin.

"Yes, sir." The moment she says it she winces. I don't think it's from the pain.

"That's good." I drop into the chair in front of her desk. "I like what you've done with the place."

She smiles, and it looks good on her. "I had to tidy up a little bit."

"I saw the before picture," I tell her. "That was more than a little bit."

Her eyes widen. "It was bad, wasn't it? I knew he was messy but..." She trails off. "I mean, my boss told me there was a lot of mess to deal with." There's a barely perceptible shift in her demeanor. Like she's closed up but is trying not to show it. "Anyway, hi. I'm sorry about this morning. Can we start over?"

"What happened this morning?" I ask.

She smiles again. I'm only half joking. She looks completely different from the woman laying helplessly prone on the locker room floor, and not just because of the bruise. Sitting behind the desk she's in control. Her hair is perfectly tied into a pony tail, her glasses are perched on the bridge of her elegantly straight nose, and her blouse is now buttoned enough so I can't see the swell of breasts that kind of entranced me earlier.

This is good, I tell myself. I have to work with this woman. I have to make sure she does nothing to harm the team. Having fantasies about burying my face in the valley of her chest isn't exactly professional.

"I'm Eli Salinger," I say, reaching my hand across the desk.

She curls her fingers around my palm. "Mackenzie Hunter."

"Have we met before?" I ask her. "It's just that you look familiar. But I can't place it." I've always had a knack for recognizing faces. Now that she's upright and my view isn't obscured by Goran's ass it's nagging at me.

Two tiny lines furrow her brow. "I don't think so."

"Where did you go to school?"

"Cornell."

"I played there a few times," I say. "Did you go to hockey games?"

She shakes her head. "No, sorry. I think I have one of those faces. People think they know me but they don't." She shrugs.

"Do you know anything about hockey."

She takes a deep breath. "Not much," she admits.

It's not the face. It's the eyes. I feel like I've seen them before. And it's annoying me now.

But it's past six and I have two matches to watch at home tonight.

"Well then, welcome to the Mavericks," I say. "You've picked an interesting time to come and mix things up. I assume you'll be concentrating on the business side of things."

"That's why I'm here." She nods. "But I need to understand the whole business, including how the team works. The first thing we need to do is cut down on expenditures. I'll be undertaking a full audit of every payment we make. Including the team."

"Our salaries are negotiated in advance. We can't cut those."

"I understand that. But we can freeze them. Look at bonuses."

I shift in my seat. "My players aren't in the NHL. They're not highly paid. Any cut including bonuses will affect them badly. Most of them are living alone for the first time. Paying their own bills."

"The team folding would affect them worse," she says.

"You have the IRS breathing down your necks. Nothing is going to be sacred until there's money to pay them."

"But you can't do anything without Wayne's agreement, right?" And I know for a fact that Wayne would never agree to anything that put the team at a disadvantage. Hockey is everything to him. Winning is paramount. You could sell every bit of furniture in the offices and he wouldn't give a damn. But touch his team?

You're dead meat.

"I have authorization to make any changes needed."

"From who?"

She doesn't blink. "The Gauthier family."

"Greg?" I ask.

"I said the family, didn't I?"

Her attitude is annoying me.

"Look," I say, trying to keep my voice reasonable. "I get it. You're a businesswoman. You know how to run regular businesses. But this isn't a regular business, it's a sport. You've already said you don't know much about hockey. So all I'm asking is please don't interfere in the way I run my team." I let out a sigh. "Or at least run it by me before you do."

Her frown deepens. Something I said was wrong but I have no idea what. I don't think I insulted her. Almost the opposite. Any other coach would be screaming right now.

"Okay. I'll do that."

"Thank you."

"Have you met with Wayne yet?" I ask her, because I'm certain he's not going to be as laid back as I am about this.

She opens her mouth then shuts it again. Those two tiny lines appear above her eyes. "I'm actually meeting with him tonight at his house."

She's so closed off she should have a red and white sign flashing in front of her. And yet I kind of like it. For the past fifteen years, I've had my fair share of relationships and had to bat off a lot of female interest. And unlike some of the guys on my team, I wasn't stupid enough to think that interest was for me as a person.

It was for me the NHL player. It attracts people. We're not gods but we're different, and different is interesting.

"Give him my best," I tell her.

"I will."

"And ice that cheek before you leave. Twenty minutes."

She gives me the tightest of smiles. "Sure."

I stand and go to leave, but then for some stupid reason I turn around at the last minute. "Oh, and by the way. If you need somebody to talk to, or if you're feeling lonely while you're in town, give me a shout."

I regret it as soon as I say it, because I don't have time and I don't really want to.

Her smile disappears completely and I regret it even more. "I'll be fine. But thank you." As if to reiterate her point, she picks up a piece of paper from the desk and starts studying it like she's got a pop quiz in ten minutes.

That's when I realize she thinks I was hitting on her. And I wasn't. I was trying to be nice. She's alone in a new city and knows nobody. I feel kind of sorry for her.

I close the door shut behind me and stomp down the corridor. Now I'm the one in a pissy mood. And it doesn't feel good.

CHAPTER
FIVE

MACKENZIE

"How's your gramps?" Rachel asks me the following week. It's so good to hear my best friend's voice, even if it's only on speaker phone. It makes me feel homesick for New York, though. I'd give anything to be sitting with her in a bar drinking cocktails right now.

It's been a week since Gramps had surgery. Because he's old they're taking things very slow with his rehabilitation. I've been in to see him every day but he's always extremely sleepy.

Dad hasn't flown down yet. They're in the middle of filming and Gramps doesn't want a fuss. So it's just me and his old friends visiting him right now.

"He's doing well. They're talking about moving him to the nursing home next week."

If only the team's finances were so resilient.

I've spent the last week combing through everything, with the help of the only staff member who seems to understand the filing system. Brian is nice, but he also quakes whenever I'm around.

He also quakes when anybody else is around. He's just a quaker, I think.

From what I've discovered so far, there really is no money anywhere. Our season ticket sales are down from last year – which isn't a surprise since the team played abysmally. I had hoped that having a former NHL player coaching might spark some interest, but the fact that Eli lost the pre-season put an end to that.

The arena will be less than half full for the first game of the season. Which isn't great for income but also isn't great for team morale. I need to talk to Eli about it but I've been avoiding him for the last week.

Ever since he found me on the floor and was an asshole. Then did a 180 switch and offered to take me around town.

"And you? Have you settled in?" Rachel asks.

I'm staying in a serviced apartment. Warner Power has a contract with the chain and it's weird because the room is exactly the same as the ones I've stayed in throughout the country. It's like a Big Mac, but for rooms.

"I'm good." I don't tell her I miss having all my things around me. And the weekend was pretty miserable. I visited Gramps and then I drove to the mall, and wandered around aimlessly for an hour before calling it quits and heading home.

I'm used to eating out on my own. Being a consultant, I go where the work is and hotels are pretty much my best friend. But it feels wrong here. This isn't a big anonymous city. It's a small one and everybody seems to know each other.

There was one moment when I thought about taking Eli up on his offer to show me around.

And then I remembered what a bad idea that would be. Not just because he works for my client – and my grandad. But also because our talk in my office unnerved me. I'm used to being the one in control but he seems like he wants to fight me for it.

And both times so far I've lost.

"How are things in the office?" I ask her.

"Busy. We're all bidding on new projects. Mark is getting twitchy because our billable hours have plummeted. Which anybody could have told him would happen since you aren't here."

"Mine would have plummeted, too. I didn't have a project to book hours to."

"You would've found one by now. You hate doing nothing. Anyway, enough about work. Tell me about the hot hockey guys."

I laugh. "They're all twenty years old."

"The perfect age. Time has not withered them." Rachel sighs. "They have so much stamina. And they're grateful, too. Like get down on their knees and pray at your lady garden grateful."

"You obviously haven't met a hockey player," I tell her. "They're not grateful. They're flooded with attention."

"Ah well. There's always the Golden Mates app," Rachel says consolingly.

I don't tell her that Allison has already sent me an email with instructions on how to load my profile onto the dating app. I'd completely forgotten about being part of the beta team. Or maybe I'd just hoped that since I agreed before I got the orders to take this project in Morgantown that she'd forget about it.

But apparently her boyfriend is delighted that I'm away from New York. He wants beta testers all over the eastern region.

So now I have this stupid profile to write and I'm too damn nice to say no.

This is the problem with me. At work I can say no without

flinching at all. I'm representing businesses and they want me to be ruthless.

But outside of work? It's like trying to push a rock up a hill. Exhausting.

A knock at the door makes me jump.

"Just a minute," I tell Rachel, because I haven't actually gotten to what I wanted to run past her. "Come in," I call out.

Goran Olssen, the Mavericks' center half, puts his head around the door. Ever since he gave me a bulls-eye view of goods, he's been bringing me coffee every day to say sorry.

"American with hot milk," he says, mispronouncing Americano. "Just how you like it."

"Thank you, but you don't have to keep doing this. It wasn't your fault." The bruise on my cheek is now a sepia shade. Like an old movie but in flesh form.

He shrugs. "My mom says if I hurt people I need to make up for it."

"You didn't hurt me. I did. I'm the one who had an argument with the door," I remind him.

"Who are you talking to?" Rachel asks, her voice echoing through the speaker.

"Um, one of the team."

"Goran," he answers at the same time.

"Hi Goran," Rachel says, her voice low. I wince, because now she's going to have so many questions. "I'm Mackenzie's friend."

"Hi Mackenzie's friend." He smiles at me and I smile back. He's a good kid. "I should go," he tells me. "I have rehab. Then we have practice."

"Sure." I nod. "Thanks for dropping by."

"I'll see you tomorrow," he says. "American again?"

"You don't have to," I remind him.

"I know. But I want to." He nods his head at me then walks out, pulling the door closed behind him.

"Oh my God," Rachel squeals.

"Don't start," I warn her.

"Seriously? You have guys bringing you coffee in the morning? How old is this one? His accent is amazing."

"Guy. One guy. And he does it because for some stupid reason he thinks he has something to do with the bruise on my face. Which he doesn't. But if it makes him feel better to bring me a drink in the morning, then all is good."

"What's his last name?" Rachel asks.

"Oh no." I know her too well. "You're not looking him up."

"Why not? Is he hot?"

"He's twenty-one."

"He's hot, isn't he?" She just won't give up. "It's okay I'm Googling him. Goran and Morgantown Mavericks. Yep, there he is. His last name is Olssen. Oh he's pretty. Look at those cheekbones. You could cut cheese on them."

"Why would you want to cut cheese on cheekbones?"

"Shut up. You should totally let him show you how sorry he is."

"He works for a client," I remind her. "Rules, remember?"

"All I'm hearing is 'I'd do him if I could'," Rachel sings out.

"I'm ending this call," I warn her.

"No you're not. You wanted to talk to me about something. You haven't yet."

"We've been talking for twenty minutes," I point out.

"Yep, and yet you still haven't said what's worrying you."

This is the problem with people who've known you for decades. They know all your tells.

"I had to lie to the coach," I tell her.

"About what?"

"He asked me if I knew anything about hockey. I couldn't say that I did. So I told him no."

"Why did you do that?"

"Because if I told him I know all the ins and outs of hockey he could guess who I am. And I don't want anybody here knowing."

"Does it matter? They might take you more seriously if they know you're part of hockey royalty."

"It matters to me." I don't want them knowing. Because if they find out then they'll assume I only got where I have thanks to nepotism. I've worked so hard to make it in my own right, and that has nothing to do with the Gauthier name.

And then there's the other thing. If anybody Googles my real name…

Ugh. I hate the thought of that.

"Then keep lying. It's fine," Rachel says.

"But he also asked me if we'd met before. What if he recognizes me? If they find out I'm lying it's going to ruin things for me." I hate this. I should never have come. I've built up a great life away from the hockey rink.

This is all my dad's fault. And Kenneth Powers'. Who – by the way – now has an impossible-to-buy rink side season ticket to the Rangers home games, courtesy of my dad.

"Chill," Rachel urges. "It's all good. Now fill in that dating profile. You need to relax, meet some guys, get some good sex. It's been way too long, honey."

Yeah it has. And maybe she's right. Not about the sex part, but about the meeting people. I've been here for two weeks and the only people I see outside of the arena are my grandpa and his cleaner.

I'm lonely. And it's making me a little paranoid.

———

ELI

· · ·

"Coach." Carter sticks his head around from the shower room. Steam flows out from the door. I turn away from the diagram I've been drawing to show the team what formation I want us to start with tomorrow night.

"Yes?"

"We have a problem."

I try not to sigh. The closer we get to the opening game the more high strung the team is getting. I'm not exactly chill as a pill myself, but I'm the coach and they need me to stay strong.

"What is it?" I ask, walking over to where he's standing.

"These towels. They're crap. They're not soaking up anything."

Max pulls the door open wider. "They don't even wrap around our waists." He demonstrates and yeah, the coverage leaves a lot to be desired.

A *lot*. I'm going to have to wash my eyes out with bleach tonight. *Again*.

"Just dry off as best you can," I tell them. This is the thing about being a coach. You end up dealing with all the little shitty complaints, no matter how unimportant they are. But at this stage of the season preparations, anything that rocks the delicate ecosystem of the team is unwanted.

And unnecessary.

And those towels definitely aren't our usual ones. I grab a spare one that hasn't been near any of the team's balls and look at the label. It's a different service. Somebody's switched up the contracts. I have a good idea who that is.

It's a minor irritant but I'm irritated all the same.

So once we've finished talking about our strategy and the team has left, I head upstairs to the office block and knock on Mackenzie Hunter's door. I don't want to have this conversation. I shouldn't have to have it.

But I'm the coach and I'll do it. Lucky me.

"Come in."

When I open the door she's by the filing cabinet, bent

down, her gray skirt tight across her behind. She has her hair pulled back and she's wearing glasses again. She's every schoolboy's librarian fantasy.

If you like that sort of thing. Which I don't but my body seems to. One reason I've been deliberately avoiding her all week.

"Is everything okay?" she asks, turning to look at me. The smile that's pulling at her lips melts away when she sees my expression.

"Did you change the towels?" I ask her, my voice more irritated than I'd planned for.

She blinks. "Yes. The service we were using was extortionate. I found another one for seventy percent of the price." She looks so damn pleased with herself.

"Can you stand up please?" Her ass is distracting me. I need to stop looking at it. And turning away to look at the wall while we're having a conversation isn't exactly going to help.

She runs her tongue along her bottom lip – not helping either –then stands. She's wearing a red blouse today. It has a v-neck and I can see the beginning of her cleavage.

What the hell is wrong with me? I'm not Goran, I don't pant like a puppy at the sight of a woman. And yet here I am, wondering how soft her skin would feel if I ran my finger down that perfect line between the swell of her breasts.

Fuck.

This is what happens when you don't get laid for way too long. I blame my experience with Cassie. My ex. When she found out I was leaving the NHL, she took me aside and told me that she was sorry, but she just wasn't down with the AHL.

I wasn't exactly attached to her – it was more of a friendship with mutual benefits – but it still stung. But I understood it, too. She's an actress and is trying to get noticed. A boyfriend in the NHL helps.

Last I heard she'd been flirting with the guy who caused the injury that ended my career. Hart and I were rivals ever since we both joined as Rookies and it grates me that he was the one to finish my knee off.

Okay, more than grates. It pisses me off. And is one more reason why I'm going to make this team into a winning one, even if it kills me.

"You promised me you'd run anything that affects the team by me first." I say to her.

"They're just towels," she points out. "Nobody cares about those."

Tell me you know nothing about hockey without telling me you know nothing about hockey. I pinch the bridge of my nose and her eyes follow my movement.

"They're not *just* towels," I say, trying not to sound as annoyed as I feel. "They're the towels the team uses before every game. The same towels. Or at least the same thread count. The same size. The same feel. And you changed them."

"I know," she says, looking confused. "Didn't we just establish that?"

"And now the team is spooked. A day before the season starts."

"Spooked?" she asks. "About towels? Seriously?"

Fucking hell. "Seriously," I say, trying to keep my annoyance hidden. "You can't just change things on us without warning. We have rituals, we have comfort objects. We don't like change so close to a game. Anything that changes the way the team works is a shitshow at this point in the season. And also, the towels are shit. I checked them."

"They're still premium towels. The provider said so." Her voice is lower now. She looks unsure.

"This is why I asked you to run things by me," I tell her. And yeah, now I sound pissed. But I have a shit ton of work to do today and talking about fucking towels wasn't part of the plan. "If they're spooked they don't have their minds a hundred percent on the game. And I need them to be focused. You could have talked to me, we could have discussed trying the towels out or maybe delaying the change." I shake my head. "Do you know *anything* about hockey at all?"

She flinches and I regret saying it.

She puts her hand to her still-yellow cheek. "I'm sorry. I didn't think…"

For one horrific moment I think she's going to cry. All that composure, that certainty, where is it now? I want it back because I feel like a dick.

"I know. I get it. Please, just run things by me. Those kids are desperate to win. They want to please. But they're also temperamental. I can't have anything veer them off their path for the next two days."

"Understood." Her voice is tight.

"Okay." I take a deep breath. Somehow I've ended up being the asshole again, so I decide to take a different tack. "Are you coming to the game tomorrow?"

"No. I wasn't planning to. I… ah…" She looks around. "Too much to do, you know?"

"There are seats in the staff box. Ask Jake at the ticket desk to reserve one for you. It'd do you good to learn a little more about the game."

Something about my words brings the life back into her. "I don't need to understand the game to figure out how to save money," she says, her eyes meeting mine. "And it's best if I keep some distance. Getting too close to employees is never a good thing in my position."

"Maybe you should tell that to Goran," I say lightly. Because, yes, I've noticed him hanging around her office, and no, I don't like it.

I've said nothing to him yet, but if it gets worse, I will.

Her cheeks flush. "I don't need to tell that to Goran. Nothing is going on."

"He has a crush on you."

She opens her mouth then hesitates.

"I'm not accusing you of anything," I add, because I'm feeling like an asshole again. Which isn't a normal feeling for me. Or at least it wasn't until Mackenzie Hunter arrived in the locker room.

I don't like how I keep opening my mouth and saying the wrong things. But here I am, still doing it.

"I just think you need to not encourage him," I finish.

"I'm not encouraging him," she tells me, her eyes narrowing. "He buys me a coffee, I drink it. I don't know what that means in your dirty, misogynistic mind, but that doesn't mean I'm about to get down on my knees and let him ram me from behind."

"Ram you from behind?" My voice is thin.

"Shut up. You know what I mean."

Yeah, I do. Somebody fucking help me because I'm picturing it right now. Only I'm the one doing the ramming.

I squeeze my eyes shut to get rid of that image.

"I'm not a misogynist," I tell her, my voice strangled.

"Do you even know what it means?"

"Do you think because I'm a hockey player that I don't have any brains? Yes, I know what it means."

It's her turn to look awkward. But she does it so much better than me. "I'm sorry. I just…" She shakes her head. "There's nothing going on between Goran and me. I'll make it clear he shouldn't bring me coffee any more."

How did we end up here? I just wanted to change the shitty towels back to our good ones. Not butt heads with the management consultant and imagine her…

No. Not going there.

"No. I'm sorry," I tell her. "He's a good kid. I don't want him put off his game. Let's just forget I ever mentioned it. Please."

"Okay," she breathes.

"You should still come to the game tomorrow night," I tell her. "I'd like to see you there."

Our eyes meet again.

"Thank you," she says quietly. "I'll see what happens tomorrow."

"You do that."

CHAPTER
SIX

MACKENZIE

"The damn nurses won't let me watch the game," Gramps complains to me over the phone. "I told them I won't shout or swear, but they don't believe me."

"I wonder why that is," I say dryly. I know for a fact that his nursing team has been explicitly told by the doctor not to let him watch because it always spikes his blood pressure. "And it's not their fault so don't give them hell for it."

"Can I stay on the line?" he asks. "You can tell me what's happening."

"No." I'm firm because he's exactly like my dad. If he sees any chink – even if it's tiny – in your armor he'll push and probe until he gets what he wants. "I'll call you afterward. How does that sound?"

"It sounds like I'm a prisoner in my own damn room," he grumbles.

"But at least you're recovering," I tell him. "That's good, right?"

"Hmm."

I've been to visit him twice this week. And every time I've had to promise that I haven't made major changes to the team. Which I haven't, mostly because I've no idea what changes I can make to actually get this team into making some money rather than hemorrhaging it.

The IRS is breathing down the team's neck. There are no savings to be made. And the one I tried caused so many problems I wish I hadn't bothered.

Yes, I'm still kicking myself about the towels. I should have known that change wouldn't go down well so close to the season opening game. I should have thought of it but I didn't.

And Eli Salinger is pissed with me.

For some reason I don't like it. Even though he tried to be nice afterward, I could still see the frustration in his eyes. I hate that he made me feel small. Like I'm not good enough. He might not have meant to do it but that's what happened.

The same way I never felt good enough when my mom tried to teach me to skate or my dad urged me to try dribbling a puck with a stick. And I always ended up flat on my ass.

I let out a sigh.

"What is it?" Gramps asks. "Is there a problem?"

"No, no problem. I need to go. I'll call you later."

"Wait! Can you call during the intermission at least?" he pleads.

"Goodbye, Gramps."

"Mackenzie!"

I disconnect, because I have my orders from his nursing team. My stomach is rumbling so I head down to one of the concession stalls, the smell of hotdogs making it do little flips of excitement.

When I was a kid, I spent my life dreaming about that smell. It was the only good thing about watching hockey. I'd stuff my change into the little Minnie Mouse purse my mom had brought home for me when she was skating for Disney, and then I'd wait until the whole family was shouting at the players before hopping off to buy myself the biggest, most delicious dog covered in onions and sauce and mustard. It was my idea of heaven.

Until the day Isabella told me I was getting a little bit pudgy.

That memory makes me feel sad as I reach the front of the line. Maybe I should head out and grab a salad instead. But then I see the line of dogs slowly rolling down the grill and I can't resist buying one and smothering it with mustard.

As soon as I bite into it I can't help but groan. It's that good. Yeah, the hot dog stands in New York are great, but this is something else.

I use my pass to get back into the staff area. Ahead of me is the locker room. I walk resolutely past it, kind of in a trance because of the goodness of the dog. That's why I don't notice Goran until I almost bump into him. He's wearing just his underclothes – the thermals that will be topped off by his gear.

"Hey." He glances at the dog. "That looks good."

"It's great," I tell him. I think I might be addicted. I swallow down the last bite and try not to groan again. Maybe game days won't be so bad after all.

"You have mustard on your mouth," he says. Then he reaches out to slide his finger along my bottom lip. His bright blue eyes catch mine and for the first time I'm wondering if what Eli said is true.

Does Goran have a crush on me? I'm old enough to be his mom. Well okay, his much older sister at least.

His finger lingers on my lip and then the locker room door opens and of course Eli has to walk out at the exact moment he's touching me.

His brows knit as he sees me and realizes that Goran and I are standing way too close.

"Team talk," he tells Goran.

I step back too late. And then Goran does the most idiotic thing imaginable.

He licks the mustard off his fingers.

Eli's face turns red. Shit shit shit.

"I should go," I say, because I have no idea how to make this look better. "Good luck with the game."

"Thanks." Goran smiles and it doesn't help. But he can't see Eli's face, which is probably a good thing right now. I turn on my heel and walk back to the door that I came through. I'll find another way up to the exec box.

Or watch the game on the television in my office. That might be the better choice.

I don't look back as I press the unlock button and grab the handle.

But I can still feel the heat of Eli's stare as he watched Goran lick his fingers. And the feeling of mortification as it washes over me.

———

ELI

Nobody says a word as we walk into the locker room at intermission. We're a goal down and haven't been getting any chances at all. The team all grabs a drink, pulls their tops off, sit down heavily on the benches, and I'm still trying to work out what to say to make them play better.

Everything we practiced has been forgotten. They look like a freshman team in high school. I'm pissed but I need to be able to bring them all together somehow.

Max looks more pissed than I am. And I don't blame him. The defense has been sloppy and he's had to save more pucks than he should. He's also let two go past him.

But he's pretty much the only one that isn't playing below his potential.

When they're all seated and rehydrated I clap my hands together. And I keep my voice even as I talk us through the game up until now. None of them are smiling, there's none of the energy in the room there would be if they were winning, but at least they're listening to me.

"You're better than this," I tell them. "Every single one of you." Sorry Max. "I need you to go back on that ice and be ready to win. The puck is yours for the taking, so take it. Be aware of who is around you. Pass when you see a break."

We talk about the plays we've practiced. I tell them who'll be on the ice after intermission.

"I'm coming onto the ice, too," I say, because I can do it for twenty minutes. I need to. I might be here primarily as the coach, but the AHL rules allow me to play, and my doctor has cleared me for twenty minutes of active play a week.

Watching them from behind the bench has been excruciating. My mind may have accepted the fact that I'm semi-retired, but my body wants to be on the ice.

My voice is hoarse from shouting at them.

"But I can't do this on my own," I tell them. "Not least because I'm old and slow."

They laugh but it's true. The AHL is mostly a young man's league. I'm forty years old. Past retirement age, even if I was firing on all cylinders.

"Are you with me?" I ask them.

"Yes Coach!"

And that's all it takes for the mood in the room to swing. They're nodding and talking to each other, as though they're actually realizing they're a team and need each other's help. I check my watch. We have seven minutes left.

"Five minutes," I say. "Conserve your energy, do what you need to do, and then let's get back on the ice and win this damn thing."

When the intermission ends, we head back out. The Zamboni has cleared up any evidence of the game so far, and as soon as my skates hit the surface it feels like I've come home. My blades are sharp, my stick is taped exactly the way I like it, and I can feel the rush of cool air come through the grill of my helmet. I take my place on the right wing and nod to Goran who's facing off against the opposition, his stick poised and ready.

Then the puck drops and blood rushes through my ears as the third period begins.

Nothing else matters but the puck and the goal. I glide across the ice, my mind calculating which team member is where, who is attacking, who is defending. It takes a millisecond because hockey is all about reactions. There's no time to take a breath, to look around and strategize.

My body knows what to do. It always has. And when I get the puck it feels like I'm complete. I head down the right wing and pass, the puck locking onto Carter's stick.

He's in front of the goal. I hold my breath.

And he slams it into the net.

Roars fill the air from the half-full arena. Carter lifts his stick in the air and promptly gets sent off the ice. He skates over and climbs off, replaced by Dubois, who vaults the wall and slides easily over to the center forward position.

We're two minutes away from the end of the period when Carter is allowed back on. He high fives Dubois and nods at me and I nod back at him.

We're down 2-1 and it's pretty much a done deal. But at least we scored. The whole team has lifted its game this period. The defense has worked so hard that Max looks almost bored in front of the goal posts. The game has been mostly at our end, but their goalie is good and he's warded off every attempt on goal since Carter's.

In the corner of my eye, I see the clock counting down. Carter has the puck and he's weaving it around the opposition's players, looking more like he's dancing than playing hockey.

And then, without even taking a breath, he slams the puck right into the center of the goal, and for a moment the whole arena is silent before they realize that he's done it again.

2-2. We're tied. Which means overtime. And this time Carter keeps his damn stick down as he basks in the sound of the crowd's adulation.

As I glide across the ice to congratulate him, my gaze lifts to the staff box. And I see Mackenzie there, watching us.

CHAPTER
SEVEN

MACKENZIE

Dad officially retired from the NHL when I was twelve-years-old, but I still have vivid memories of him coming home after a defeat. My brothers would be fast asleep in bed, and my mom would usher Isabella and me to our bedrooms, waving off our protests that we wanted to see our dad before we went to bed.

You could always tell when he got home. The sound of the engine on his sleek Ferrari would echo as he pulled into the driveway and then the garage door would whirr. It could take him any time from a minute to an hour to walk through the connecting door into the kitchen.

And my mom would just wait. For as long as it took.

I know all this because one night I snuck down to watch him come home. I'd finished my book and I was bored. So I sat on the stair that gave the best view of the kitchen and watched the back of my mom's head as she waited, too.

I don't know how long it took for him to walk in. But I do

remember the tightness of his face, the narrowness of his eyes and the way he held his body.

Anger radiated off him. And for a moment I was scared.

But then mom stood and walked over to him, not saying a word. He closed the door behind him and watched her with wary eyes. And though I couldn't see her face, I could see her hands as they reached up to cup his jaw. Something in his eyes flashed.

And then he kissed her. Hard and desperate. At that moment I knew I should go. This was private stuff. Mom and Dad stuff.

I was eight then. I didn't know exactly what was going on. By the time I was twelve, I knew and I was embarrassed.

She soothed him the only way she knew how. And in the morning he'd be okay. He'd eat breakfast with us, talk about the game, about our day ahead.

Because Mom always knew exactly how to deal with him.

For some reason I'm thinking about those nights as I watch Max let the golden goal in and throw his stick down in disgust onto the ice.

Everybody in the staff box lets out a groan. And I'm groaning internally too because I'm going to have to tell Gramps that we lost.

The other team celebrates to muted applause – this is the AHL and there's not a huge contingent of away fans who've come to support them – as our own team bump their fists half-heartedly and head to the tunnel.

The last one to leave the ice is Eli. And though I'm too far away to see his expression, even though he's taken his helmet off – I know exactly what it looks like.

Because I know how important it is to win.

From that early age I learned that nothing else matters. Coming second is for saps. There are no awards for taking part or even for doing your best.

You win or die.

That's it.

Brian and the rest of the office staff say their goodbyes and leave. I'm the last one sitting here, staring out at the ice.

And I know it's because I don't want to go to my office and phone Gramps. I don't want to go downstairs either. I'd forgotten how much I hate it when a team loses. The atmosphere makes me feel uncomfortable. I don't know what to say.

It isn't until the arena is empty that I finally stand and walk back to my office. There are emails to send and invoices to pay, and I have to review this week's staff payroll to make sure they will all get some money in their banks. It's almost ten-thirty by the time I pick up the phone and tap out the number for Gramps' nursing home.

When I speak to the nurse in charge she tells me that he's already asleep but she'll let him know in the morning. I let out a huge breath of relief. There's nothing more for me to do but to go home, go to sleep, and face this all again in the morning.

The arena is in darkness as I make my way down the stairs to the staff exit that leads out to the parking lot. It's only when I hear a thud of something against the floor that I turn around.

And see Eli Salinger walking out of the locker room, wearing jeans and a hoodie. His hair is dry but it looks fluffy, like he showered an hour ago and didn't bother doing anything with it.

I wonder if he's been sitting there alone in the locker room, the same way I've been sitting in my office. I feel a weird pull to him. It's like an itch I can't scratch.

He doesn't notice me standing there. His jaw is so tight I'm wondering if it's wired shut. I hold my breath as he presses his lips together then shakes his head, stalking with intent toward the door.

And toward me.

He stops short when he finally realizes he's not alone. His eyes look so dark as they reach mine. I part my lips but really, I can't think of a word to say.

Nothing that makes losing feel better. Because nothing can. Dad taught me that.

I step toward him, and he doesn't move. His gaze is wary but still on me. My heart hammers against my ribcage as I lift my hands and press my palms softly to his bearded cheeks.

This is all kinds of messed up. I'm so aware that I barely know him. And apart from knowing what my panties look like when I'm laying prone on the locker room floor, he doesn't know me either.

And yet touching him feels natural. It feels good.

It makes me want things I shouldn't.

I open my lips again, this time to say something. But he gives a barely perceptible shake of his head.

Maybe he's right. Whatever I say is going to ruin this moment. I let out a long, ragged breath.

As the last of it escapes, his mouth comes crashing down on mine.

His lips are warm, hard, needy. Without even thinking I kiss him back, my fingers curling into his hair. His tongue slides against the seam of my lips, requesting entrance, and I part them, sliding my own against him. There's a vibration from his throat – a grunt – and then my back is against the wall and his body is pressing against me. I feel a throb between my legs that matches the rhythm of his kisses.

I feel the hard planes of his stomach as it presses against mine. I clutch onto his arms, my fingers no match for the iron of his biceps as he holds me close.

His hand slides down my side, fingers feathering my hips, then he hitches my skirt up and touches my leg. His hand curls around my skin, lifting it, until my calf brushes against his hip.

And he's there. Hard and thick. Pressing against the part

of me that's pulsing with need. My nipples pebble as he pulls his mouth from mine, kissing my jaw, my neck, the little dip where it meets my chest.

My breath catches in my throat as he kisses down. Even through the fabric layers of my blouse and bra I feel it as his lips close around my nipple. Moistening the silk, tugging, the roughness of his beard against my breast making me arch my back and let out a cry.

He drops to his knees and presses his face between my thighs. Somewhere in my hazy mind there's a voice telling me to stop this. Because I'm the one who started it. He might be making me gasp right now, but there's no doubt who has the power here.

He breathes in and groans. Neither of us has said a word. I'm not sure I could. My entire being is focused on the apex of my legs and the way his nose is pressing against it. My fingers are still tangled in his hair, the tips touching and caressing his scalp. While his are tracing the line of my panties, his index finger sliding them aside, and he lets out another low groan as he feels how wet I am.

His breath is warm against my skin. And this whole thing feels inevitable. He's going to devour me. I'm going to let him.

I'm going to love it.

I don't think about what will happen afterward. How embarrassing it will be to face him tomorrow. How I'm jeopardizing every piece of professional repute I've built up over the years.

All I can think about is how to soothe him. How to be soothed.

A light flickers overhead, buzzing like a fly caught in a net. And I tense, half-expecting to see a member of staff walking toward us.

We're in the hallway, in full view. My skirt is hitched

around my hips, my thighs are pressed against his cheeks and there is no way to explain this away if we get caught.

Eli must be thinking the same thing. He lets go of my thighs and slowly stands, pulling at my skirt, smoothing it.

Oh God.

I've spent my life giving presentations. Telling people how I can make their companies run better, how I can save them money, make them succeed.

But right now I can't string two words together. It's like he's stolen my voice along with my common sense.

Oh no, honey. He didn't steal them. You practically threw them at him.

"I'm so fucking sorry," he rasps.

I shake my head, still mute.

"I shouldn't have…" He trails off, his face full of horror. "Jesus, I'm sorry."

I need to tell him it's okay. That I started it. And I wanted him to keep going. That if the light hadn't flickered he'd be face deep in me right now.

"Eli," I finally manage to say, my cheeks flaming hot.

He looks at me as though I'm about to give the Gettysburg Address. His eyes don't leave my face.

But I have nothing. No words of wisdom. No apologies. Just a throat that feels like it's got the Hoover Dam halfway down it.

So I do the only thing a self-respecting woman who's just gyrated her body on a hot coach's face can do.

I get the hell out of there.

ELI

. . .

As soon as I walk through my front door I slam my bag on the floor and lean against the wall, banging my head against the painted brick.

I'm a fucking idiot. I want to punch something, probably myself. What the hell was I thinking, touching her.

You weren't thinking. Or at least your brain wasn't.

I toe my sneakers off and kick them against the other wall, all too aware that throwing a hissy fit at forty-years-old is fucking stupid. Not least because if I dent the wall I'll have to repair it myself.

Having a tantrum is less exciting when you've learned to have some modicum of responsibility.

Still pissed with myself, I stomp into the kitchen and open up the refrigerator to grab some fresh water.

This is bad. Really bad. I actually feel worse than the day I was told I couldn't play in the NHL again. More angry than I was at fucking Hart for deliberately fouling me.

I put my fingers to my face and fuck if they don't still smell like her.

And there's the other thing. I'm horny as fuck because I somehow cock blocked myself and all I can think of are those little sounds she made as I ran my finger along her wetness.

She mewled like a damn kitten. The memory of it sends blood rushing where it shouldn't. I think about her wide eyes and the softness of her fingers as they raked through my hair and I think I might be losing my mind.

To top it all off, we lost the first game of the season. Funny how that's not the first thing on my mind right now.

And it should be. I'm the coach. I should be watching the game and making notes, ready for our early start tomorrow because I'm the idiot who insisted on early training every time we lose.

My phone rings and my brother's name appears on the screen. I tell myself to get a grip and slide my finger across the glass.

"Hey. Aren't you working?" I ask him. Holden's the brother closest to my age, and also a doctor in New York. I've never gotten my head around his shifts, but nearly every time I talk to him he's working.

"On call," he said, clearing his throat. "I saw the final score. I'm sorry."

I pinch my nose. I don't want to talk about this now. I don't want to hear the empathy in his voice. "Yeah. We played like shit."

"You went to overtime. That isn't shit."

"That's like saying you took somebody into surgery but couldn't save their life," I tell him. Holden always understands medical metaphors. He doesn't understand hockey at all.

My older brothers – by a couple of years – Liam and Myles – have already sent me messages saying they watched the game on television and they're sorry.

I haven't responded to them yet. I will when I calm down.

"It was always going to be a tough match," Holden says. "Especially as it's your first."

"Third."

He clears his throat. "The other two were pre-season, they don't count. You have time to turn things around."

"Sure." I lean against the kitchen counter. "So what's up with you?"

"Nothing. Just working."

"You're always working."

"That's because I'm a doctor," he says. "It's what we do."

Funny thing is, working is what all of us Salingers do. To the detriment of nearly everything else. It's a minor miracle that Myles and Liam are both married – for a while there it looked like they were going to be perpetual bachelors.

Before I can say anything more, there's a beep and Holden huffs. "I have to go, sorry, bro."

"It's all good." Or it will be. Once I chop my own head off.

"Speak soon." He disconnects and I throw my phone onto the counter. Our little conversation hasn't helped take my mind off of what happened back in the arena though.

And no, I don't mean the loss. I mean Mackenzie Goddamned Hunter.

The team will expect me to give them words of advice. To tell them how to improve things.

And right now the only thing I can think of is that I wish I'd put my tongue against her just once.

I throw my now-empty bottle of water into the recycling and grab an energy bar because I probably spent two thousand calories on the ice and I'd like to wake up tomorrow and not feel like I'm dying.

And then I head upstairs because it's late and I have a hard on that won't go away so I'm going to beat myself off to the memory of the way she parted her mouth as she cupped my face and the fantasy of sliding myself between those pretty lips as her tongue flutters against me until I explode inside of her.

Tonight I beat myself off like crazy. Tomorrow I apologize.

Maybe by next week I won't feel like punching myself in the face.

CHAPTER
EIGHT

MACKENZIE

Team practice is in full swing as I tiptoe my way up to my office the next morning. And yep, I'm completely avoiding the man who buried his face between my thighs yesterday, because I still don't know what to say to him.

What was I thinking? Just because my mom knew how to soothe my dad doesn't mean that I need to use the same moves on a guy I barely know. My parents were married. They'd been doing the horizontal tango for years – four kids as a testament to that.

I can't remember the last time I reacted like that to a man touching me. I felt like putty in his hands. Like I'd do anything he told me to. I wanted to.

I wanted to feel him everywhere.

This is what happens when you don't have any kind of physical contact for months. The last time anybody hugged me was Rachel when we were at work. The last time anybody touched me was when I got my black eye in the locker room.

And I miss it. I miss being touched. I miss being wanted. For a few minutes last night I felt like a goddess.

Now I just feel lost.

At ten my phone pings with a message and I'm glad for the distraction. At least until I see it's the family chat.

Team talk tonight – 9pm. Dad

Great. I've already decided to go see Gramps on the way home, so this should top my night off nicely.

Maybe when the call is done I can pull my nails out one by one with some pliers just for fun.

By the time lunch comes around, I've barely gotten any work done. I haven't eaten since last night's hot dog either, so I grab my purse, deciding to head out to the mall where there's a sandwich shop that does the best salads I've ever tasted. But before I can slide on my jacket, Eli Salinger knocks on the door.

I open it, and just like last night neither of us can find our voices. He looks as awkward as I feel. No, maybe ten percent less awkward.

Because he still has this hockey player confidence that's impossible to miss. All muscles and intimidation. My heart starts to slam on my ribcage.

"You heading out somewhere?" he asks, his voice low.

"I need some lunch," I tell him, still not meeting his eyes.

He clears his throat. "Ah. Can we talk before you go?"

The urge to run is strong. But this conversation is inevitable. And also already excruciating.

I try not to sigh too loudly. "Close the door," I tell him, reluctantly walking back to my desk to put my purse down.

I hear the lock click and take a deep breath. When I turn to look at him his eyes are on me. It makes me jump.

The dark beard on his jaw makes him look even more dangerous. For a second I swear I can feel the roughness of his face between my thighs.

I open my mouth and his gaze dips to my lips.

"I'm sorry for last night," he says. There's a thickness to his voice that he has to clear away with another cough. "If you need me to quit I'll talk to Wayne."

"Why would you quit?" I ask him, genuinely confused. "I started it."

"You touched me. I took it too far. We work together." He blinks. "I'm not even sure if you're my boss, but if you are that makes it worse."

"I'm not," I blurt out. "Gr... Wayne Gauthier is still your boss. I'm just a consultant."

"Either way it shouldn't have happened."

He's right. We're on the same page. But instead of feeling relief something else pulls at my gut. I'm... disappointed? Which is stupid because this could have turned out so much worse.

"It was a game night," I said. "Emotions were high. Tensions hit the roof." I pull my lip between my teeth. "Why don't we both forget about it?"

He blinks. "You don't want to talk about it?"

I shake my head.

"Or reprimand me?"

"No," I whisper.

He looks at me carefully. "So that's it?"

"Yep. How was the team this morning?"

He runs his thumb along his bearded jaw. "Pissed."

"It was a hard match. You could have won it."

He winces. Ouch, wrong thing to say.

"Yeah, well we need to play better next time."

It would help with funds if they won, that's for sure. Spectators like winning teams. Wisely, I don't voice that thought.

"You will," I say. "The potential is there. They just need to start working as a team."

A ghost of a smile passes his lips. And I'm looking at him again, realizing that I don't just find him attractive. I'm starting to like him.

No, I *do* like him. And that's wrong and dangerous and it will only end in tears if I let it.

Which I won't, because I'm grown up and I know better than to mess with things that make me sad.

"I should head out," I say, pointedly picking up my purse again, because I need some space. I'm lonely, I'm somewhere I don't want to be, and I'm grasping at any bit of friendship somebody offers me. "I need some lunch."

"Oh yeah. Sure." He nods. I hate that he still looks relieved.

"You want me to pick you up anything?" I ask.

He blinks. "Like what?"

"A sub. Or a salad. What did you think I meant?"

"I've no idea." He shrugs. "I just wasn't expecting you to offer me something to eat."

My cheeks flush as I remember offering him something to eat last night. And when I bring myself to look at him that darkness is back again.

"No sub then?"

He shakes his head. "No sub. But thank you."

I brush past him and reach for the door. "You're welcome."

There, that wasn't so bad, was it? Now that it's over and done with, maybe we can forget it ever happened. That thought lasts until I reach my car and let out a long, agonizing breath.

My heart is still slamming against my ribcage. And I'm still remembering him dropping to his knees in front of me.

It's simultaneously the hottest and most embarrassing thing that's happened to me.

But hot seems to be winning out.

———

"You dirty minx," Rachel says when we're talking on the phone that evening. She sounds like she's trying to keep from laughing. "You've hardly been there five minutes and you're already hooking up with a hockey player, even though you told me you hated them. What else has been going on? Orgies on the ice? Horny stuff with hotdogs? I need to get out of New York and find me some provincial guy."

"He's AHL not NHL," I point out. It was a mistake to tell her about last night. I probably shouldn't have called her at all. But I'm sitting in my beautifully sterile serviced apartment with nobody to talk to. I literally don't trust anybody else not to spread the gossip and I needed to let it out to somebody.

It's killing me that I was such an idiot.

The good news is that I know where Rachel's skeletons are. Like the time she hooked up in an elevator at our Christmas party. *With the guy who was repairing the elevator.*

"Wait," she says. "I've got his picture on my phone now. He's hot."

"Hmm." This isn't helping. Because yes, Eli is hot if you like that kind of thing. Which I don't because me and hockey players don't go together.

"And he really dropped to his knees and put his face in your crotch?"

I grimace. "You make it sound crude."

This time she really does laugh. "Honey, of course I do. Because it *is* crude. In the sexiest of ways. When was the last time a guy breathed you in like that?"

"Um, never?" With most of my exes – and there haven't been many – oral sex was a one-way street. They definitely didn't seem to love breathing me in.

My cheeks flame because Eli looked like he enjoyed it a lot. At least for a brief second. And for that moment it felt so good.

"You think it would have continued if the lights hadn't flickered?"

"I don't know," I admit. "Hopefully one of us would have come to our senses." Preferably me, because I'm not good at rejection.

Ah yeah, but he rejected me later anyway.

It shouldn't have happened. That's what he said. Along with offering to quit.

And now I'm panicking again, because maybe I'm the one who should quit. I *want* to quit. To get away from here. Don't I?

"Why would you have come to your senses?" Rachel asks, genuinely confused. "If a guy like that dropped to his knees for me…"

"Because he's a client."

"Pah. Not really. Isn't your granddad your client?" she counters.

"Yes. But he works for the client. You know the rules." We both know them. If my boss got wind of what happened outside of the locker room, he'd haul me back to New York and fire my ass.

I'm a grown up. I know better than this.

"It's a shame though. He really is beautiful."

"Yeah." He really is. And kind. That's the weird thing, it's his rugged kindness that's killing me. Making me want things that are way too bad to say out loud.

"And I bet he has a huge—"

"Okay! Enough."

"I'm just saying. Or maybe asking. Did you feel it?" There's a hopeful note to her voice.

The memory of his thick ridge pressing against me flashes into my mind. And I have to shift in my seat. "So, what's happening in New York?" I ask, because I really don't want to talk about Eli Salinger anymore. I don't want to think about him, I don't want to fantasize about him.

I just want to do my job and get back to New York.

"Spoilsport."

"I'm serious. Any new projects on the horizon?" I feel so out of touch. While I'm here I can't be working on bids which means I don't know what's happening. I hate the thought that the other consultants are going to get a head start on me if we win a great project and they can put themselves forward.

"A few things are coming in, but nothing major," Rachel tells me. "Relax. Enjoy the break. How's your gramps doing?"

"Funny you should ask. I visited him about an hour ago." And he's feeling better because he ranted at me about the team's loss. "He's slowly healing. But I don't think he understands that he's never going to be back to full fitness again."

"Poor guy," Rachel says. "It must be awful growing old."

"You sound like Allison when she's talking about us,"

"Ugh, don't remind me," Rachel pleads. "Don't you hate it when people call us old?"

"Pretty much." And I know for a fact that Gramps hates it, too. It's probably harder for him than most since he's been so physical for most of his life. Even in his eighties he's still been able to skate.

Until now, that is.

"How are you finding her boyfriend's dating app?" I ask.

Rachel groans. "I forgot all about it until Monday. She pleaded with me to fill everything in so I did and then nothing. Like no matches at all. How about you?"

"I've had a few," I tell her.

"WHAT?" She sounds outraged. "How many exactly?"

"Um, five I think." I got the fifth through last night. They all seem like nice guys. Two of them are insurance, one runs his own business, one is a lawyer, and I have no idea what the other one does.

"What are they like?" she asks. "I can't believe I haven't had one."

"You only just downloaded the app," I point out. "And anyway, these aren't real matches. We're all just beta testing it, right?"

"Of course they're real matches," she says. "It's only the women who are beta testing it."

"What do you mean?"

"I mean the guys are real sign ups. Didn't she tell you?"

I frown. "No." There are five messages in my inbox that I've ignored because I assumed they're generated by the app. "She didn't send me any instructions on what to do."

Rachel laughs. "Maybe that's because she assumed you've used a dating app before. You're supposed to be chatting with them and providing feedback." Rachel pauses. "Hey, you could go on a date."

"She said nothing about a date."

"I know. But if you want Mr. On His Knees to get the message that you're definitely not interested then going on a date should spell it out to him."

"A minute ago you seemed intent on me letting him get on his knees again," I point out.

"Yeah, but I know you. You never would, you're too straight laced."

"I'm not," I protest. "I'm just professional."

"Sure," she says smoothly. "And to make it clear how professional you are, go on this date. You said it yourself that you're lonely. What's wrong with going out for dinner with somebody? When you get back to New York you won't have time again, so do it now while you can."

The sad thing is, she's right. I'm usually okay with my own company but coming home every night to an empty house has been difficult. I miss having friends around to catch up with over a coffee, or colleagues to grab a bite of dinner with after work.

After three years of working our asses off, this free time in the evening is making me feel antsy.

"I'll check with Allison if that should even happen."

"Funnily enough, we're working late tonight and Allison is sitting about three feet away from me," Rachel says, sounding smug. "I'll check with her myself. Wait." So I do and she's back in an unseemly short time. "She says yes. She's ecstatic that you have matches. Her boyfriend wants to know how good the matching algorithm is, and the only way to do that is for you to meet up. She'll want a full report afterward."

"Let's hope none of them are serial killers," I say.

"It's okay, her boyfriend has all of their details. I'll run a background check."

"Don't run a thing. That's illegal."

"Yeah, but it'd be fun," Rachel says.

"How about you just let me take care of it?" I'm not an idiot, I know to not meet them anywhere unsafe. "And you go find your own matches." I check my watch. I need to get going anyway. I have to prepare myself for our family chat in twenty minutes. And it won't be good. I've already sent them an interim report. There's no money to be found. I can't even change the damn towel service without there being major heartache. "I have another call to take. I'll catch you later."

"Yes, you will. Now reply to those messages. You'll be Allison's star pupil."

———

"That can't be right," Dad says. He's looking casual in a hoodie and a cap. He's in Toronto with my brothers who had a game tonight. My mom and Isabella are on another screen, both in white fluffy gowns with their hair in curlers. They're having a mom and daughter spa day on their day off from filming for their reality show.

"It is," I tell them. "There's no money and no way to save

anywhere near enough," I tell him. That's the truth of it. Yes, I can scrape around and find some minor savings, but that won't pay the IRS bill. "Maybe we should look at putting the team up for sale."

"What about the Razors?" Dad asks, referring to the NHL team the Mavericks are affiliated to. "We could ask them for a loan."

"They already gave one last year." They have a good reason to want to keep the Mavericks going, since we're the team that feeds them new players. But they're also a business and they're not going to inject any money into the team without getting something back for it. I take a deep breath. "We could look at offering to sell at least part of the team to them."

"That would kill Gramps," my dad says, looking pensive.

"I know, but our options are limited. I can make some savings, turn some things around. Enough to make it profitable in the future. But to pay that IRS bill we need cash flow now and that's something that takes time to make."

My dad's head drops into his hands and I know he's genuinely upset. He may be a pain in my ass at times but he always idolized his own dad, the same way Brad and Johnny idolize him.

And I'm frustrated that I can't make this work. But unless he pays that bill, Grandpa will have to sell the team, declare bankruptcy, or – and this worries me the most – go to jail.

The thing is, he wouldn't have to. There are ways to pay this bill. But he's stubborn as a mule and he won't sell the team. I know it.

"Maybe I could take out a loan," my dad says.

My mom sighs. "But who will pay it back?"

Neither of them have been great with money over the years. Or rather, they don't save a lot. They get it and they spend it. Which is great until you need a lump sum.

"How soon do we need to pay the IRS?" Mom asks.

"I can negotiate it," I tell them, relieved that at least that's something I can do. "If we can show them we have a plan, they may give us a few months."

"Okay. Then that's what we need to do." My dad nods. "I'll work out how to raise the money."

"I'm sorry," I say, because I hate being the barer of bad news to them. Yes, they drive me up the wall but nobody wants to hear that your father's team is about to fold.

"It's not your fault, honey," my mom says.

Yeah, but sometimes it feels that way.

CHAPTER
NINE

ELI

After winning our next two games the atmosphere in the locker room has done a one-eighty degree flip. Everybody is smiling, turning up early for practice. Even I manage to crack a smirk when Goran comes in with coffee for everybody then insists on taking one upstairs to Mackenzie, because he still thinks he's her best friend.

And yeah, I don't like it. Not because I think there's anything going on between them, but because I've been actively avoiding her and I feel like an ass about it. I saw her in the hallway after our first win and she smiled widely at me and I just nodded and walked away.

Yep. Asshole.

And now I'm annoyed with my twenty-one-year-old Swedish center half because he can go up and give her coffee and joke around with her and I can't.

When he comes back down, he's grinning and it annoys me even more. "Get your kit on and get out on the ice," I tell him. "You missed some simple passes last night."

The smile melts from his face. "Sorry. I didn't…" He shakes his head. "What passes?"

I pinch my nose with my finger and thumb. "It doesn't matter."

"No, seriously, what passes? Should I look at the recording first?" He's so earnest and I feel even worse.

He's a good kid. He doesn't deserve me taking my annoyance out on him. "It's okay. You just need to spend a little less time in the offices and a little more time practicing."

"Sorry. I was just giving Mac some advice about her clothes."

When did he start calling her Mac? And why would she ask for his sartorial advice? It's not as though he's some kind of fashion icon. He wears sweats and hoodies to the rink every day.

"She has a date," Goran adds, as though he can read my thoughts. "She wanted to know which dress looked the best."

My brows pull in tight. "A date with who?" I ask him.

He shrugs. "Some guy."

"Did she try the clothes on in front of you?"

"No." He looks at me as though I'm an idiot. "She held them up. They're both pretty."

I open my mouth to ask for more information. And then I close it pretty fucking fast. It's none of my business. What do I care if she's going out with another guy? She's a free agent, she can do what she likes.

"Did she say where she's going on this date?" I ask Goran.

He makes a face that tells me he has no idea. "I only want to know that she'll be safe," I tell him. The same way I'd want to know that about anybody in the backroom.

"Yeah." He nods. "I should have asked her."

"It doesn't matter," I tell him. "Just go get on the ice," I tell him. "I'll be out in a minute." The others are already out there warming up.

"Sure." He flashes me a smile. The kid has the whitest teeth I've ever seen. "You doing okay, boss?"

"I'm absolutely fine." I tell him. "I just want you to connect with every pass you get."

————

MACKENZIE

I'm already regretting agreeing to this date. I replied to all five messages after talking to Rachel. Two of them didn't reply back – maybe I pissed them off that I didn't respond right away – and two of them didn't seem that interested in meeting up at all.

The fifth – Andrew Casinger – is a lawyer, working for a firm in the center of Morgantown. He's suggested we meet up for dinner at a bar around the corner from his office.

I look at my watch then head into the bathroom to check that my hair and makeup are still okay. They are, which isn't any surprise since it's only twenty minutes since I did them, but still.

I'm nervous. And I'm also enjoying dressing up for once. It's a strange combination.

It's almost seven-thirty by the time I head down the stairs to the staff entrance. I hear talking in the locker room so I walk on by, but then I hear my name being called.

Goran jogs to catch up with me. "You look great," he tells me. "I knew that red dress would work."

I'd been trying to decide between this one and a little black dress when he came in with my coffee this morning. Since I'd promised Eli I'd make it clear to Goran that I wasn't interested I didn't think it would do any harm to tell him about my date and get some clothing advice at the same time.

And he was actually helpful. The red dress works better.

It's more casual which works for a mid-week date. It's made of soft jersey and wraps around my body, tying at the side and then flaring down to my knees. I've teamed it with some strappy heels and for once I have my hair down.

"Thanks for your help with it." I felt better once I got a second opinion, especially as Rachel wasn't answering her phone.

"Any time." He shifts his feet. "Ah, did you tell somebody where you're going?"

My brows pinch. "I told you," I say.

Goran shakes his head, and his golden hair shakes with him. "I mean where you'll be. In case anything happens on your date."

I'm still bemused. "In case what happens?"

"I don't know." He grimaces. "Eli just said that I should have asked."

"Eli said you should ask me?" I blink. "Why?"

"He wants you to be safe."

Color me confused. "How does Eli know about my date?"

"I told him." Goran looks down at his sneakers. They're the popular ones with the white soles that all the athletes are wearing. "Was that wrong?"

"No, it's fine." There's a weird prickly feeling on my neck though. I reach back and touch it, half expecting it to be damp with sweat. I'm trying to decide if I'm annoyed he knows about the date or if I'm annoyed he hasn't said anything about it.

I'm not sure which one is true.

"I'm going to Wine and Dine," I say. Because actually he's right. It's a good idea that somebody knows where I'll be. I should message Rachel, too. Goran's a lovely kid but he could definitely forget if he doesn't write it down.

"I know you are. But where will you be doing it?" he asks.

I laugh. "That's the name of the place I'm going to. Wine and Dine on the corner of Laurel and Krepps."

"Oh." His eyes widen. "It's a name and a description. Cool."

"Yep. Let's hope they make good food, too." I give him a wave. "I should go before I'm late." Who am I kidding, I'm already late. I don't want to be the one sitting at the table waiting for my date to arrive. "Have a good evening."

"You too."

I'm almost at the door to the parking lot when I see Eli stalking down the hallway looking like a man on a mission. He's wearing gray sweatpants and a Mavericks t-shirt that clings to his chest showing every ridge of muscle. His eyes catch mine and sweep down and I immediately blush because he's looking at my dress. It's tight, probably too tight, but I haven't been on a date in months. Okay, years. And I wanted to feel good.

"Going somewhere nice?" he asks. There's a tic in his cheek.

He knows I'm going on a date. Goran told me that. But if I say anything he'll know that I know and...

This is way too complicated and I don't have time.

"To meet a friend."

"Hmm."

It's stupid because I want him to tell me I look pretty. Part of me even wants him to beg me not to go, because there's still this weird pull between us I can't name. But he doesn't. He just stares at me for a moment too long.

"You should probably put a jacket on. It's getting cooler out there."

I lift a brow. "It'd ruin the line of my dress."

And he's looking at my body.

Again.

And I'm blushing.

Again.

This is stupid. I'm going to be even later.

"Have a good evening." I reach for the door knowing I'm

making the right decision. This thing between me and the coach has to stop. We work together. More than that, I work for his boss.

My career always comes first.

"Mackenzie?"

Surprised that he's still there, I look over my shoulder at him. "Yes?"

"I'll be here until late," he says. "If you get into any trouble, call me."

"I won't get into any trouble."

A ghost of a smile passes his lips. "Yeah, well just in case. You have my number, right?"

I nod, because I have everybody's number.

"Good." He nods, his eyes narrow for a moment as he looks at me. I don't break his stare because... well, I don't want to appear weak.

His lips twitch again before he turns away and stalks his way back up the hallway, and I pull the door open, trying to ignore the way my heart is speeding in my chest.

———

ELI

I spend the next hour alone on the ice, slamming puck after puck into the net to wear off the energy that's driving me mad.

The rink is covered in shaved ice. I'm going to have to call the rink manager to come in early. But I still can't stop because I'm pissed with myself for caring that she's out with somebody else.

Which is stupid. I made it clear to her I'm not interested. That I regretted what happened between us that night outside the locker room. But I didn't expect to feel this fucking annoyance at her taking me at my word and meeting up with another guy.

I whack the puck toward the goal one more time. It hits the net, and the goal shakes for a moment. Then I let out a sigh because this is all messed up.

I should follow Mackenzie's lead. Go out. Find somebody who doesn't want to be lonely tonight. Bury myself in them until every emotion is numb.

But I don't want just anybody. For some stupid reason every time I touch myself it's *her* that I see. That I smell. I've touched myself, imagining what it would feel like to make her come on my tongue. To keep doing it until she's wrung out and as empty as I am.

Okay. That's it. I'm officially messed up. And I'm going home. I skate over to remove the goal because it's the least I can do to make our rink keeper's life easier tomorrow morning when he has to clean up the ice. Then I step over the boards and take off my skates, sitting on a bench to pull on my shoes.

It's only then that I feel a weird sensation. A prickle on the back of my neck. I reach up to rub it, and then I turn my head to see that she's there.

In that fucking dress. Her hair curling down around her shoulders instead of up in that bun she always wears. She's standing in the center of the tunnel, her heels in her hands as though her feet hurt from wearing them, her legs bare and glistening in the harsh light radiating from the overhead strip.

"Hey." I stand, confused because she's supposed to be in a wine bar. Pleased because she's not.

Scrap that. I'm fucking jubilant.

"Hey you," she says. Then she starts to cry.

CHAPTER
TEN

MACKENZIE

"I'm not crying because I'm upset, I'm crying because I'm mad." It's mostly true. I'm also mortified and disbelieving but the overwhelming emotion is dry.

"Okay," he says, looking at me carefully. He's wearing sweats and a t-shirt which is plastered to his chest. His hair is damp from perspiration. He balances his hockey stick against the board and gives me his full attention.

"Why are men such assholes?" I ask him, wiping my cheeks with the back of my hand. It comes back sheared with mascara. Ugh, I must look a distressed state in my messed-up makeup and try-hard dress.

"What did he do to you?" he asks, his voice thick with some kind of emotion I can't quite fathom.

"It's not like that," I say quickly. "He didn't hurt me." Well other than my feelings. But that's bad enough. "He just wasn't who he said he was."

"Who was he then?"

"An asshole," I growl and the faintest of smiles pulls at his lips. And I feel this need to unload on the only other person in this building who seems to get me.

We're like the two grown ups constantly marshalling the kids around. There's a kinship in that. The loneliness I've been feeling pulls at my chest.

"It was a blind date," I tell him. "Through an app."

I expect him to tease me but he doesn't blink an eyelid.

"With a lawyer. Or at least that's what I thought." I clear my throat because the embarrassment is starting to wash over me. "I'm doing it for a friend. Her boyfriend designed the app. It's for… ah… older people."

"Older people?" His brows knit. "Why are you using it then?"

I want to hug the guy. "Allison, my friend, doesn't know many people over thirty. So I agreed to beta test it."

He says nothing, but it feels good to talk. Yes, I could call Rachel but I want to talk to a real live person. I want to get it all out and feel better.

"So I arranged to meet this guy – Andrew Casinger – at the wine bar. Except when I walked in there was only a young guy waiting in there."

"How young?" He looks interested now.

"I'm not sure. Twenty-five tops."

Eli lifts a brow.

"So I'm about to leave and this guy – the young one – comes up to me and says my name. So I assume maybe he works for Andrew or something and is there to tell me that he can't make it."

"But he didn't?" Eli guesses.

I shake my head. "He insisted on buying me a drink and then told me he was using the app to find older women who might invest in his business."

"What kind of business?" Eli asks. I can't tell if he's amused or not.

"Another app." The irony isn't lost on me. "He's developing something to do with the medical field. I don't know, I kind of tuned it out."

"Why's he using a dating app to find investors?" Eli runs his hand through his hair, his biceps bulging at the movement.

"Because the dating app is targeted at older women. And apparently they have the kind of money he wants. And he thinks he can charm it out of them."

"He's catfishing for money?" Eli's mouth drops open. "Jesus."

"And I fell for it." I feel stupid. Embarrassed. And yeah, a little bit like I'm over the hill. "Hook, line, and sinker." I put my hand on my face. "I'm such an idiot."

Gently, Eli pulls my hand away. "No you're not. You were doing your friend a favor, that's all." He's still holding my hand. "Tell me you made him pay for your drink at least."

For the first time I laugh. "I didn't even get that far. I just shouted at him and left."

"Good." His eyes are warm. He finally lets go of my hand. "Did you get this guy's real name?"

I nod. "Ben Dickson. Why?"

"Because I'm going to rip his fucking head off."

I laugh again. And it feels good. "No, you're not."

"Okay, his balls."

"I'm not sure he has any. Anyway, he's just some stupid kid."

"He's twenty-five. He knows better."

"Everybody at work told me it gets like this. The older you are, the harder it is to find somebody to date. But I didn't listen." I was too busy working. The last time I really dated – when I was thirty-three, before our three years of over-working on a project began – I hadn't noticed this phenomenon.

Is it something that suddenly happens the day you turn thirty-five? Why did nobody tell me?

"Look, there are assholes everywhere. I bet you met a few of them when you were in your twenties."

He's right, I did. The memory of one particular asshole rushes into my mind.

"Were you an asshole back then?" I ask him, really hoping he wasn't.

"I tried not to be. My exes would probably tell you otherwise."

I tip my head. "And now? Are you an asshole to women now?"

The corner of his lip quirks. "I still try not to be. But again, you'd need to ask the women I've dated."

"Are there a lot of them?" There's a weird ringing in my ears. High pitched. Like a siren.

"Women I've dated?"

"Yeah." The need to know tugs at me. Eli's brows knit and I take a moment to enjoy looking at him.

Because Eli Salinger is a handsome man. Dark hair, dark eyes, a lightly bearded jawline you could crack eggs on. And that's when I realize that of course there are a lot of women he's dated.

He must fight them off.

"A few. I haven't dated since I left Boston, though."

"Why not?"

He shrugs. "Haven't wanted to."

"I know a superb dating app you could try."

He laughs and there's that frisson of excitement again. I feel it curl around me like a chiffon blanket. Soft. Teasing. Enticing.

"I'm more of a long term kind of guy," he says softly.

My heart is hammering against my chest. "So you don't usually go around dropping to your knees in front of women then?" I keep my voice light. Teasing.

Because I'm afraid. There is a weird vibe between us. My heart is hammering against my chest.

I want this man and it's not right.

"No. Just with you."

I want you to do it again. That thought hangs in the air like a flashing neon sign between us. Can he read it? Does he know what I'm thinking?

His eyes turn even darker. I think he does.

"You look beautiful in that dress, Mackenzie."

His words feel like seduction. Praise has always been my weakness. I didn't get enough as a child. Textbook Freud.

Doesn't stop my skin from tingling though.

"I wish I hadn't worn it," I tell him. Because I do. I'm embarrassed that I made the effort for a guy who only saw me as a dollar sign.

"I'm glad you did."

My heart is galloping now. Like a racehorse desperate to win. "He offered to have sex with me." There's the last confession. I didn't tell him that before. It was just too mortifying. "When I said I'd dressed up for him he said we could have sex if I wanted."

"If you wanted…" Eli repeats my words. He looks like he's about to explode.

"I guess in return for… payment."

"Don't go there, Mackenzie," Eli says. "This is on him, not you. It's not a reflection of who you are, or of your attractiveness. Because you're fucking beautiful."

His words are like honey, making every part of me feel soft. Sugary.

Is this why I came here? For Eli to make me feel better? To make me feel wanted? Honestly, I'm not sure. I could have driven home. I could have gone to another bar and drowned my sorrows.

Instead, I drove right here and looked for him everywhere until I found him on the ice.

Hitting the puck into the goal like he was on a mission.

Not wearing a helmet or padding. Just this man and his body, perfectly aligned with the hockey stick he was holding.

"The other night. When you were between my thighs, when you breathed me in," I say, my voice husky. "I liked it."

CHAPTER
ELEVEN

ELI

We're standing by the boards on the edge of the rink, but there's only the two of us here, nobody else. Once we leave I'll call security and they'll lock up and patrol the way they do every night.

But for now, we're alone.

I smell of sweat. I wasn't wearing padding when I was doing my anger management version of hockey, but I'd still worked up a lot of heat by slamming the puck into the goal.

But all I can think about is this woman in front of me. The one I've been fantasizing about since I felt her thighs against my cheeks.

The one who's telling me she liked it when I did it.

Her cheeks are flaming. I can tell she's embarrassed at admitting it. And I don't want her to be embarrassed. I want her to say it again.

"Ignore that," she says instead. "I'm tired and I'm feeling old and rejected and—"

"You're not old," I say, because it's a scientific fact.

That earns me a smile.

"And he didn't reject you," I point out. "He's an asshole. A predator who thinks the world owes him everything he wants." I've met a few of those myself. My voice softens as I take in her bright red cheeks.

So I put myself out there. "For what it's worth, I liked it too. You smelled amazing."

Her voice lifts an octave. "That's not true. Guys hate the way women smell."

Where the hell has she been getting this information? "No, they don't."

Two adorable lines form between her brows. "Yeah, they do. There's a reason why guys won't go down on a woman unless she's freshly showered."

My eyes narrow. I'm torn between amusement because she looks so serious about this and annoyance because honestly, she has a terrible guy radar. Why does she find it so hard to believe the lies but not the truth? "You've been talking to the wrong guys. A real man wants to smell the real you. Not the sanitized version." Don't get me wrong, I'm all for hygiene. And upkeep. As long as it applies to both sides.

And I've been thinking about how good she smelled for weeks. And it has nothing to do with her damn shower gel.

She's still looking at me like she doesn't believe me. And I hate being called a liar. An asshole, okay. Moody bastard. Fine.

Liar? No way.

"There's nothing dirty about smelling like a woman," I tell her. My voice is lower now. Thicker. "It's every man's fucking fantasy."

You're every man's fantasy. That's what I want to say. But I don't. Because this push pull thing is making me be careful. I'm not going to overstep any marks or go where she doesn't want to lead me.

She opens her lips then closes them again. I get a flashback to how soft they were when we kissed.

Then she shivers. And no wonder. She's wearing that red dress with nothing on her arms and we're standing in an ice rink with an ambient temperature of around forty degrees Fahrenheit.

"Come here," I say, holding out my arms. I expect her to shake her head and remind me that we're colleagues and that isn't happening.

Or even better, to remind me that I promised her nothing would happen between us again.

But she doesn't. She steps forward, her teeth chattering as her face rests against my chest. I wrap my arms around her until the shuddering stops

"I'm kind of sweaty," I tell her as she relaxes into me.

"Every woman's fantasy," she says, her voice muffled by my chest.

I laugh, and she laughs too, tipping her head until her eyes lock with mine. My heart is hammering against my chest. I'm reminded of that familiarity again. Why do I recognize those eyes? It feels like the answer is at the edge of my consciousness.

It's annoying me.

The atmosphere between us has twisted again. Yes, I'm still sporting a semi-hard-on but this is softer. More like comfort. More like friends.

I like that, too.

"Tech bros are assholes," she says. I grin because yeah, I've met a few who've wanted investment or endorsement and that's the feeling I got, too.

"They are," I agree. "And when you get home, I want you to let your friend know, so they kick him off the app."

"Don't worry, I will."

"And then I want you to delete the app."

Her brows lift. "Why would I do that? I promised my friend I'd beta test it for her."

"And you have. Job done," I point out. "Why would you put yourself through that again?"

She stiffens in my arms. "Because maybe I want to make a connection. It's almost impossible in New York and it's even more impossible here. Tonight's the first time I've been out to dinner since I got here."

"You didn't get to dinner," I point out, and it doesn't seem to help.

She huffs and steps back from my hold. Then she huffs again, but this time, I think, because she's realizing how cold it is.

"No I didn't," she says, looking hurt. "And I want to. I really want to. I want somebody to take me to dinner. And not because I might invest in their stupid business idea, or even because they think I might put out on the first date. I want them to do it because they like me. Because they want to spend time with me. Because they know they'll have a good time doing it."

There's something about her voice that makes my chest ache. "I get that."

"Do you?" She blinks, sounding almost hopeful.

I nod my head. "Yeah, I do. I was the same, when I was playing for the Razors. You have no idea how hard it is to find somebody who's actually interested in you, the person, not you the hockey player. Somebody who wants to hear what you think, not just take selfies and post them to Instagram because it might boost their profile."

She runs her tongue along her bottom lip. "Did you get that a lot?"

"Yeah. And I guess at first it's fun. In your twenties when you don't want to settle down and you think you're gonna rule the world."

"And now?"

I give her a half smile. "Now it's not fun. And it doesn't happen as much anymore. As much as I love the Mavericks, they don't have the same effect as an NHL team."

She gives a little laugh. "You're losing your touch."

"So it would seem."

Her hair shines beneath the bright lights of the arena. Her eyes are bright, her lips and chin pink from the cold.

The cold. She needs to get out of here.

"Come on, let's go," I say, inclining my head at the tunnel. "You're cold."

"I'm fine."

"No you're not."

"You have this annoying habit of thinking you know me better than I do," she complains.

"I don't know you better," I tell her, hustling her away from the rink. "I know bodies better. And they don't react well to hypothermia."

"I won't catch hypothermia in here. It's not even freezing." She frowns. "Why is that? How does the ice freeze when the air is above freezing?"

I push down a smile. Does she know how fucking adorable she is? "The air is cooler near the surface of the ice," I tell her, relieved because we've made it to the tunnel and the air is much warmer in here. "The ice temperature is below freezing. About twenty-four degrees. Wait here," I tell her and run into the locker room. The door – as fucking always – almost whips my ass it's so eager to close.

I walk over to my locker and grab one of the three clean hoodies stashed in there. When I turn to walk back out to the tunnel, I jump like a damn kangaroo because she followed me inside.

I've never seen anybody look so out of place in a locker room. She's put her shoes back on and is standing in the center of the painted M.

"You've mastered the door," I say softly.

Her lips quirk. "I'm a quick learner." She glances at the hoodie in my hands. "I guess you're cold too, huh?"

"This is for you." I hold it out. She looks at it strangely.

"It's too big for me."

"I know. But it's this or you freeze. Lift your arms up."

By some fucking miracle she does as she's told and I slide the hoodie over her head, all too aware of the irony that I'm putting more clothes on this woman that I've fantasized about nearly every night.

If my brothers were here, they'd laugh their asses off.

"You know you have to undress a woman to have sex, right?"

Yes, dickwads, I know. But right now she doesn't need me to seduce her. She needs to warm up.

She needs somebody to be kind to her.

I thought I was lonely here, but it's different. I have family, I have friends. When I'm really bored, I have the team to hang out with.

She has nothing. And I hate that. I hate that she's alone.

I don't want her to be.

I realize that's weird. That maybe I need to stop thinking about this stuff. But then I look at her in my hoodie and blood rushes fast through my veins.

She looks swamped. Her dark hair is fluffed from me pulling the sweater over her head. Her cheeks are still pink, her lips still full.

And for a moment she's looking up at me like I'm some kind of God.

I want to fuck her. And then I want to talk to her. All night. I'm not sure which I want the most right now.

My cock hardens as if it's trying to help me decide.

I'm way beyond that high school need to mark a woman with my clothing. And yet I'm imagining scooping her up and taking her home.

Seeing her wearing nothing but that hoodie.

Then I'd lift her onto my kitchen counter and bury my

head between her thighs until she's calling out my name while wearing my hoodie.

"Thank you," she says. "This is lovely."

"You're welcome," I grunt, putting the dirty thoughts out of my mind.

"I'll bring it back tomorrow," she promises, as though that's the problem here.

I shake my head. "Keep it."

She lifts the hood to her face. "It smells like you," she says, smiling.

It's like I'm in the middle of a game. Every synapse in my body fires up. I'm in fight-or-flight mode. I'm in 'lift this woman up and fuck her against the wall' mode.

I'm a neanderthal. A fucking geriatric caveman.

"Are you sure you're okay with me having it?" she asks. I must be grimacing again.

"What age did cavemen die?" I don't realize I've said it out loud until she replies.

"I'm not sure. Early thirties, maybe?" Her nose scrunches up as she thinks. "Why?"

"That would make a fifteen-year-old middle-aged."

She looks amused. "Imagine going through puberty and a mid-life crisis all at once."

I laugh, but I'm still on edge. Mid-life crisis, is that what this is? Just a simple reaction to getting older. My body's feeling it and it wants to fuck whatever it can.

Nope. Just this woman. All the time.

That voice sounds exactly like my brother, Liam. I hate that.

I blow out a mouthful of air. "I want to take you out for dinner."

"Now?" She blinks. "Isn't it a little late?"

She didn't say no. "Not now. Tomorrow. Next week. You name the day. I want to take you out."

Her voice is soft. "That isn't a good idea. We work together."

"So we won't do it on work time."

"You have a game next week."

"And I'm free every other night."

It's her turn to breathe out. "I'm not allowed to fraternize with clients. My company frowns on it."

"Would you say yes otherwise?" I ask her.

She gives the slightest of nods.

"Then we'll make it a business meeting. Talk boring work all night. Thread count of towels. Whether Goran's driving you crazy or making you happy bringing you coffee every day. You choose the topic, I'm good with that."

There's that smile again. I want to press my mouth against it. See if it tastes as good as I remember. "And after?" she asks.

"I'll drive you home."

"And then what?"

"I'll make sure you've gotten in safely and I'll turn my car around and drive myself home."

Her eyes flicker. She looks almost... disappointed? "It's still not a good idea."

"You still didn't say no."

"I'll think about it," she tells me. I notice her pull the the fabric of the hoodie close to her nose again.

Weird how much I like that.

"You do that."

She's still smiling. And so am I. Our eyes are locked like we can't move them. She takes a step forward and presses her lips against my cheek. "Thank you for cheering me up," she whispers.

I close my eyes and breathe her in. She's warm and soft and smells like sheets on a summer day.

"Did you just sniff me?" she asks.

"You keep sniffing my hoodie. It's only fair."

"Do I smell good?" Her voice is light.

I inhale her again. "Like you wouldn't believe."

She kisses me again. This time on the corner of my mouth. It's like she's trying to see how far she can push me before I break.

It takes every ounce of self-control I have not to turn my head, to take control of the kiss. To push her against the wall and let her know how she affects me.

But I don't want to do this the wrong way. I already regret pushing things too far that first night. Not because I don't want her but because I do.

So no, I'm not going to kiss her. Even though I'm almost certain that's what she wants right now. I stroke her hair then step back, and this time when our eyes catch her gaze is hazy. A little dazed. It dips down to my chest and back up again.

"I'm still thinking," she whispers.

I give her a grin. "Good."

CHAPTER
TWELVE

MACKENZIE

"We're going to have an exhibition game," my dad says through the phone line. I blink at the clock beside my bed. It's six a.m. and I was dead to the world when my phone started blaring incessantly. I'd answered it thinking there was something wrong with Gramps. While I'm here, I'm the first point of contact for the nursing home.

"A what?" I croak, trying to blink the sleep out of my eyes.

"To raise money for the IRS. We'll have a big exhibition game. Charge premium for the seats. An all-stars versus the Mavericks game. It'll be fantastic."

I sit up in my bed, my sleep-heavy mind reminding me it's a Saturday morning. The one day I let myself sleep in until I wake up naturally. Which is usually by nine, anyway. I have yoga at eleven and this afternoon I need to do some grocery shopping and drop in on Gramps for dinner.

It's been two days since Eli asked me out on a date and I haven't seen him since. The Mavericks had an away game and I was kind of thankful for that.

I need time to think.

The truth is, I'm attracted to Eli. But I also know it's a very, very bad idea to get involved with somebody at work. The fact that he's a hockey player makes it worse.

Ex-hockey player. *Whatever*.

But really, I want to say yes to his offer. I want to spend time with him. I want him to touch me. I can't stop thinking about him.

It wouldn't be forever, anyway. I'm leaving for New York as soon as Gramps' IRS matter is settled. And he's clearly here for the long term.

Would it be so wrong to have a fling?

"So that's great, right?"

I blink. I'd forgotten about Dad. "Um, you cut out for a minute there. Can you tell me again?"

"I said I've already got a team in mind for the All-Stars side. I have connections, so we'll make sure the best come to Morgantown. We'll sell it out in no time."

"We're in the middle of the season," I tell him. "We can't fit that kind of game in between our fixtures."

"We'll do it during Bye Week."

Every team gets a week off mid-season. "Most of the team will want to go home then," I tell him. It's their one chance to decompress during a hugely over scheduled season.

My dad sighs, letting me know I'm annoying him. "I know the owner. We'll make it work."

"We don't have the staff to do this," I warn him. I know I'm being a Negative Nancy but the kind of event he wants to put on is huge. "To deal with ticket sales and publicity and then to man the arena." We're small fry compared to the NHL. We don't have the steward and security that those big guys have.

"I've got that covered."

"How?"

"The production company is going to do all that."

"The production company?" I say slowly, my skin prickling. "What production company?"

"I, ah, they're interested in making a documentary. About me and your mom and the family business." He gives a little high-pitched laugh. "Skating, I mean."

"It's going to be filmed?" Alarm washes through me. There's no way this team or this arena is fit for public consumption. "Is that a good idea?"

"It'll mean all the profits we make go straight to Gramps' IRS bill."

I let out a long breath. I hate to admit that staging an exhibition match is a good idea. But it is. Better than any I've had. It could actually come close to paying the government off in one lump sum, especially if filming rights are involved.

But somewhere along the line I've become a little protective of this team. I don't want them to be used for publicity. I've had too much experience of how it can go wrong.

"Let me talk to Gramps when I see him today."

"Sure." He doesn't sound at all perturbed. "He'll be fine with it."

Yeah, he will. But I still need to get my head around it. It's one thing having my parents be famous while they're over in L.A. But to have them where I work? That's something different.

Especially since the team has no idea I'm related to them.

So now I have two things to think about. Eli's offer of a date and my dad's plan to invade Morgantown. And somehow they feel linked in my brain.

———

ELI

. . .

"You haven't charmed this woman into bed yet?" Liam asks. "You're losing your touch."

"I don't have a touch," I tell him, placing my golf ball on the tee. Myles – my eldest brother – has decided the three of us need to spend some time together now that I'm living closer to him and Liam. So we're playing a round of golf at Liam's club just outside of Charleston.

Myles is already in a bad mood. He's currently trying – and failing – to hit his ball out of a sand trap. I don't know why he decided playing golf with us was a good idea, because he's spectacularly bad at it.

I've got a pretty good handicap. Golf was one of the few pastimes we were insured to play during the NHL season, so I'd have a round most weeks when I was living in Boston. And Liam's spent half his life on one course or another making business deals.

Myles, on the other hand, has spent way too much time staring at a computer screen.

"Yeah you do," Liam says. "There was a time when I never saw you without a woman."

"In my twenties," I tell him. "And you were no better."

"Who was no better?" Myles asks. He's finally hit his ball onto the fairway. We all climb into the golf cart and head toward it.

"Liam," I tell him. "Remember his little black book?"

"I remember you asked if you could have it after I started dating Sophie," Liam retorts.

"I was joking." I really was. I never have and never will be interested in my brother's ex-girlfriends.

"Yeah, well it wasn't a book, anyway. I just had a lot of friends." Liam's jaw is tight. He taps his fingers on the wheel as he drives. We drew straws to see who would drive, and I'm still kind of annoyed that Liam won.

That's the problem with being one of six brothers. The competition is intense. As kids we'd fight about anything. It used to drive our mom crazy. And our dad, when he actually had time to spend with us.

Myles ended up inventing the Salinger Olympics so we could compete against each other for real every summer at our dad's estate in Virginia. An organized way for us all to beat the hell out of each other.

"Anyway, stop changing the subject. Why haven't you gotten this woman to fall for you yet?"

"What woman?" Myles frowns.

"If you'd hit your ball onto the green occasionally you'd know," Liam tells him. "Eli's falling for a woman."

"I didn't say I was falling for her. I said I liked her."

"You gave her your hoodie."

Myles turns around from the seat next to Liam and lifts a brow. "You gave her your hoodie? That's awesome!" He says it in a Californian accent, as though we're all at middle school.

I put my hands up in exasperation. I knew I shouldn't have said anything. "She was cold and I had a sweatshirt she could wear. We're not fifteen, it meant nothing."

"Yeah," Liam says. "It's not like he gave her his sperm." He draws that last word out, making Myles wince.

"You make it sound like a sordid transaction," he mutters. "Ava and I are married."

"But you weren't when you first gave her your little tadpoles," Liam grins. He's enjoying himself. He's never happier than when he's riling our oldest brother.

"I was in love with her. She wanted a baby." Myles gives him a pointed look.

It's a long story, but Myles and his wife met at work. And at first they hated each other, but somehow Myles found out that Ava was trying for a baby alone and offered to help. Between donations they fell in love.

"I'm not in love with Mackenzie," I say.

Liam stops the cart abruptly.

"Then why are you chasing her? You're forty-years-old, aren't you getting tired of no-strings sex."

I groan because that's not what I meant. "I like her," I tell him. "And I want to get to know her better."

"And you want to bone her." Liam smirks.

"Can we go to the green now?" I ask him. "I'd like to be out of here before dark."

"Myles needs to get out of the cart first," Liam says.

"Why do I need to get out?" Myles asks. *Is he pouting?*

"Because your ball is there," Liam says, pointing at the fairway. "And ours is on the green. So go hit your ball and we'll see you there."

"I'm not walking to the green," Myles says. "Wait for me here."

"Didn't you hear what Eli said? He wants to get out of here before the sun sets. If we wait around for you it'll be tomorrow by the time we're done."

Myles reaches over him, muttering to himself as he grabs a wedge from his golf bag and stomps to his ball.

I miss Holden. He's the peacemaker in our family. He'd have butted their heads together by now.

Liam whistles as we watch Myles look at the ball and then at the green. "He's gonna take all day," he says. "Just to piss me off."

"Are you two this bad at work?" I ask him. They run a company together in Charleston, and I can only imagine the way they must bitch at each other in the boardroom. I feel sorry for the staff they've recruited to work for them.

"Nope. We save it for when we're with you."

"Gee, thanks," I say. I love these guys but I want to be at home. Or at the arena. I idly wonder what Mackenzie is doing.

Liam gets out of the cart and stretches his arms up, letting out a groan. "You know where I should be right now?" he asks me.

"Where?"

"In bed with my damn wife."

I glance at my watch. "It's the middle of the afternoon."

"Exactly. Nothing better than Saturday afternoon sex."

I wrinkle my nose. I don't need to know about their between the sheets activities. "Can you stop?"

"Nope. She's too beautiful." He has the grin of a man who's made all the right choices in life. "And I'm gonna say something to you now, but you can't tell Myles."

"I hate secrets," I remind him.

"It's not a secret. I just don't want him butting in. This is between us. Man to man." He points at his chest then mine.

"You'd better hurry up then." We watch as Myles swings the club high above his shoulder, then stops mid-movement. He takes a step back and inspects the grass. He's slower than a snail in molasses. "Okay, scratch that," I say, trying not to sigh. "Take your time."

Liam's face turns serious. He rolls his shoulders then looks me in the eye, clearing his throat. "There comes a moment in, a man's life when he has to stop messing around." He frowns and shakes his head. "Actually no. When he *wants* to stop messing around. When he meets the woman he knows he can't live without. And I don't know if this woman is it for you, or if it'll be somebody else, but she's out there. And you need to be ready."

This might be the most bizarre conversation I've had with Liam to date. "Um, okay."

"I mean it. If she's it, don't give up. You need to woo her until she's yours."

"What if she doesn't want to be wooed?" I ask him, thinking about my conversation with Mackenzie the other night. "What if she doesn't even want to go to dinner with you because she thinks it might cause problems with her job?"

Liam whistles again. Long and low. "Oh, that's a Myles question."

"Myles," Liam calls out just as he swings again. His wedge hits the ball awkwardly, sending it flying out to the left, toward the trees.

"For fuck's sake," Myles shouts. "I'm sick of this game."

"Tell you what," Liam says. "Get back in here and we'll pretend you hit it on the green."

I look at him and Liam shrugs. Then we both smile because it's actually nice to find something Myles isn't good at.

"Eli's girl works with him and isn't sure it's a good idea for them to date," Liam says as Myles climbs in next to him. He doesn't bother trying to find his errant ball.

Myles looks over his shoulder at me again. "Are you going to let that stop you?"

"No."

"Good." Myles nods.

And it's weird but also a relief to say it out loud. I know that she's worried but I don't think it's that big of a deal if I take her out to dinner. Or do more. I'll just run it past Wayne first, since it's his team.

In fact, I'll do it on the way home. Because I want this woman and I won't let anything stop me.

I've spent my life competing in order to get what I want. If I have to compete with her job, I will.

"Now, can we finish this round so I can get the hell out of here?"

CHAPTER
THIRTEEN

MACKENZIE

Gramps' nursing home is really lovely. Fifty older residents are housed in a low-level sprawling building surrounded by lush gardens where they're encouraged to either walk or be pushed around each day, admiring the late blooming pink coneflowers that are planted along the wheelchair friendly paths.

When I enter the lobby to sign in, I'm greeted by the receptionist, who knows me by name now. "Hey, Mackenzie," she calls out. "Your grandpa's in the sunroom." She lifts a brow. "He's in an excellent mood."

"Has my dad called him today?" I ask her, trying to work out if he's been told about Dad's grand idea.

"Yes, how did you know?"

"Just a lucky guess."

I find Gramps sitting at a table, staring at the sports pages of the newspaper. He has his glasses on and his walker is next to his seat. He hates it, but he can't move around without it or a wheelchair yet.

"Hi," I say, sitting down in the chair opposite his. "I brought you some treats." He asked for Tootsie Rolls of all things, so I bought a bag of them, along with some cookies he loves from the local bakery. "I'll put them in the kitchen when I leave."

"No, leave them with me," Gramps says, his voice raspy. "People steal things from the kitchen."

"They do?"

"Yep. I took somebody's cheese sandwich from there the other day."

I try not to laugh. "How are you feeling?"

"Like I want to go home."

"You can't yet," I say lightly. "There's no way you can deal with the stairs."

"I don't like my bed here. And the nurses keep treating me like I'm old."

I press my lips together.

"Don't laugh," he says. "I'm not so old that I can't wipe my own ass."

Eeek. Way too much information.

"I got your afternoon cup of tea for you, Wayne," the nurse says, sliding a cup and saucer in front of Gramps.

"Thank you, sweetheart," he says, smiling at her. I swear she blushes. My dad got his charm from his dad. They both know how to sweet talk anybody.

"Any time." She smiles at him and walks away.

"Stop looking at her ass," I whisper as his eyes follow her every move.

"I can't help it. There's nothing else to do." Then he tips his head to the side, as though remembering something. "So your dad called, We're gonna put on a show."

"An exhibition match," I correct.

"Whatever. Great news, huh?" He's grinning now. "We get to raise some money and put the team on the map, too." He looks at his walker. "And now I have a deadline to get up and about. I want to be there in person to watch the game."

"You should talk to Eli about it," I tell him. "Decide if the Mavericks are up to playing another game. It's a busy season for them."

"Of course they're up for it," he says. "They're young and hungry. Giving them a chance to play against some hockey legends is going to make them even hungrier."

"Do you think they're ready?" I ask. "What if it's completely one sided?"

He looks at me as though I'm an idiot.

"We need the money, Mackenzie. That's why you're here."

He's right. It's the only reason I'm here. I don't care about the team. Or at least I'm not supposed to. But I've seen how hard Eli's worked with them. I know how much they want to succeed. I don't want them to sacrifice everything just to pay off the IRS.

Gramps picks up his cup and puts it to his mouth, still looking at me. Except he's not, his eyes are trained over my shoulder. He winks and blows a kiss and I don't have to turn around to assume that his favorite nurse is behind me, still serving people drinks.

How is it that my eighty-eight-year-old grandfather can flirt without embarrassment yet I'm finding it impossible to say yes to a date with Eli?

It's annoying. I seem to have skipped the gene for that the same way I skipped the gene for being able to stand up straight on an ice rink.

———

ELI

. . .

The parking lot is almost full when I pull into the Sunnyside Nursing Home. It's not my first trip – I've been coming once a week since they discharged Wayne from the hospital. He likes me to catch him up on all the team gossip, and he's actually great at talking through plays and strategies.

He's seen and done everything. Nothing phases him at all.

"Hello," the receptionist says, smiling brightly. "He's in the sunroom. His granddaughter is with him."

"His granddaughter?" I thought all his family was in L.A. "Did she fly in today?"

"I don't think so." The receptionist frowns. "She's been coming regularly."

That's weird. Because Wayne told me his granddaughter is doing some *Ice Stars* show on the television. Either way it's nice for Wayne. I put on my best smile as I walk into the sunroom and look around the room. It's full of guests and their visitors – Saturday afternoon must be the most popular time to visit.

And then I see *her*. And everything fits into place. Mackenzie Hunter isn't just some woman from New York. She's Wayne's granddaughter.

Of course she is. It's those damn eyes. They're the same as Wayne's.

Why would she lie about something like that? Didn't she know it would come out eventually?

Her back is to me. Her dark hair is down again, the same way it was the other night. There's a wave to it, and it's shiny like she just washed it.

And it's like I can feel it in my hands. The silkiness sliding through my fingertips. The same way I remember how soft her lips were. How good she smelled.

Any time in the past few weeks she could have told me the truth. Especially the other night when I asked her out for dinner.

But she lied.

I reach the table and she still doesn't seem to know I'm here. Wayne's noticed me though, because he's smiling and lifting his brows.

She turns around slowly. Slow enough for me to actually enjoy the anticipation. Her pretty hazel eyes meet mine and I have to force myself not to react.

"Eli," Wayne says. "Have you met my..." he trails off. "You know Mackenzie from work, of course."

"Your granddaughter," I say and Mackenzie winces. "Yeah, we've met."

———

MACKENZIE

Eli's jaw is tight. There's a tic in it, too. He also looks really good in a dark blue polo shirt and a pair of chinos. They're completely different to his usual clothes, but I like them.

I take a deep breath and smile at him. He doesn't smile back.

"Can I borrow Mackenzie for a minute?" he asks Gramps, who's still distracted by the nurse.

"Sure." Gramps shrugs.

"I was leaving anyway," I say, standing. "We can talk on my way out." I lean over and kiss Gramps then hand him the bag of goodies. "Don't eat them all at once."

Eli doesn't say a word but I can feel him following behind me as I push through the doors to the reception area. The woman behind the desk waves at me and I smile back, but my heart is hammering against my ribcage.

The air is cool when I step outside and my jacket is way too thin to keep out the chill.

I turn to look at Eli, putting my arms around my waist to keep warm.

"Why are you never dressed for the weather?" Eli asks, looking genuinely perplexed. "You live in New York. It's cold there. You must have coats and sweaters."

It's the strangest question, yet it's completely Eli. "I don't like the winter."

"You think by not wearing a coat you're gonna stop it from coming?" he asks. "Like King Canute and the tide?"

"No. I just…" This conversation is futile and I'm not sure where it's going, so I sigh. "I'll wear a coat next time."

"Good." He shrugs off his jacket and holds it out to me. "I only have so many fucking clothes I'm willing to give up." He's only wearing that distracting polo shirt beneath it, and it's freezing out here. I can't take it from him so I shake my head.

"Put it on, Mackenzie." His voice is low. He's annoyed with me.

"No."

His brow crinkles as though I'm the first person to say that word to him. "Put. It. On."

"What am I, your kid? You can't talk to me like that." And I know it's not about the coat. Even so, he's pissing me off. Just shout so we can be done with this, okay?

He lifts his hands up in what looks like frustration. "Just put the coat on so I can talk to you." He pauses. "Please." He sounds beseeching now, and I'm feeling sorry for him.

"That's all I needed," I mutter, taking it from him and sliding my arms through it. Like his hoodie, it's ridiculously large on me, but the warmth is enticing.

"I know what your thinking, and I didn't lie. I just didn't tell the truth."

He gives me one of *those* looks. A tip-his-head to the side, eyebrows lifted kind of stare. "Didn't you trust me with the truth?"

Oh. He's *hurt*. And I don't like that one bit. In fact, my heart does a weird clenching thing. "Nobody at the Mavericks knows," I tell him. "Almost nobody outside of the Mavericks knows either."

"So I'm nobody now?"

I open my mouth and close it again. I have no idea what to say to that.

"I get it." He steps back. "I understand. You're not interested." He rakes his fingers through his hair, and his polo shirt lifts enough to expose a sliver of his stomach.

"I'm a fucking idiot," he says, shaking his head. "I'm sorry for bothering you. It won't happen again."

My mouth drops open as he turns and walks away. That hammering of my heart against my chest feels like a full on assault now, it's so fast I'm finding it hard to breathe.

"Eli!" I call out. Okay, it's more of a scream. *Whatever*. It does the trick because he stops walking and turns to look at me. And I realize I actually need to say something now other than scream his name.

I take a deep breath, all too aware of his eyes scrutinizing my face.

"I hate people knowing who I am because they treat me differently," I tell him, having to shout because he's half way across the lot. "And when they know my name, they Google me, and the stuff that comes up…" I trail off. I don't want him to look at me differently. I don't want him to see me as Wayne's granddaughter or Greg's daughter or – even worse – the woman who exposed her uncovered nether regions to the nation.

He walks back toward me, reaching out, his hand touching my face. It's so tender it makes my heart ache even more. His brows are pulled tight, his gaze intense.

And I'm overwhelmed by his closeness. And scared. Of getting hurt by this man who seems to be my friend. Who wants to be more. But being scared isn't getting me anywhere. It's just hurting him, too.

"And the thing is, I am interested," I whisper. "Really interested."

Breath escapes his lips as he lowers his brow to touch mine. I can feel the flicker of his eyelashes as he blinks.

"But I'm leaving as soon as this job is over," I tell him. "This thing between us, whatever it is, could only be short term."

"Just for now." He nods. "Okay."

"Okay?"

"Yeah, I'll take that."

I inhale sharply. I don't know whether I'm pleased he's being so amenable or annoyed that he's not fighting for more. But I don't want to play games. I want to be real.

I'm so sick of hiding away.

"I need you to do three things though," I tell him. "Before we do anything else."

His fingers caress my jaw. "What?"

"First, I want you to Google me." My chest hurts at the thought of it, but it's necessary. If he's annoyed that I kept my family name from him, he'd go crazy about this. "And second, I want you to promise not to tell anybody who I really am."

"Why would I tell anybody?" he asks me. "It's not my story to tell."

I don't answer him. He'll find out soon enough. Taking a deep breath, I look straight at him. "And thirdly, I don't want anyone to know about this. Us, I mean. I don't want us to be subjected to stupid gossip."

"You want me to be your secret?"

"No. I just want to keep it separate from work. I like you, Eli. I like spending time with you." A hint of a smile curls my lips. "And I enjoy wearing your clothes. A lot."

He laughs.

"But I've learned the hard way that dating in public is difficult for women. We get judged in a way men don't.

There's a reason I've never dated at work." My eyes catch his. "And a reason we're not allowed to sleep with clients."

"I'm not your client."

"But you work for him."

"I work for your grandpa."

"Is that any better?" I ask him.

He smiles. "Not really. Because if he finds out what I've been thinking about doing to you he's gonna kick my ass."

"What have you been thinking?" I ask him.

"Dirty, dirty thoughts."

My face heats. So do other parts of my body. I want to hear those thoughts so badly. I want him to play them out on my body, the way he plays hockey on the ice. Strong, sure, always on target.

"Can you do those three things for me?" I ask him with a whisper.

"Yeah, I can." He runs his hand down my back, pushes it up beneath his coat.

"And do you need me to do anything for you?"

He's drawing circles on my spine.

"I can think of a few things." His lips twitch. "But no, I don't need anything. I'm a what you see is what you get kind of guy. No secrets, no issues. Just a huge need to throw you over my shoulder and carry you back to my place."

He's smiling now. And I am, too. A little shiver wracks down my spine.

"Thank you," I whisper. And I mean it. He's the first man that's listened to my feelings today and not ridden completely over them.

I'm starting to think he's the real deal.

CHAPTER
FOURTEEN

ELI

I've always been a sucker for discipline. In my career, following the rules can make the difference between scoring the winning goal and being benched for a game. Sure, I make mistakes sometimes. Get a little heated, have a little scrap on the ice.

But there's a reason for my longevity as a hockey player. I've always kept my head in the game.

So when I agreed to Mackenzie's three requests I meant it. The only problem is, I don't have time to think about them because I get a panic call from Myles whose babysitter hasn't turned up.

"Can't Liam help?" I ask.

"Liam's otherwise engaged."

"How about Sophie?" Liam and his wife are Charlie's godparents. She adores my nephew. I can't see her giving up a chance to take care of him for a few hours.

"She's also otherwise engaged."

Ah. I remember Liam's plans for Saturday afternoon. I guess they've stretched into the evening.

"It'll take me an hour to get to your place," I point out.

"That's fine. I'll change our reservations," Myles says. "Please, Eli. I wouldn't ask you if I wasn't desperate."

There are so many replies I could make to that. But I like Myles and I love Charlie. And Ava's near the top of my favorite people list.

"Do you need me to stay overnight?"

"Oh god, no," Myles blurts. "Two hours max. We'll go out for dinner and then you can make yourself scarce. Charlie will sleep the whole time. I'll make sure he's down before we go."

"Okay," I say. "But you owe me."

"Of course I do," Myles says smoothly. "And I promise. Charlie won't cause you any problems at all."

———

An hour and a half later, Charlie is causing problems.

Okay, not problems exactly. But as soon as Myles and Ava are out of the door, he's crying. I go in to see him, looking cute as hell in his little sleep suit, his toddler face red from screaming.

"Hey bud," I whisper. "What's up?"

He reaches his hands out for me and I lift him up. His little arms curl around my neck.

"I see monsters," he sobs.

"Your dad's gone out."

He doesn't get the joke. Just keeps sobbing against my neck. I rub his back and murmur softly to him, telling him there's nothing to be afraid of.

I don't have a lot of experience with kids. Sure, I help coach some older ones with the help of Goran, but the little versions, the ones who believe in monsters, I'm not sure how to handle them.

"You want a drink?" I ask him.

He shakes his head.

"Something to eat?"

That gets his interest. "Yes."

"What do you want?"

His face crumples in concentration. Damn, he looks like Myles sometimes. "Pasta."

I try not to laugh. "I meant a snack, buddy. Dinner time is over."

"Want pasta."

Damn, I walked right into that one. "How about a cookie?" I suggest. Because I know Ava has those. I might have helped myself to a few.

But there are at least two left in the packet.

Charlie nods and I carry him to the kitchen, putting him on the counter with a warning not to move. He takes my instruction seriously, sitting as still as a statue while I pull the almost-empty cookie jar from the cupboard.

"Okay, so here's the thing," I tell him. "If I give this to you, we don't mention it again. Uncle and nephew rules, okay?"

He nods, still looking serious.

"Because your mom will give me a lecture about not giving you cookies at nighttime."

He nods again.

"And your dad will..." Ah, Myles will do nothing. I decide to stop talking and give the kid a cookie.

He takes his time eating it. I never noticed what tiny teeth he had before. They're like a chipmunk's, nibbling around the edges, his tongue licking the crumbs from his lips.

About ten hours later he finishes it and I carry him back to bed.

"Story?" he asks.

"It's late. You need to sleep."

"Story. Please."

And damn if I don't cave. I pull some picture book from his shelf and sit next to his crib, reading it out loud.

By the time I've finished, he's asleep again. His eyelids so delicate I can see blue veins crossing them. He also has crumbs on his lips, but it's too late to hide the evidence now. If I brush at them I'll wake him up, so I'll just have to hope he licks them away in his sleep.

Tiptoeing out of the room, I pull the door gently shut then walk over to the couch. I'm tired. I got up at stupid o'clock this morning to meet Myles and Liam for golf. And then I drove over to tell Wayne that I want to date his consultant, only to find out she's his damn granddaughter.

And then she told me she was interested, too.

I let my head fall back on the cushions, thinking about the way she looked today. She has this dignity, this strength. But she's also vulnerable. When I was holding her today there was this look in her eyes that made me want her more.

This tenderness, this ache. I felt it, too.

And you made a promise.

I reach for my phone. There's no time like the present to keep it. Sliding my thumb across the screen I open up Safari and type her name into the search box.

The first result is her LinkedIn profile. She has this kick-ass profile picture that's somewhere between a schoolteacher and a movie star. I linger on it a bit too long before I scroll down to her experience. She went to high school in L.A., followed by college in New York, as she told me. Straight into a job at Warner Power, where she's been climbing the ranks ever since.

She has an MBA. She's intelligent, I knew that much. More so than me and I like it.

Reluctantly closing LinkedIn, I look through the other

results. Her social media is locked down tight, if she has it at all. I'll have to ask her. The rest of the links are articles about how she transformed companies, how she volunteers at the local women's shelter, all stuff that makes her look better than ever.

And to be honest, there isn't that much. She seemed so intent on me Googling her and I have no idea why. That's when I remember she's Greg's daughter. So I delete the search and type *Mackenzie Gauthier* into the box.

The first few results are websites for Wayne and Greg. It's an unusual name and they get all the top hits.

But then I scroll down and there are some older links. Like the stone age of the internet.

Most of the hits are from a video. I click on the first one and it takes me to some old-looking website. It hasn't been updated in years, but it reminds me a bit of MySpace. The video is at the top and there are about a billion comments below, but I don't bother reading them before I click on the little play symbol and the video loads.

A girl appears on the screen. It takes me a moment to realize it's Mackenzie. She's standing by the boards of an ice rink which I recognize right away. It's home to the L.A. Kings. I haven't played there a lot – I've always been in the Eastern divisions – but I'd know it anywhere.

The seats are absolutely full. The game must be over because there are only a few people in the middle of the rink, like there's some kind of prize giving going on. There's a voice blasting through the speakers but the sound is distorted and I can't make out what they're saying, but then I see Mackenzie start to skate onto the rink.

Okay, you couldn't really describe what she's doing as skating. It's more of a walk-slide – panic thing. But that doesn't matter. What matters is that she only takes a couple of steps out before she does an amazing slip, her legs flying up into the air, her skirt flying out, her body landing with a thump on the frozen rink.

The camera zooms in. Really, really close. Whoever did this must have been using professional equipment because I don't remember phones having great cameras back then.

My chest tightens as I realize why the camera is so intent on zooming in on her legs. Her skirt is over her waist. Baring all.

She's not wearing panties. Christ.

I quickly close the video and try to ignore the sick feeling in the pit of my stomach. Instead, I scroll down to see more results. So many gossip pages, so many forums. Are they all talking about Mackenzie? My stomach twists.

How can I not remember this? The results are from 2007. What was I doing then? I frown, trying to think. I was twenty-four. Mackenzie must have been twenty.

Then it comes to me. I was playing in Sweden that year. On a loan from the Razors. The gossip didn't make it over the Atlantic.

I turn my phone off. I've seen enough. No wonder she changed her name. No wonder she doesn't want people associating her with her family. One Google search and you'd know her intimately.

And now all I can think about was the way she looked at me when she asked me to do three things.

Like she expected to scare me away.

MACKENZIE

On the way home from visiting Gramps, I picked up a bottle of wine and an enormous bar of chocolate and I've been steadily demolishing them both throughout the night. As soon as I got into the apartment, I showered and changed into my pajamas – and yeah, I put Eli's hoodie on, too.

It's warm and it's comfortable and I need all the comfort I can get.

I told him to Google me. Which means he'll see that video.

He'll probably read all the comments, too. And find out that I was supposed to skate onto the ice with the rest of my family to congratulate my dad on getting an award. I hadn't wanted to do it. But he'd wanted us all there, and I was twenty years old. I felt I was old enough to skate over to meet him.

The lack of panties thing was something else entirely. Unknown to my parents, I was dating a hockey player a few years older than me. He'd asked me to go bare for him because it was sexy, and being the idiot I was, I did it.

It doesn't matter that it was almost sixteen years ago. Or that I'm a grown woman who's built a career she loves. When I think of that video, I'm back there in that arena, wanting the guy to love me.

Wanting my family to love me, too.

But instead I had to deal with having my face, and other parts, splashed all over the internet. Not to mention those damn magazines you used to get at the front of the aisle.

Mostly, I don't think about it anymore. It's in the past, where it needs to stay. But now and then I see the video getting shared again.

It's low level gossip. We're not the Kardashians and it's not a sex-tape. But it still mortifies me. And if people find out at work, they'll look at me differently.

Maybe Eli will, too.

I pour another glass of wine and swallow a big mouthful, telling myself that everything's going to be okay. If Eli's put off by the video, then this wasn't supposed to be.

So why does my chest hurt? Why do I want to throw myself on my bed and let the comforter muffle my screams?

The door buzzes, and I glance at my watch. It's almost eleven. I walk to the intercom to see a grainy image of Eli Salinger on the video screen. And my heart does a little leap.

"Hi," I mumble. Because I can only assume he's here about the video.

"Can I come up?" he asks through the speaker.

It must be raining outside. His hair is wet and so is his jacket and I know he's here to tell me that it's too much. He doesn't want me anymore.

I press the button to open the door. "I'm on the second floor."

By the time I slide open all the locks and check my hair in the mirror to make sure it's not sticking out ten different ways, he's here. I open the door and he's standing there, his eyes soft as they meet mine.

He's definitely seen it. He knows. I wrap my arms around my waist, ready to get it over with and get back to my chocolate.

I should have bought more wine.

"Nice hoodie," he says.

I look down at my ridiculous attire. I'm wearing short pajamas because my legs always get overheated in bed. But my feet don't so they're clad in fluffy socks. On top is his hoodie and although my hair is neat, it's tied back in a high ponytail like I'm trying out for a role in *Grease*.

"Come in." I step aside. "Can I get you a towel?"

He rubs his wet hair. "It's fine. It only just started when I got out of the car." He looks at my coffee table. Half-drunk wine and half-eaten chocolates. I must look like a loser.

I take a deep breath. "Okay then, hit me with it."

"With what?"

"You've seen the video, right?"

He nods.

I curl my fingers into my palms, ready for the brush off. "There are jokes. Viral ones. *Ice beavers invading the rink* have been mentioned," I tell him. "*Beavertown looks colder than I remember* is another. I think that one made Letterman."

"Mac…"

The way he says my name is like a caress.

"You know the worst ones though?" I ask, not waiting for an answer. "All the people that accused me of having some kind of relationship with my dad because I fell over and bared it all. That made me feel sick."

He says nothing. Just looks at me. I feel raw and exposed.

"I don't usually go around showing my body off. My boyfriend told me it would be hot." I blink. "Actually, I don't think he was *technically* my boyfriend. I thought he was then, but he wasn't." There's no point in explaining it. It was a long time ago and I was stupidly naïve. Just stupid, actually.

But I've grown up and moved on. Mostly.

Eli's lips part. He breathes out. Still saying nothing.

So I keep on rambling. "I guess I'm lucky it happened then. Before Twitter and Instagram were a thing. Before people went viral in a matter of seconds." I try to smile but my cheeks won't play ball. "Anyway, so now you know. I'm an idiot who can't skate for shit and everybody knows what I look like with no clothes on."

"You were wearing clothes."

I will not cry. Not over something that's old history.

"And I don't know what you look like," he tells me.

"Of course you do. You saw the video."

"When I realized what was happening, I turned it off. I barely saw anything."

"Why?" I don't understand.

"Because if you want me to see you, you'll show me. I don't get off watching somebody get humiliated."

"You really didn't watch it all?" I ask, my voice small.

Because there were some pretty intense close up shots. *The Hair of Beavertown.* That was another favorite.

He shakes his head. "Nope."

There's a little spark of hope in my heart. And a feeling that Eli is a good, good man. A man I want to wrap my body around.

And that's when I launch myself at him.

CHAPTER
FIFTEEN

ELI

She lands in my arms, her legs curling around my hips. Her hands cup my face, her palms warm on my bearded jaw.

"You didn't look," she says again, as though it's some kind of miracle and not the normal reaction of a grown man who respects the hell out of the woman he's been pursuing.

"That's what good guys do," I tell her. "They don't look."

"Where can I find one of those?" She sounds like she's teasing. Her poise is recovered – or as much as it can be when I'm holding her up against me.

My poise, however, is on a hair trigger. Her chest is pressed against mine. She smells of flowers and me, with that hoodie covering most of her body. Her legs are smooth as they wrap even tighter around me and I grasp them to keep her from sliding down.

"I'm gonna kiss you now," I tell her, just in case she wants to escape.

"Yes, please."

Our eyes catch and we're both grinning like loons. I'm not sure who laughs first, but suddenly we're both almost doubling over. It takes all the strength I have not to drop her, and I'm glad I don't because she looks glorious, her head tipped back, her eyes pleading.

To prevent the kind of injury that could put me out of action for months, I carry her over to the sofa and sit. Mackenzie wiggles until she's straddling my thighs.

The laughter abates. The grins don't. We stare at each other and somehow it feels more intimate than a kiss. I reach out and stroke that silky hair I keep fantasizing about. Then I curl my fingers around it and yank until her head is tipped back and her neck is exposed to me.

Her chest hitches. She likes it a little rough then. I do, too. Not all out pain but a little edge.

I lean forward and scrape my lips and teeth against her neck. Then I lick, feeling her pulse against my tongue.

Fuck, I'm hard as steel.

I slide my hand beneath the hoodie she's wearing, feeling the warmth of her skin leaching through her cotton top. My palm caresses her waist as I kiss my way up her throat, along her jaw, to her parted lips.

Her eyes are already hazy. Her breath fast. "I'm really going to kiss you this time," I warn.

She laughs again. It's an aphrodisiac. I want to make this girl laugh as she comes. I want to make her laugh over breakfast in the morning and while she brushes her teeth at night.

I push that thought out of my mind and concentrate on her lips. My mouth claims them, my hand sliding under her pajama top, my palm pressing against her bare skin. The kiss is hot and hard, her body squirming against mine as she curls her arms around my neck. It's like we can't get close enough to each other. We lick and kiss and touch and grind but it's still not enough.

The hoodie comes off, revealing a gray tank that does nothing to hide her sweet breasts and her hard nipples.

"It's winter," I mutter. "Most people wear flannel."

She scrapes her nails against my neck, where my hair meets skin. It feels so damn good I want to let out a purr. "I get hot in bed."

"You're about to get hotter."

"Shut up and kiss me again, Salinger." I like the way my name sounds on her lips. Way too much.

So I do exactly what she asks. Taking my time, kissing the corner of her lips, the soft center, before sliding my tongue against hers. This time when she grinds against me it's slow and deep. I want to take my clothes off. I want to feel her skin against mine. Somewhere, deep inside of me there's the teenage Eli who wanted everything *now*.

But I also want to savor her like a fine whiskey that's at its very best. I kiss her neck again, her shoulder, dragging my tongue over the swell of her breasts. Then I push the straps down, exposing them to me.

"You're beautiful," I mutter, taking them into my hands. She's a damn work of art. Her breasts are heavy against my palms, her nipples tight as I run the pad of my thumb over them. She lets out a deep groan and I like that, too.

I like everything about this woman. Her squirms are getting desperate, hard against me. Then she reaches down, her fingers stumbling as she unfastens the button on my fly, then pushes her hand down inside my shorts.

Her fingers curl, her palm caresses. My eyes roll into the back of my head. She kisses my neck the same way I kissed hers. Hard and fast and with teeth.

It's my turn to groan.

"Eli," she whispers frantically, lifting her gaze to mine.

"Yes?"

"I'm too old to get off on your thighs on a sofa. Take me to bed."

Before the last word is out of her mouth, I'm standing, holding her against me, walking over to what I think is the door to her bedroom.

It's not. It's the laundry room. *Shit.*

"The next one," she whispers in my ear, trying not to laugh. "And you can put me down if I'm too heavy."

"You're not too heavy."

"Yes I am."

"You're not. And even if you were I'm not putting you down. I'm too old to fall into that trap."

"What trap?" she asks innocently, trying not to smile. I let out a victory grunt as I find the right room and stride over to the bed, throwing her onto the mattress.

"The weight trap."

"There's a weight trap?" Her eyes widen with interest. And I feel like I'm walking right into said trap without even thinking.

I clear my throat. "There's a media trap that makes women think that they have to weigh a certain amount or look a certain way to be desirable. Which is fucking nuts." I curl my hands around her thighs, pulling her toward me. I'm still standing at the end of the bed, but as soon as her knees hit my waist I drop to my own, pulling her shorts off on my way down.

She sits up, leaning back on her elbows. "What are you doing?"

"What do you think?"

"I… Oh…" Her breath catches as I bury my face between her legs. The last time I breathed her in layers separated us.

This time it's pure, unhindered Mackenzie. And it's amazing.

"Are you smelling me?"

"Shut up." I slide my tongue against her and it seems to do the trick. She stops asking questions and lets out a long, soft moan.

She tastes even better than she smells. I devour her, licking her to the edge, teasing her with the bend of my fingers, coaxing out her pleasure. She's so tight against me, her breath stuttering, her body undulating, and then she lets out a loud cry as she soars.

It's glorious.

Her eyes meet mine as I slowly bring her back down from her high, kissing her thigh, her hip, wanting to kiss every part of her. I can still taste her on my tongue.

"Come here." Her voice is raspy. I do as I'm told, climbing up over her, kissing her lips this time.

She slides her fingers through my hair, kissing me back like she can't ever get enough. Her body arches off the bed to get closer. Then she pulls my shorts down and that's when I remember.

"I don't have anything." *Goddamn it.*

She blinks. "But you're a hockey player."

I lift a brow. "I didn't come here thinking something was going to happen. Please tell me you have some?" I pray to the God of contraception that she does. But she shakes her head and I think I might cry.

"It's okay," I tell her. "This was enough."

"I have an IUD," she whispers. "And I'm clean."

I say nothing, because I've never gone bareback. And there's nothing I want more right now. But this is her choice. I can't influence her. She's taking more risks than I am.

"It's okay, we don't have to," she whispers, taking my silence for rejection in a way only she can. "I'll just touch you."

"I want to," I tell her. "I'm clean, too." I fist myself, drag the head against her. Her eyes widen and she looks down.

"Oh."

"What?"

"It's been a while."

"Yeah. I've not exactly been painting the town red either," I tell her.

"No, you don't understand. I mean a *long* while."

I blink. "How long?"

"Three years." She looks down again. "Be gentle."

I nod, cupping her jaw with my palm. "I won't hurt you," I whisper, because it feels like this conversation is about more than just sex.

There's a depth to her gaze that makes me want to carry her away and protect her forever. She's never looked more vulnerable or more beautiful. I kiss her lips, her cheek, the tip of her nose. "I'll never hurt you," I tell her.

And I mean it. She's a strong woman. I know she doesn't need my protection. She doesn't need my promises, either.

But I want to give them, anyway.

She slides her hand between us, curling her fingers over mine. With the gentlest of movements she pulls me against her until I'm nudging at her entrance.

She's warm and she's wet and I have to take a minute to center myself. I'm forty years old. Coming before I even enter her isn't an option.

"Okay?" I ask her.

"More than okay." She nods.

I slide inside of her slowly until she's full of me. I take a breath to let her get used to me, but also for me to get used to her.

I'm going to come so fast it's not going to be funny.

I drag my hips back, reaching between us, circling her with my finger until she groans. Her legs wrap around me, pulling me back in, and our mouths clash as my hips find the rhythm they need. She pulls my bottom lip between her teeth and bites softly.

"Harder," she whispers. "Please."

This woman is going to kill me. She's the perfect mix of polite and dirty.

Still, I do as I'm told, like I'm a slave to Mackenzie Hunter, moving inside of her until our bodies clash. Her fingers dig into me, her nails sharp and delightful. Every nerve ending in my body is on fire.

"Eli," she whispers, and my name on her lips is like an aphrodisiac. I'm not going to last long here.

"I'm so close."

"Good," I grunt. Because I'm on a damn hairtrigger here.

And then her head tips back and she calls out my name, her body convulsing around me. It's as good as I thought it would be.

Better than anything I've ever felt.

"I'm gonna come," I rasp, trying to pull out. But she clings to me harder.

"Do it inside me."

And I do, inside this woman who already owns me and doesn't know it. I collapse on top of her, bracing my weight with my arms because I don't want to crush her.

I come and I come, my breath ragged. She drags her nails down my back and I hope she's marked me.

And when I slowly float down from the high, my eyes catch hers. I check that she's okay, that she's still breathing.

Our lips brush and my chest feels so tight I'm wondering if I'm about to have a heart attack.

"So good," I mutter against her lips. "You're killing me."

"I died first."

I slowly pull out of her, aware of her stickiness, the mess I left behind. I kiss her again and roll out of bed.

"Are you going?"

I sit on the mattress and look at her. "What?"

"Are you leaving?"

Is she serious? Who hurt this woman?

"No. I'm going to find something to clean you up with." I look at the door on the far side of her bedroom. "Is that your bathroom?"

She nods.

"Stay here. I'll be right back."

On the shelves where her towels are stacked I find a wash-cloth and put it under the faucet, wetting it with warm water. I take it back to her, along with a towel, and slowly wipe away the pleasure I just left.

"Why would you ask me if I'm leaving?" I dry her with the towel. She has the prettiest pussy. I want to kiss it again.

"I just thought…" She shakes her head. "It doesn't matter."

"What did you think?"

"That maybe you didn't enjoy it."

"You felt me come, didn't you?" I ask her. "You heard me roar like a fucking lion. What part of that makes you think I didn't enjoy it?"

Her cheeks are red. "I don't know."

"Has somebody left you right after sex before?"

She nods. And I'm feeling like an animal again, but in all the wrong ways. She's so vulnerable right now. And the last thing she needs is to see how pissed I am. Because I know she'll think it's because of her.

And it isn't. It's because of all the assholes who've made her feel less than she is.

Who haven't appreciated what they have.

The irony of it is, if they'd appreciated her she wouldn't be here. They would have snapped her up and kept her with them, the same way I want to.

"I don't want to leave," I tell her. "Right now, I'm wondering how sore you are and how long I need to wait before I can bury my face between your legs again."

I take her hand and put it on me. Her eyes widen when she feels how hard I am.

"I'm not twenty anymore," I tell her. "I'm not supposed to get hard right again after sex, but that's what you do to me."

She runs her tongue along her bottom lip. "I'm not that

sore," she whispers, sending a tremor of anticipation right through me.

I push it away.

"I can wait." I smile at her. But before I can roll over and pull her into my arms she's scooting down, and I close my eyes as she takes me to heaven again.

CHAPTER
SIXTEEN

MACKENZIE

Eli is still next to me when the glow of the clock on the bedside table tells me it's almost three in the morning. After I made him see heaven with my mouth he collapsed against the pillows, pulling me against him as he crashed into sleep.

I dozed, too. But now I'm awake and staring at his pretty face.

He looks young when he sleeps. Like there's not a care to etch lines on his face. His eyes flutter and his lips part to let him breathe but he barely moves.

My gaze continues down to his chest. I look at the smattering of hair across his muscles and it makes me want to kiss him.

So I do. I kiss the skin stretched across his defined pectoral muscles, breathing him in like he does to me.

And yeah, it's intoxicating.

He has these tight, masculine nipples that I already know are overly sensitive. I sucked them after I sucked him and I swear he purred like a cat. I touch one with the tip of my tongue and even though he's asleep, he lets out a groan.

Then I pull at it with my teeth and he slides his fingers into my hair. I guess he's awake.

I look up at him. "Hey."

"Hey." The warmth in his voice is like a blanket. "You okay?"

"Yep." I smile at him. "Just wanted to see how sensitive your body is."

He scratches my scalp with his short fingertips. "Everything about me is sensitive where you're concerned. What time is it?"

"Just after three."

He blinks. Long languid sweeps of his lashes make me realize he's only half awake. "It's okay. You can go back to sleep. I'll just amuse myself with your nipples."

His chest rumbles with laughter. He pulls me up against him. "You need sleep, too," he points out.

I lay my head on his chest, curling against him. He strokes my hair and I can't lie, I let out a little purr. "I'm not sleepy," I tell him. It's the truth. So many thoughts are whirring around my mind right now. And if I'm being truly honest, I want to enjoy laying here in his arms.

Eli Salinger gives good hugs. It's a revelation. I never knew how starved I was of human contact. Yes, I have friends who hug me, and yes, I love them to bits.

But this skin against skin? When did I last feel this? It should be available on prescription. Eli could rent himself daily to do this.

No, he shouldn't. I don't want him holding anybody else like he's holding me.

I blink. Because I shouldn't be thinking that. This is strictly for now. In a few months I'll be going back to New York and Eli will be here.

"What are you thinking about?" he murmurs. "Your muscles have all tightened up."

"Did Gramps tell you about the exhibition game?" I ask him, even though that's not what's on my mind right now.

"Yeah." He strokes my back, his finger tracing a line down my spine. "The team will be stoked."

"Do you think it's a good idea?" I lift my head up. "Your schedule is already tight and the team is stretched thin."

His fingers reach the base of my spine, caressing the myriad of nerve endings all bundled there. I arch my back and he chuckles.

"You're worried about the team's fitness?" he asks.

"I don't know. I just…" I trail off. "I guess I'm weirded out by the fact my family will be here along with TV cameras." I look up at him. His eyes are soft, still sleepy. He looks so contented. "I guess you're used to the cameras."

He shrugs. "When I'm playing hockey I don't even think about them. Don't think about anything except getting the puck in the goal."

"That's because you're good at it," I tell him.

That earns me a smile. "Well, thank you."

It must be so nice to glide across the ice without giving a damn. Without feeling like you're constantly going to fall on your ass.

"You're doing it again," he murmurs.

"What?"

"Over thinking."

I bite down a smile. "It's a bad habit."

"What are you thinking about now?" he asks me.

This time I'm completely honest. "That it must be nice to enjoy skating."

Eli tips his head to the side. "I don't really think about that, either. Like I don't think about walking."

"You'd think about walking if you fell over every time your feet hit the concrete."

"Is that what you think when you see the ice?"

"Pretty much." I trace the hard curve of his bicep. "Or really, I think about how to avoid going anywhere near it." I lift a brow. "Now that you know who my family is, you probably think I'm a changeling."

He looks pensive. "I know your dad, of course. Who doesn't? And I've played against your brothers a few times."

I grimace. "Sorry." They're famous for being assholes on the ice.

"They're good kids."

And it's weird, but I like that he likes them. Brad and Johnny are my closest siblings. With mom and dad so busy all the time, and Isabella being at practice any time she wasn't at school, I felt like their stand-in-mom.

His fingers have made their way back up my spine. He kneads the muscles just above my shoulder blades and I groan.

"You need to relax," he whispers. "So much tension."

"This is me relaxed," I say and he laughs again, before sliding his hands down to my waist and hitching me up.

"What are you doing?" I ask, surprised by the sudden jerk of his palms.

"Helping you relax. Move up here. Sit on my face."

"Eli!" My eyes widen. Nobody's ever asked me to do that before and I'm embarrassed.

"I'm serious," he tells me. "Sit on it. I'm gonna make you come and then you're gonna let whatever thoughts you have going on disappear so you can curl up in my arms to sleep."

"I'll squash you," I protest.

He quirks a brow. "You're not gonna squash me." His hands curl around my hips and damn if he doesn't practically lift me over his chest. I squeal and scoot on my legs until my knees are on either side of his biceps.

I look down at him. His eyes are dark. "I'm hungry," he tells me. "Now get your ass up here."

Though I'm embarrassed, I do as I'm told, reaching for the top of my headboard as he lets out a long groan.

"I'm never gonna get bored with the way you smell."

If I felt exposed with him kneeling in front of me earlier, it's nothing compared to this. I'm straddling his head, his fingers digging into my thighs to steady me, as he slowly slides his tongue along my neediest part. And he's right, all thoughts about ice and failure fly out of my head. All I can think about is his tongue, his fingers, the way his beard feels against my thighs.

He makes me feel safe and alive. Like I could do anything and he wouldn't judge me. I've never felt like that before.

It's just me and this stupidly attractive hockey player, who's fisting himself as he devours me, letting out groans like I'm the best meal he's ever eaten.

I close my eyes, bracing myself against the headboard and let out my own aching groan, embarrassment forgotten as he teases me until I'm screaming.

This man is going to be the death of me.

———

MACKENZIE

"Why did you take the dating app off your phone?" Rachel asks. It's Monday morning and I'm drinking my Goran-delivered coffee, trying not to wince because I'm kind of tender down there.

No wonder. I spent most of yesterday in bed with Eli. Every time we talked about getting up we ended up having sex again.

My lady parts have been seriously overworked.

"Who told you?" I ask her.

"I overheard Allison on the phone to her boyfriend. She's

promised him she'll find some other sucker to test it. Anyway, stop changing the subject. Was it your date that put you off?"

"Kind of."

"What do you mean *kind of*? What else would make you do that—" She trails off. "Oh. My. God. Have you been seeing somebody without telling me?"

"No." I shift in my chair.

"Is it that delicious Swede who brings you coffee?"

"Goran? No." I frown. "I'm nearly old enough to be his mom."

"That shouldn't stop you. Who else then? Wait. Eli Salinger?"

How did she get there so fast? Maybe it's the distinct lack of men my age in the local region. "Maybe," I concede.

"EEEEK!" Her cry makes me wince. "You and the coach?"

"Please tell me nobody in the office heard that."

"I'm not in the office," she tells me. "I'm walking out of the coffee shop onto the sidewalk. Nobody can hear me. Well, nobody from work anyway. The donut guy just gave me a funny look though." There's a slurping sound. "Anyway, don't change the subject. I need all the details. Right now."

"What details?" I ask her. "It was one night." And a day. But she doesn't need to know that.

"Was he good?"

I roll my eyes. "Um, yeah."

She lets out a groan. "Talking to you is like getting blood from a stone. I need enthusiasm here. Marks out of ten. That kind of thing. My dry spell has been as long as yours. I need to live vicariously through you."

I check that the door to my office is closed. This isn't the kind of conversation I want anybody to hear.

Not even the donut guy.

"He didn't watch the whole video," I tell her.

"What?"

"I told him before we could do anything he needed to

watch the video of me on the ice. He started watching it then stopped when he realized what had happened."

"You told him to watch a video of your coochie?" Rachel asks. "Why would you do that? Some kind of weird foreplay?"

"No. I wanted him to know what he was getting into. That I have history. If it ever comes out, he should know in advance."

She sniggers.

"Not like that. You have a dirty mind."

"Oh honey, I'm not the one who's been making the beast with two backs with a hottie hockey player." She clears her throat. "So was it good?"

I take a breath. "Yes."

She squeals again. Louder this time. I send out a silent apology to the people of Manhattan. "I knew it. He's a hockey player. They're notorious for being the best kind of lovers."

"My dad's a hockey player," I point out, feeling icky. "And my brothers."

"Except them," she adds quickly. "They're crap."

"I don't know if that's any better."

She lets out a sigh. "We're getting off track here. Fuck your family – not literally because eww – can we get back to Eli Salinger?"

"Why do you keep saying his whole name?" I ask her. "It sounds weird."

"Because he's Eli Salinger," she whispers. "There are fan sites devoted to him."

"What kind of fan sites?" I ask, because I haven't actually Googled him. Maybe I should.

But then I'd be as bad as all the people who watched my video, wouldn't I?

"Ones that Photoshop his head onto naked bodies."

I wrinkle my nose. I'm definitely not looking now. "Why would they do that?"

"Because most women don't get to see his naked body in real life. Is it awesome? Is he buff?" She lets out a laugh. "Of course he is. Do you think he'd mind if you took a picture and sent it to me?"

"I'd mind," I tell her. "So no."

"I was just kidding. Ask Goran to do it instead."

"Shut up." There's a beep on my phone, and I've never been happier to hear it. "I've got to go. There's another call coming in." It's actually an Instant Message. The alert sounds are different, but Rachel doesn't need to know that.

"Just draw me an approximation," she says quickly. "In fact, don't bother. I'm going to search for hockey porn."

"Goodbye, Rachel," I say dryly, ending the call. I pull the phone back to see the message, a stupidly big smile pulling at my lips when I see the author.

Meet me in the locker room at seven tonight. – Eli

It's stupid how happy that small message makes me.

And then I remind myself not to get too excited. This is just a casual thing. That's what I wanted, isn't it?

What if I'm busy? – Mackenzie

Three little dots appear on the screen. He's typing back.

Are you busy? – Eli

. . .

I mean, no. And he almost certainly knows that. I just like teasing him. It feels good. Normal.

This flirting makes me feel like a woman.

Not really. I just read that a woman shouldn't make herself too available to a guy. – Mackenzie

You been reading those 1980s issues of Vogue again, Hunter? – Eli

Ah, you got me. Tomorrow I'm starting the grapefruit diet. – Mackenzie

Don't change a thing about that beautiful body of yours. I've been fantasizing about it all day – Eli

It's been thinking about you, too. When it's not aching. Or chafing. – Mackenzie

Chafing? Ouch. You should follow the cure for that in the April 1982 edition. – Eli

I left that one at home. What does it say? – Mackenzie

Sex. – Eli

. . .

Just one word? That's poor writing. Also, they must have used big type. – Mackenzie

I'm paraphrasing. But also happy to volunteer as tribute. – Eli

Shut up. I'm busy. – Mackenzie

Meet me at seven? – Eli

You forgot to ask nicely. – Mackenzie

Please. – Eli

Ah, I'm a sucker for a guy with good manners. They make the most considerate lovers according to the December 1988 edition. – Mackenzie

Shut up. I'm busy. – Eli

I wish I could see his face. But this office doesn't have a view of the rink, where I assume he's watching practice. Part of me – the part that I know Rachel would approve of – tries to think of an excuse to go down there.

I could annoy him with some new towels. Or push his patience by talking to Goran about the new blend he brought me today. Which was actually delicious. The coffee shop on the corner apparently changes its guest blend monthly.

But then my phone rings, and I'm brought back down to earth with a bump.

"Hi Dad," I say.

"Hi sweetheart. Did you talk to Gramps? We need to make some plans."

I push those lovely thoughts of handsome hockey players with senses of humor from my mind and try not to sigh.

"Yes," I tell him. "He's excited. Let me grab a pen and we'll talk."

CHAPTER
SEVENTEEN

ELI

"What's going on? Why haven't you all gone home?" I ask Goran. Half of them are still in the locker room despite the fact I told them to call it a day an hour ago. I check my watch. It's almost six-thirty. I have things to do.

Telling them about the exhibition match was a mistake. I should have saved that little bombshell for tomorrow. They've all been behaving like overexcited kids, trying to guess who'll be playing on the All-Star team, and then pretending to beat them.

It's exhausting.

"Just waiting on Carter," Goran says. "He has a minor problem."

An icy shiver wracks down my spine. "What kind of problem?" I ask, my voice low. We have two games this week. We can't afford to be without our best center forward.

"His girlfriend is pregnant."

"What?"

"We don't know if she's pregnant," Max points out.

"Good point." Goran shrugs. "She thinks she's pregnant. He's on FaceTime with her while she does the test."

"Where is he?" I look around the locker room. It's a damn mess. I'm going to have to read them the riot act again tomorrow.

Make them write it out on a chalkboard a hundred times.

My mess is nobody's responsibility but mine.

I pinch the bridge of my nose. Was I as much of a punk as these guys when I was starting out in my career? Probably. But I was drafted straight into the NHL and we had all the support money could buy. Your apartment needs cleaning? Great, the team has a list of cleaners to choose from. You need some clothes for a night out? We'll hook you up with our stylist.

Seriously, I was more babied than these guys could even imagine. I find it embarrassing to think about now.

"He's in the bathroom," Goran says, pointing at the door. "We're giving him some privacy."

A loud whoop comes from said bathroom. Then the door flings open and Carter comes running out.

"You're gonna be a daddy?" Goran asks.

"Nope! A single line, baby." Carter does a little dance. "No little Carters for me."

I clear my throat. His eyes slowly scan the room before landing on me. "Uh, hi Coach."

"Do I need to give you a lecture on condoms?" I ask him.

"No, sir."

"Good." Because I'd feel like a fraud. I was bareback in a woman who gave me her word she has a contraceptive implant last night. Who the hell am I to talk?

But it was Mackenzie. And you trust her.

Yeah, isn't that the kicker? I trust her so much I want to do it all over again. Multiple times.

"Now clear up this mess and get your asses home." I pull my phone out and write a quick message to Mackenzie to make it 7:15 and not 7. There's no way I'm having her walk into a locker room that smells of sweaty hockey balls.

Carter is so hyper than he does most of the cleaning by himself, all the while giving the others a running commentary on how he would have made a great dad if his girlfriend really had been knocked up. I sit in the corner and stare at my notes for plays this week, pretending I'm not listening, but eventually it grates on my nerves.

"Okay," I say, standing up. "You're all done. You can go."

"But there are still clothes to pick up," Carter points out. Doesn't stop him from looking hopeful.

"I'll finish."

He frowns. "Really?"

"Yes, really. Just go!" Before I lose my damn mind.

They take their time packing up. Too much time. My teeth grit as they finally agree on where they're going – out to a steakhouse because they need to celebrate the fact that Carter's sperm aren't working – but then before they can walk out of the locker room Goran remembers he left his phone on a chair by the rink.

The door to the locker room opens and Mackenzie walks in, holding it so it doesn't slap her in the face.

"Oh," she says, looking at the team surrounding me. "Sorry, I should have knocked."

"It's fine," I tell her, trying not to stare at the way her skirt curves over her hips. The same hips I held on to yesterday as I made her scream with my tongue. "Everybody's just leaving."

Goran gives her the biggest smile and she smiles back. A little jolt of jealousy rushes through me.

"We're heading out for a drink," he tells her. "Carter has something to celebrate. Why don't you join us?"

Her gaze flickers to mine. She's still smiling but this time it feels like it's all for me.

"Actually, I'm here for Eli," she says. "We have a meeting."

"To talk about the exhibition game?" Goran asks. "Want me to stay and help."

"It's fine," I say, my eyes not leaving hers. "You have a good time. We've got this."

They take five more minutes to leave. I swear they do it on purpose because every second that passes makes my blood heat just a little more. Finally they troop out, Goran at the rear, and he looks back one more time before leaving.

When the door finally closes I let out a low breath.

"Sorry. They were supposed to leave an hour ago."

"What's Carter celebrating?" she asks. Damn she looks gorgeous in her white blouse and gray pin striped skirt. I picture myself unfastening the buttons one by one and immediately get hard.

"It doesn't matter." My voice is husky. "Come here."

She looks over her shoulder. I get it; I do. She's scared somebody might walk in on us. And yes, part of me is pissed about that because I don't give a damn who knows. But I'm more pissed because it wouldn't be me who'd suffer, it'd be her.

I'd get the high fives. She'd get the knowing looks and the people gossiping behind her back. The world shouldn't be like that.

She steps into my arms and every muscle in my body relaxes. She's warm and soft and she smells so good.

"Hey," I say, kissing the tip of her nose.

"Hey." She lifts her face up and I take the hint, pressing my mouth against hers. She opens her lips, her breath soft against mine, and I groan because maybe some parts of me aren't so relaxed.

They're very much standing to attention.

"Did you bring me here for locker room sex?" she asks breathlessly.

"Nope."

Her eyes narrow. "Have you ever had locker room sex?"

"Nope."

This time her expression is disbelieving. "I thought that was a rite of passage."

"You been reading hockey romances or something?" I ask her.

She smirks. "No."

"So why are you smiling?" Not that I'm complaining. Her smile is one of the best things about her. Along with other things.

"My friend said something about watching hockey porn."

I frown. "Hockey porn? Is that a thing?"

"Apparently." She wrinkles her nose.

"Have you watched any?" I'm curious now. How sexy can hockey be? We smell like animals when we get off the ice. Seriously bad. That's why the locker room has such a powerful ventilation system.

"No." She shakes her head. "Why would I watch porn when I have the real thing?"

I swallow hard. We're here for a reason. And it's not for locker room sex. Though now that I'm thinking about it...

"So why am I here then?" she asks me.

I hold my hand out to her. "Come with me."

Blinking, she takes my hand and I pull her to the bench, sitting her down. I kneel in front of her and her eyes do that little hazy thing, making me want her more than ever.

Then I reach for her gorgeously high-heeled shoes and pull them off.

Her breath catches.

My thumbs slide along her nylon-covered feet. Smooth and warm. There's a steady pulse between my thighs.

I lift her foot to my lips and kiss the arch of her sole. Her toes curl up.

"I thought you said…" It's her turn to sound husky.

"I did." I put her foot down and reach into the bag I stashed here earlier. "You need to get changed."

"Changed?"

I hand her a pair of tight leggings and a Mavericks t-shirt, along with another one of my old game jerseys.

"Okay, this porn is turning seriously weird," she mutters, taking the clothes. "Is it some kind of reverse thing? You want to fuck the hockey player?"

I chuckle. "No. I just don't think you can skate in that skirt of yours."

She looks down at her skirt and then up again. "Wait. Skate?"

"Yeah, we're going skating."

Her eyes widen. "Oh no we're not." She shakes her head vehemently. "I'd rather do the locker room sex."

I take her face between my hands. "Do this for me, please."

She looks at me for a moment, tiny furrows appearing between her brows. "Is this because you don't want to date somebody who can't skate?"

"Are we dating now?" I ask her.

"I don't know. Are we?"

"Yes we are." We really fucking are. "And for the record, I don't give a shit if you can skate or not. But I do give a shit that it hurt you that you couldn't. But I can teach you."

"You can't. Nobody can. My mom tried."

"How hard did she try?"

Mackenzie blinks. "I don't know. Isabella was already competing by then."

I nod. "I'm not going to teach you to dance. Just skate. That's all." I run my hand along her jaw. "Do you trust me?"

She looks at the clothes she's still holding then back up at me. "I think so."

My lip quirks. "I'll take it. Now go change."

She puts the clothes on the slatted bench and unbuttons her blouse, her fingers deft but slow. My eyes are glued to the movements. She pulls the silk fabric from her waistband and unfastens the rest, then her blouse gapes open.

And I'm almost in pain.

I inhale raggedly. "I'll meet you rinkside. I've got our skates there."

Because if I don't leave now the locker room sex is going to be happening.

MACKENZIE

I can't believe I agreed to this. I teeter on the skates Eli bought me, trying not to fall before I get on the ice.

"If I end up in the hospital, I expect you to sit by my bed looking guilty," I tell him.

He smiles and holds out his hand.

Before my blades even hit the ice I get a flashback. Me at nine or ten years old, sitting on the bleachers with a book and a packet of chips, my legs swinging as Isabella and Mom skated like demons, gliding gracefully across the ice, Isabella jumping and twirling and smiling.

By that point we'd learned that ice and I didn't mix. But I was still too young to be left at home when it was time for practice. Brad and Johnny were young enough to go to the daycare in the big sports arena, but I'd long since outgrown that.

Nobody skates as beautifully as Mom. Isabella came in a close second, but Mom was always more comfortable on the ice than she was on the ground.

She'd call me her little changeling. Tease me that I was probably swapped at birth.

For a while I'd scrutinize every competition that Isabella competed at, watching the girls who were my age, trying to see if there was any family resemblance.

"You need to move," Eli says. I blink and see him standing there patiently, his hand still wrapped around mine.

"This is only going to end one way," I mutter. "Badly."

Gingerly, I put one skate on the ice, telling myself that the faster I do this and fall over the quicker we can leave and have some passionate sex.

He'll owe me a massage or two, as well. I smile at the thought of that.

The other skate hits the slippery surface. My heart races. The smile melts from my face.

"You're on the ice," he murmurs. "And you're upright."

"For now."

"Trust me," he says again.

"I do. It's me I don't trust." My free hand wraps around the wooden board on the edge of the rink. I'm shaking.

"Look at me please," he says, his voice soft.

I do. He's gazing right into my eyes and it gives me a little jolt. He smiles and nods. "That's it. Now let go of the board."

"I'll fall."

"I won't let you."

I take a deep breath and do as I'm told. As soon as I've prized my hand away from the wood he takes it in his other hand. "Okay?"

Not really, but I nod anyway.

"I hate being bad at things," I mutter.

"That's because you're so good at everything else," he tells me. "But luckily for you I'm good at this, and I've got it for both of us. I'm going to skate backward now. You need to come with me."

"Don't let go of me." I tighten my grip on his hands. My heart is hammering against my chest.

"I won't."

"And if I fall, don't you dare laugh."

His thumb caresses my palm. "If you fall I'll owe you an orgasm."

My head snaps up. "Really? So I get an orgasm for every time I fall? You're not exactly motivating me to stay upright. What if I fall a hundred times? I'll be getting off for days. You really need to restructure the benefits you offer."

He grins. "You're moving."

"I'm what?" Then I realize what he means. While I've been babbling, he started skating backward, pulling me along for the ride. Then I look down at my feet and dizziness over-whelms me. I feel myself wobble. More than wobble, I'm flailing.

He lets go of my hands and I know it's going to hurt.

But instead of my head slamming against the ice, his hands grab my waist and pull me against him. Yes, his chest is hard, but not as hard as the rink.

Instinctively, I wrap my arms around him.

"Don't look down," he advises.

"Now you tell me."

"You need to look straight ahead," he continues. "Looking down will put you off balance."

"Sure." It doesn't matter because I'm not intending on letting go of him. If he wants to skate he's going to have to get used to me being a limpet.

"Mackenzie?"

"Yeah?"

He strokes my face. It feels good. But it also means he isn't holding onto me, so I tighten my grip on him.

"We're moving again," he says. He's so damn nonchalant,

skating backward, a thirty-something woman attached to him.

"*You're* moving," I tell him. "I'm just along for the ride."

He turns, the show off, and I keep clinging. Then he dips his head to brush my lips with his. "You're doing great."

The stupid thing is, I flush with pride. Just because I'm staying upright by clinging onto him. I'm a sucker for praise and by the way he's smiling at me he's worked that out.

"If you call me a good girl I'll scrape your eyes out," I warn him.

"Will you? I wonder." He kisses me again, still skating backward. How the hell does he know what's behind him? I glance over his shoulder and see the barrier rapidly approaching us.

Or rather us rapidly approaching the boards.

But then he curves on his right skate and pulls me seamlessly along with him. Clearly, he has eyes in the back of his head.

"As much as I like having your body pressed against mine," he says as he completes a backward circuit of the rink. "I think we're going to have to take it to the next level."

"It's fine," I say, gripping the back of his jersey. "I'm quite comfortable here." I put my cheek against his chest and look up at him. "Let's not push it."

Ignoring my protests, he unwraps my arms from his waist and slides his hands along them, until my palms are against his again. "If you stay upright I'll fuck you until you see stars," he tells me.

"You've changed the bonus system without consultation," I protest. "That's bad business."

"Move your skates, Hunter."

I go to glance at my feet and he immediately reprimands me. "Don't look down, remember."

Yeah, I remember. But maybe a little too late, because this time my blades go out from under me before he can catch me, and I end up ass down on the icy cold rink. I groan as I see him looming over me.

He's still smiling as he reaches a hand out.

"It's fine. I like it here," I tell him. "Nice view."

"Get up."

"No." I'm not completely mortified. He isn't laughing, for one. Just smiling like I'm the prettiest thing he's seen.

And yeah, I quite like that.

Two hands slide under me and I'm suddenly lifted through the air. "Hey, what's going on…"

"You're getting up." But he doesn't let go. Just skates around with me in his arms.

"You're going to give yourself a hernia," I tell him.

"I'm giving myself a hard-on." He doesn't even wobble as he skates. The man has muscles of steel.

"I'm not having sex with you on the ice."

He grins. "We'll save that for the next lesson." He moves his arms, adjusting his hold on me until I'm vertical and facing him. I'm scared of cutting him with my skates so bend my knees and tighten them on his waist, keeping my feet away from his body. It has the added advantage of pushing me closer to all the right places

"Not helping, Hunter," he tells me.

"Don't you just want to take me home? Do dirty things to me?"

"I do," he says seriously. "Very much so."

"Then let's go," I tell him. "It's cold and my ass is wet."

Gently, he puts me back on the ice. "Not until you can skate for five seconds. Without holding onto me."

I pout.

"Then we'll leave," he promises.

It takes half an hour and more falls than I care to think about, but eventually I manage to skate for five seconds without touching Eli or the boards. I still feel wobbly, and keep to the edge of the rink with half an eye on the exit. But the smile on his face makes up for the fear rushing through my body.

He's standing by the exit to the rink so I deliberately slam into him, using him as a brake because if I use my skates I'm going to end up on the floor again.

He catches me and laughs, putting his hands on me to twirl me around the ice. I still hate it and grip onto his sweater like I'm holding on for dear life, but I'm also feeling kind of jubilant.

"Can we go home now?" I plead.

"Yep. Your place or mine?"

"Whichever is warmest," I grumble. And then I add. "Mine." Because my toothbrush is there. And my pajamas. I'm hoping he might stay the night again.

Strictly for now.

I ignore that voice and let him lead me off the ice.

CHAPTER
EIGHTEEN

ELI

"Mac?" I whisper. She's dead to the world, her hair a mess of waves as she lies on the sheets. It's a mess because of me. I kind of overshot. And then we had to shower, and one thing led to another.

I trace the bridge of her nose. Then the outline of her lips. She groans and lifts her hand, trying to bat me off like I'm a fly.

I hate waking her up. Over our nights together I've realized that she's not a great sleeper. I, however, am, and I really don't want to be awake right now. I want to be back in bed, her body curled around mine.

But here I am in my fucking clothes at stupid o'clock in the morning.

"Hunter," I try again. "I have to go."

"Huh?" Her eyes blink open. As soon as they land on me, they soften. I like that way too much.

"I have to go to practice." It's game day and we're starting early. This one is important. Against our closest rivals. There's been a beef between the Mavericks and the Fairview Phantoms for years and because we're so close geographically it's one of the few games that sells out.

She sits up, rubbing her eyes. She has bruises down her side from hitting the ice hard on our last lesson. I've been rubbing arnica into them every day and though they're yellowing they still look obvious.

"What time is it?" she asks.

"Six-thirty."

"I thought practice was at eight." Her voice is groggy.

"It is, but I want to go over a few things before the team arrives." I kiss her brow. "Go back to sleep."

"You just woke me up," she points out, not unreasonably.

"Yeah, but I didn't want to leave without saying goodbye."

Her lips curl. She leans forward and puts her arms around me, pulling me in for a soft kiss. One that gets harder. And then so do I. It takes more willpower than I realized I had to pull back.

"Will you be watching the game tonight?" I ask her.

"Yep."

"I'll see you then." I kiss her again, reluctantly standing and stretching my arms. I've been staying at her place most nights. Apart from her skating lessons we leave the arena separately every evening, then I call her from my car to decide whose place we're going to.

She prefers hers which is fine by me. I don't have to clean. Plus I don't mind putting on yesterday's clothes and showering in the locker room. Another reason to get there before the team.

The building still feels like it's asleep when I arrive. I walk into the locker room and grab a towel, heading to the shower. The water is hot and steamy, but I'd still prefer to be in bed with Mackenzie. I'm dressed and drying my hair with a towel when Goran and Carter arrive, neither of them looking fully awake.

Luckily, they're both here for rehab. They'll get stretched and pummeled then join us on the ice at nine. "Everything okay?" I ask them.

They both nod. "Need coffee," Goran says. "The shop doesn't open until eight."

"He wants to flirt with Mackenzie again." Carter grins.

I lift a brow but say nothing. I've been careful as fuck not to be seen with her because I know she'd hate that. Which is pretty annoying because whenever I see her in the hallways she's always looking delectable and all I want to do is push her against the wall and kiss her until she's breathless.

It's even more annoying seeing Goran take her coffee every day when I want that to be me.

The guys get changed then head over to the rehab room and I grab my phone and groan when I see the notification on there.

It's my nephew's birthday. I haven't sent him a damn card.

I quickly tap out a message to Myles, telling him to wish Charlie a happy birthday and that I'll bring his gift over this weekend.

Three little dots come up. I'm not surprised because Myles is an early riser, always has been. Unlike Liam, Linc, and Brooks who'd stay in bed all day if they could.

Being a doctor, Holden just doesn't sleep. He's too busy saving lives for that.

Great. You can give it to him at his party on Sunday. – Myles

I blink. I love Charlie, I do. But spending time at a kid's birthday party when I could be in bed with Mackenzie?

. . .

Not sure I can stay for the party. I may have to drop his gift and run. – Eli

You can't do that. Everybody will be here. They all want to see you. – Myles

I wrinkle my nose. I haven't been the most communicative with them in the past few weeks, but then I've been busy.

Mostly with Mac.

Another message pops up.

Even Holden's coming. If you don't show up we'll be a brother short. – Myles

Guilt washes over me. Holden tried to call me last week and I meant to call back but I didn't. Yes, I've been busy, but I've always had time for my brothers.

Especially Myles. He was the one who would drive me back and forth from hockey practice without complaint. Who came to look at colleges with me and Mom because our dad was always busy at work or on a cruise with his latest wife. Myles has always had time for us, despite being a busy bastard himself.

I slide my fingers over the screen to send a fast reply.

I'll be there. – Eli

. . .

Thank you. – Myles

Then I put my phone in the locker and pull out my uniform and skates, ready to put them on before I read through today's game strategy and get the team started on drills.

Because today's the day we're going to beat the Phantoms. It's going to be a good day.

———

MACKENZIE

I'm running late. I spent this morning negotiating with the IRS on Gramps' behalf, pleading for a small extension until after the exhibition game when the income from the ticket sales has been released. And this afternoon I've been holed up in my office having conference call after conference call with the production company that will film my parents and the exhibition game and everything that comes with it.

I expected it to be easy. A discussion about accessibility, timings, where the best place will be for the cameras. But they wanted full details of the team, and who I thought would be the best players to record and be part of the promo for the game.

It ended five minutes ago, with them telling me they'd be sending a scout down to check out locations. And they also want to meet with Gramps' nursing home to see if they can record there.

By the time I get to the staff box, the first period is about to start. Brian's saved me a seat and he pats it so I slide in next to him.

"What have I missed?" I whisper.

"Nothing yet. The team is looking good."

Eli is behind the bench and instead of watching the team face off against the Phantoms on the ice, I look at him.

He's wearing his full kit but his helmet is off. I don't know if he intends to put himself on the ice today or not, though he's obviously ready for it. He's leaning forward, his elbows resting on his padded knees, shouting out something to Carter who nods.

And then he lifts his head and even though there's a distance between us I swear our gazes connect. I want to lift my hand up and wave, but I'm surrounded by staff and I don't want them to know what's going on.

Two minutes later, we score. I jump to my feet and scream and clap, a huge smile pulling at my lips because I know Eli wanted to get the advantage. He looks up again, grinning this time.

And I find myself breathless at the sight of this man.

Last night he carried me into the bathroom after, ah, we had some fun in the kitchen, resulting in me getting more messy than I'd planned. He'd shampooed my hair, then brushed conditioner through it, before he ended up getting us both even messier again.

Sex with him is great. Like unbelievably so. But it's more than that. I enjoy talking to him. I enjoy being with him.

He makes me laugh and I love that. I don't feel alone anymore and I like that a damn lot.

The first period ends and the Zamboni comes onto the ice, so I sneak out of the box and head down to the concession stalls. I'm still in love with the hotdogs. There's a line at the vendor so I join the end and pull out my phone, idly scrolling as I wait for my turn.

There's a message from my dad, that I'll reply to later, asking me how the production meeting went. Another from my brother, Brad, who wants to know how often to feed a puppy. That sends a shiver down my spine and I reply asking for more information because Brad can barely keep himself alive, let alone a poor dog.

And then there's one from Rachel.

Check this out. – R xx

There's a link. I click on it then immediately regret it. Because it's taken me to a webpage called SexiestHockeyPlayers.com and damn if Eli isn't number seven on the list.

I make a mental note to tease him about the other six, then I stare at his picture. It was taken when he was playing for the Razors because he's wearing their jersey. He's on the ice but not wearing a helmet, so I'm guessing it was taken after a game or during a break. He's staring at something off to the left. And he's smiling. His hair is wet from exertion, he's got scruff on his face, and I'm kind of mesmerized by him.

I know how that scruff feels. I know how his lips feel on mine. I know the weight of his body as he moves inside of me.

My cheeks heat.

And this one. – R xx

I roll my eyes but click on it anyway. This time Eli is wearing a pair of shorts and a baseball cap and nothing else, running along the sand. The sun is hitting him in a way where every muscle of his stomach looks even more defined than usual. The woman standing behind me lets out a whistle.

"That man is hot stuff."

My staff lanyard is still around my neck. One glance and

she'll know that I work here and I'm perving on the coach. I quickly close it down.

"A friend sent it as a joke," I tell her.

"Everybody needs friends like that," the woman says. "What's that website again?"

I don't answer because nobody is allowed to perv on Eli Salinger but me.

Luckily, I've made it to the front of the line so I put my order in, asking for extra onions on my dog because I haven't eaten all day. And as always, I can't stop myself from biting into it before I've even left the concourse.

The arena is extra busy with all the Phantoms fans, so I push past them into the staff area, walking past the locker room as I stuff my face with hot dog.

"Mac."

I turn to see Eli standing there in his uniform and socks. I hold my hotdog mid air, all too aware that I've got ketchup on my lip. Sauces and me just don't mix.

"Hey." I smile at him. "You're all doing great."

"You coming back to mine or am I coming to you?" he asks.

I like that he doesn't ask if we're going to be together. But that's because he's not being presumptuous. He knows I want to be with him.

"Mine?"

He winks and heads back into the locker room. And I wipe the ketchup from my face and lick my finger because I'm not wasting a single bit.

———

The noise is deafening. Half of the arena is standing and cheering. The other half are trying to push past them to head toward the exit because their team lost.

Luckily, I'm in the cheering half. Every member of staff in the box is jumping up and down, high fiving each other.

Some of them even high five me.

I'm beginning to understand why people follow teams. The high is very high. And I'm so excited to celebrate with Eli. I'm so damn proud of him. He's worked hard with the players and he's turning them into a winning unit. Something they can all be proud of.

It means a lot to him after being pushed out of the NHL due to his knee injury. One night in bed he told me he didn't want to leave so early.

That he's still pissed he didn't get to retire when he wanted to.

My phone buzzes and I pull it out, expecting it to be another message from Rachel, who's apparently following the game at home, while Googling for photos of Eli. She actually sent me a link to hockey porn, because she wasn't lying, it really is a thing. I got a glimpse of a girl in her guy's hockey uniform, knelt between his knees, before I realized what it was and quickly turned it off.

It still made me hot though. The thought of pleasing Eli while wearing his jersey.

Rachel must have tired herself out, because it's from Eli, not from her.

Come meet us in the locker room. – Eli x

You sure? – Mackenzie x

Yes. All of you. The team wants to celebrate with everyone. – Eli x

. . .

So the staff and I squeeze into the elevator because Pam from accounts has a bad foot and we want to arrive together. As soon as the locker room door opens, I can smell sweat and pheromones. There's shouting and laughing and it makes me smile.

"Brian!" Carter calls out. "Come over here and give us a hug."

Brian smiles nervously but lets them envelop him as the team circles up and pulls him into their group.

They're only half dressed. Some of them have had showers, some haven't, but they all look jubilant. When the group hug breaks up Goran spots me and calls me over, enveloping me in a bare-chested bear hug. Then I get passed from player to player, squished in their brawny arms, before I end up face to face with Eli.

"Hi." I smile at him. He's grinning and I love how happy he looks. I want to throw my arms around him, let him lift me up against his chest.

But there would be too many questions. Ones I'm not ready to answer.

So I do something really stupid.

I hold my hand out for a handshake.

He looks at it, then back up at me, my hand dangling in mid air. There's a tic in his cheek that's moving in and out rapidly.

My chest tightens because I've messed up.

I hugged every single player but him. I should have hugged him. In fact I do, but it's too late, he's stiff in my arms. Does nothing to hug me back.

And I want to say sorry. I want to take it back. He's just won the most important match of his career so far as a coach and I feel like I've ruined it.

CHAPTER
NINETEEN

MACKENZIE

Eli is completely ignoring me.

Right now he's talking to Pam about the best way to ice her foot. Then he asks her about her new grandbaby and she gets out her phone to show him some photos.

And then he reciprocates, showing photos of his two year old nephew who's apparently cute as a button.

He has a nephew? Why didn't I know this? I can't ask because Goran is trying to tell me about some beef he has with a player from the other side, plus the blood is rushing too fast past my ears.

"You're coming out with us, right?" Goran asks. "To celebrate?"

"I ah…" I look for Eli to try to work out what he's doing. But he's still ignoring me. "I don't know," I say lamely.

"Yes, come," Carter says. "I can impress you with my dance moves."

"You can't dance for shit," Goran says. "No American can."

"Yeah, because Swedes are so well known for their dancing skills," Carter says, rolling his eyes. "Actually, what are you famous for?"

"Having the best center halves in hockey," Goran says. "Naturally." He tips his head to the side. "And of course we can dance. Have you heard of ABBA?"

"No, but I think my Grandma has," Carter says. "Okay, you and me at the club. Dance off."

I look over at Eli again. This time he's talking to Max, the first goalkeeper and still not looking at me.

"You're on," Goran says. "Mackenzie can choose the winner."

I bring my attention back to them. "Oh no, I'm not coming out. I'm gonna head home."

"Of course you're coming," Goran says, taking my hand. "Eli, tell her she's coming with us."

Eli turns and finally looks at me. But his expression is painfully blank. "What?"

"Mackenzie is coming with us to the club."

"No, I'm…"

"Okay," Eli says, shrugging as if he couldn't care less.

And now I'm the one who's annoyed. Because yes, I should have hugged him. But there's no need for him to ignore me like this.

Especially since I hate the taste of my own medicine.

"Sure," I say to Goran. "I'll come with you. I love dancing."

Eli's expression flickers then turns back to neutral.

It's actually true. I have rhythm when I'm not on the ice. When I was in college, going to clubs was my way of winding down. And it'll be funny to watch Carter and Goran trying to one up each other on the dance floor.

But I'm also aware that Eli now looks more annoyed than ever.

"Great. You can catch a cab with me," Goran tells me,

looking happy. Then he grabs Carter's hand and tries to dance with him.

It's another hour before we're outside. The guys have all showered and changed, and most of the supporters have gone home, though there's a small crowd that cheers as the guys walk outside. Eli hasn't said a word to me yet. He's scowling at his phone and it's only when my own vibrates in my pocket that I realize he's messaging me.

You're NOT dancing with Goran. – Eli

I was going to apologize to you, you ass. But now he's annoying me and I don't want to.

I'll dance with whomever I want. – Mackenzie

I give myself extra points for being grammatically correct. That M is working overtime.

Anybody but me, right? – Eli

I stare at the words. There's hurt there. And I hate it because I know why he's hurting. I treated him differently. Worse. When I should have treated him better.

I want to dance with you. – Mackenzie

. . .

I don't dance. – Eli

I lift a brow and look over at him. He's still ignoring me, physically at least. The big baby. He's still hot though.

Then I'll dance for you. All night. – Mackenzie

I make a show of putting my phone in my pocket, and smile at Goran when he tells me the cab he's ordered is almost here. We're behaving like kids, Eli and I, but in a weird way I like it. He's angry but I'll make it up to him. And then he'll take me home.

There's a rush of heat in my blood that I haven't felt for the longest time.

After college I didn't go dancing any more. I certainly didn't annoy hot hockey players who have a jealous streak.

And I didn't promise to dance for them afterward.

I spent my twenties and thirties building up my career. Proving I was more than my name. Maybe I was trying to prove something to myself, too. That I wasn't some nepo baby who was famous for baring all on a stupid ice rink.

The cab arrives and four of us pile in. I'm sandwiched between Goran and Ryan, with Carter opting to sit in the front. Eli gets into the next cab, looking way too delectable in a pair of dark gray pants and a white shirt, and he still doesn't look at me.

Goran and Carter trash talk each other the whole way. Ryan is on his phone, tapping out messages like he's using a manual typewriter, his fingers crashing against the screen.

"Boyfriend trouble," Goran whispers in my ear during a break from bitching with Carter.

"Oh." I give Ryan a sympathetic smile, but he's too busy frowning at his screen for that.

When we get to the club Goran gets out first, offering me a hand to pull me to the sidewalk, which I appreciate because the skirt I'm wearing is tight and liable to shift up my thighs. Eli's cab beat ours and they're already at the door. He turns around and his eyes meet mine for a moment.

I stare back, unruffled. I'm going to dance so hard for this man he won't know what hit him. I'm stupidly excited about it.

Security waves us in through the roped area. There's thirty of us in all. Eli puts his card behind the bar and whispers in the server's ear, I assume about a limit. Then the first round arrives, shots and beers. Goran insists that I take one of each.

"We down the shot then we down the beer," he tells me.

"Is that a Swedish tradition?" I ask him.

He laughs. "No, we just need to get the party started."

It works. Another round comes out and I turn it down. The music is pumping, the dancefloor is full, and the guys are getting a lot of attention from the customers who know exactly who they are.

Three girls surround Goran. He's grinning like a loon. Some others approach Carter and he waves them off. That's when I remember his girlfriend and her pregnancy scare. My estimation of him goes up. He knows where his boundaries are and I like that.

Eli is talking to Brian when a woman comes up with a piece of paper. She whispers in his ear and slides the paper into his shirt pocket.

And all my amusement disappears in that one tiny movement, replaced by a searing heat in my stomach. Yes, I'm pissed with him and I know he's furious with me, but there's no way I'm letting somebody put their number in his pocket. I'm about half a second away from stomping over there when

Eli shakes his head and takes the piece of paper from his pocket and hands it back to her.

She leans forward and says something else but Eli isn't looking at her anymore.

He's looking at me.

The woman flounces back to the dance floor and joins her group of friends who all laugh and shake their heads. My gaze turns back to Eli.

He lifts his phone.

I take my own out and read it.

Want to go home yet? – Eli

How can he read my mind so easily? Yes, I do. I want to finish this day because somehow it's ended wrongly. What should have been happy has turned sad. And I know that it happens – that's what life is made of after all.

But I still want it to be over and to start afresh.

Yes I do. But I'm going to dance for you first. – Mackenzie

You can do it for me at home. – Eli

Nice try. – Mackenzie

"So is this dance off happening or what?" I ask Carter.

He glances at Goran who has his arms around two of the girls. I'm pretty sure if he had three arms he'd be hugging all of them.

"I think he's busy."

"I'm going to dance anyway," I tell him. "Want to join me?"

"I have a girlfriend," he says, shifting awkwardly.

"I know," I tell him. It's sweet that he's being careful. "That's why I asked. I want to dance with someone who has no interest in anything but making some shapes."

He smiles. "Okay, sounds good."

"You could check with your girlfriend first," I say, because if I was her I'd want to know.

He texts her. And he tells her I'm old, because I can read his messages over his shoulder. She tells him to go for it with a thumbs up.

Well okay then.

Pushing our way through the team, we make it to the dance floor, finding a space at the edge. The music is low and pumping, some club tune I don't recognize. But my body does, it feels the beat and my pulse matches it.

Carter holds out his hand and I take it. He pulls me in and spins me out. I kind of totter because I'm wearing this stupid tight skirt.

"Wait a minute," I tell him, taking off my shoes. I lose a couple of inches in height but damn does it feel better.

This time when he spins me I let the movement take over. My body becomes one with the music. I look at Eli, who's holding a beer, his gaze on me. He's leaning on one of those high tables, away from the rest of the team.

I turn myself to face him. Put my arms up and let my body undulate in time to the music. It's sensual and sexy knowing I'm doing this just for him.

It's like he's the only man in the room. And I want him to know how much he affects me.

A pair of hands clasp my hips. I turn, expecting to see Carter there, but it's a man I don't know.

"What are you doing?" I ask.

Before he has time to answer, Eli is storming toward us. My heart is hammering against my chest.

"My boyfriend," I murmur, nodding my head at the most beautiful man in the room.

Grabby hands immediately lets go. "Sorry, my mistake."

"Don't touch women without asking," I tell him. "It's rude."

"You okay?" Eli asks, eyeing the man who's still behind me.

"You shouldn't let your girlfriend dance alone," Grabby tells him.

"My girlfriend does what she wants," Eli says, his voice low. "It's assholes like you who shouldn't be touching her."

"Yeah, well piss off." Grabby turns and storms off. I look at Eli. His eyes are dark, his jaw tight, but he's sensible enough not to look for a fight.

"I'm sorry," I tell him. "I didn't ask him to touch me."

"No need to be sorry. Not your fault. You should be able to dance if you want to without people touching you."

"I thought it was Carter for a minute," I tell him. Then I smile. "I just wanted to dance for you."

"I liked it." Eli's voice is thick. Gritty. "You want to continue this at home?"

I do. I want to dance for this man like Salome danced for Herod. Without the chopping off John the Baptist's head part. "I'll tell Carter," I say, sliding my shoes back on.

"Goran's grabbed him. Their dance off is starting."

Sure enough, the two of them are in the middle of the dancefloor, surrounded by the team. Goran is waving me over.

I shake my head. "Gotta go," I mouth. "Shall we?" I ask Eli, turning back to him.

"Yeah." He doesn't make a show of leaving with me. Just puts his hand softly in the curve of my back as we walk out of the club. Maybe people noticed. Maybe they didn't. I can't bring myself to care. I just want to go home with this man.

And I do.

———

ELI

We're having sleepy morning sex when my phone buzzes. It's the best kind of sex. Mackenzie's in front of me on her side, her body warm and inviting, so tight as I slide in and out of her. I'm kissing her neck, her jaw, whispering in her ear how beautiful she is.

She lets out little soft breaths as I circle her with my finger. I loved last night – the part when we got home and she danced for me. We fucked on the floor like animals and it felt like an apology. She said it too. That she was sorry for making me feel bad.

It was enough.

This morning feels like heaven. If I ever end up there, this is how I want every morning to be. Soft and warm and sensual.

Making love to my girl.

Without the damn phone that keeps vibrating.

"You want to get that?" Mackenzie looks over her shoulder. Her lips are swollen from how much we kissed last night. Her cheeks are pink from how much I'm rubbing her this morning.

"Nope."

It buzzes again, damn it. I snatch it up and groan. The brother's group chat.

Why didn't I turn my phone off when we went to sleep?

"Problems?" Mackenzie asks, her voice ragged.

This time I turn it off. "No. Just assholes."

She giggles, and it does amazing things to my dick. I'm going to have to make her laugh when I'm inside of her more often. I kiss her throat again, moving my other hand to her breasts, sliding slowly in and out of her like we have all the time in the world.

Hearing her breath hitch is my jam. Making her cry out my name is my life's work. Feeling her come reminds me, again, that I'd like to die like this.

Inside Mackenzie Hunter. Feeling her orgasm around me.

I take my time, riding out her pleasure, letting it mix with my own. When I finally come inside of her, it feels like every cell in my body is on fire. She turns to kiss me, and it's awkward as fuck because she's still facing away, but I love it anyway.

I clean her up – because that's also my thing – then I get back into bed and pull her against me. I'm sleepy again. It's the weekend and we deserve to rest, damn it.

But then she looks up at me. "Do you want to reply to that message?"

"What message?"

"The one that made your phone go crazy."

I blink. My brothers. Damn. Exactly the people I don't want to be thinking about right now.

"It's okay, it's probably Holden."

"Your doctor brother?"

"That's the one." I nod. "He's in town for my nephew's birthday party. He's probably pissed that I'm not there today."

Her mouth drops open. "You're missing your nephew's birthday party?"

I try not to laugh at her expression of horror. "No, that's tomorrow. But Holden came for the weekend. I'm guessing it's one of his rare times off."

"Then you should go be with him."

"I want to be with you." I'm not going anywhere. Not

today, anyway. I'm going to nap and fuck and maybe eventually the two of us will get up. "Anyway, the party's tomorrow. I'll see them all then."

"That's nice." She smiles. "I bet they'll be happy to see you."

I stroke her hair. "Come with me."

Mackenzie blinks. "What?"

"Come with me to the party. Meet my family." It's weird how much I want her to say yes. I want her there with me. I want her to meet my brothers and their wives. She's becoming important to me. I don't want to hide this thing away anymore.

"I want to." She doesn't look sure though. "But won't I be intruding?"

I laugh.

"What?" she asks.

"You haven't met my family. It's one big intrusion." It takes me five minutes, but I manage to explain how Myles, Liam, Holden, and I have one mom, while Brooks and Linc have another, and then we have a little sister from my dad's latest wife.

"And your mom and your dad's other wives are best friends?" she asks. "Seriously?"

"Seriously. They go on vacations together. They celebrate holidays as one big happy family. It's weird."

"But also nice. You don't have to choose between them." She draws a circle with her finger on my bare chest. "All my friends with divorced parents hated the holidays. Being shuttled from one house to another."

I look at her. "How about you? Do you hate holidays?"

"I love them. They were the one time of year that we were all in the same place."

"You said that in the past tense," I point out.

"Well, for the last three years, I've kind of worked through the holidays. We had this huge project and most of the other consultants have families. I volunteered to cover things while they traveled home." She doesn't look unhappy about it. "Brad and Johnny barely get time off during the season, anyway. And Mom and Dad and Isabella have been busy with their Holiday specials for the last couple of years."

I keep forgetting her parents and her sister are on TV. I so rarely watch it. I make a note to check it out. I'm curious about them all.

"Well you get to spend one day with my family," I tell her. "That should put you off holidays for good."

She laughs. "I'm looking forward to it."

The weird thing is she sounds like she means it. The even weirder thing is that I'm looking forward to it as well.

"What do you want to do about my family?" I ask her.

She blinks. "What do you mean?"

"You want to pretend we're just friends?" I don't like it, but I'll do it for her if I have to.

"No." She shakes her head. "Let's do this right." She looks at me. "Whatever this is."

"You know what it is," I say, tracing her jaw with my fingertip.

"Do I?" She breathes softly as my finger reaches her lips. She's always so skittish. And if I'm being truthful, I like the challenge. I like the chase.

And I like to win. *Always*.

She flicks my finger with her tongue and I groan.

"You're mine," I tell her. "That's what it is."

She sucks me in and I'm gone. I pull my hand away and grab her hips, hitching her up until she's straddling me. "These lips," I say, sitting up and brushing her mouth with my own. "Mine."

I kiss down her throat and her chest, to the swell of her breasts. "These are mine, too."

And I pull her into my favorite position. Thighs pressed against my cheeks, her hands braced against the headboard.

"And this?" I mutter. "Mine too." I slide my tongue along her seam, and she clenches her thighs.

"Eli…"

"Shut up and let me eat my breakfast."

And for once – to my surprise – she does.

CHAPTER
TWENTY

MACKENZIE

Eli's brother lives in a beautiful old house on the outskirts of Charleston. It has a touch of old-world glamor to it. If I wasn't sitting in Eli's Mercedes right now, the heat blasting because he noticed I was shivering and he's actually quite the gentleman, I could pretend I was in a horse drawn carriage with my Victorian suitor, ready to meet his parents.

Although I don't think that's how it happened in those days. Didn't men and women have chaperones whenever they were together? I try to imagine that now. Eli constantly cockblocked by a knowing older woman.

"What are you smiling at?" he asks me.

"Just admiring your brother's house."

"Yeah, it's nice. Liam lived in the guest house for a while. We'd stay there whenever we visited. It was like *Porky's* but so much worse."

"*Porkys*?" I say. "What's that?"

"You haven't seen *Porky's*?"

I shake my head.

"Probably for the best," he says. "It'd put you off guys for good."

He pulls in next to a huge black BMW and shuts off the engine. "We should agree on a signal," he says.

"What for?"

"In case you want to leave. Like a codeword."

"How about, Eli, I need to leave?"

He laughs. "That would work."

"But I'm sure it'll be fine. I'm excited to meet your family."

He looks at me with warm eyes. "You've been warned."

As soon as we're in sight of the front door, it flings open and two younger men come out.

"Thought you weren't coming," the first says.

"He brought a girl," the second replies. "He's been coming a lot."

"Shut the hell up," Eli says, shaking his head. "Mackenzie, these are my younger brothers, Brooks and Lincoln." He looks at them with an eyebrow raised. "Boys, this is Mackenzie."

They both wince at being called boys. I probably would, too. They must be in their late twenties or early thirties. They remind me of my brothers and from the way they tease Eli, I'm guessing their love language is the same as Johnny and Brad's - shit talking. My chest twinges. I miss them.

A woman walks out and a smile splits her face. "You're here," she says. She's wearing a dark blue wrap dress that emphasizes her curves. Her cheeks are plump with a smile, and she looks at Eli with warm eyes before she slides her gaze to me.

"Hey, Mom," Eli says, taking my hand in his. "This is Mackenzie."

Her eyes are the same color as his. They have the same color hair, too. But where he's all masculine jaw, she has a heart-shaped face.

"Mackenzie, this is my mom," Eli says.

"Linda," she says, reaching forward to hug me. "It's so lovely to meet you."

Eli reluctantly lets go of my hand. Then a little girl toddles out of the door with her hands held up to him. "Lie," she says, jumping up and down in the way kids do when they want to be picked up.

He swings her up into his arms, blowing a raspberry on her cheek. She giggles and my ovaries do a little dance.

"This is my sister," he tells me, which seems so ludicrous because she can't be much older than two or three and he's forty. "Francie, say hi to Mackenzie."

She waves and hides her head. Her shyness makes me smile.

"Don't worry," Linda says. "She won't stop talking as soon as she gets to know you." She holds her hands out to Francie – who I know isn't her daughter, but her ex-husband's child – and Francie happily slides into her arms, as Eli's mom carries her inside.

We follow them in and another wave of Eli's relatives welcome us. Eli tells me their names and I immediately forget them. I thought I had a big family, but it's tiny compared to this.

And everybody seems so relaxed and happy to see him. His older brother – Myles – asks Eli about the game on Friday night, and the one who looks just like Myles – Liam – comes over and introduces himself and his wife, Sophie, to me.

Sophie hugs me. "They're all a bit much," she whispers. "But they're lovely. Want to come meet Myles' wife?"

"Sure." I let her lead me down the hallway that's adorned with what looks like expensive art. It doesn't feel pretentious, though. It feels like a home full of love.

Myles' wife is a lovely woman named Ava, and she's in the kitchen with a little boy who looks like he's having a tantrum. She looks up as we walk in and lets out a long sigh.

And then she sees me and smiles. "Oh, hi! You must be Eli's friend."

"Mackenzie."

She hugs me, too. They're a cuddly family, unlike mine, but I throw myself into it.

"Your house is beautiful," I tell her. "And this must be the birthday boy."

"Charlie," she says. "And he's a little overwhelmed."

Myles walks in. "Problems?"

"You could say that. He wants everybody to go home."

"Not Daddy. Daddy stay," Charlie says, his voice vibrating with a suppressed sob.

"Well, at least I have permission to stay in my own house." Myles scoops Charlie up in his arms. "What's up, bud?"

"Francie opened one of his gifts," Ava says. She looks at me. "Sorry, you've just walked into Toddlermageddon."

"Not Fancy's," Charlie says, leaving out the 'r'. "Mine."

"That's right, but we share, don't we?" Myles asks. "Even on birthdays."

"Mine," Charlie says again. And I'm reminded of last night. Of Eli calling me his.

My heart does a little clenching thing.

I liked it. And it also scared the hell out of me. How can I go back to New York knowing what it's like to be Eli Salinger's girl?

I can't do long-distance. He'll break my heart.

"Are you okay?" Sophie asks.

"Oh, I'm fine." I smile. "Actually, Eli brought Charlie a gift. Do you think it'll help if he gives it to him?"

As though he hears me say his name, Eli walks into the kitchen. Ava hugs him tightly then whispers something in his ear. He looks over at me and smiles.

And my legs go a little weak.

Somebody tugs on my hand and I look down to see Eli's little sister looking up at me. "Hi," I say, scooting down.

She leans forward and whispers in my ear. "Charlie don't like me."

"Oh I'm sure he does, sweetie," I tell her. "He's just a little sad."

"I stole his gifts."

"I know." I nod. "But you gave it back, right?"

She nods, looking so serious. "Not mine," she whispers.

I look around for her mom, who I think I met in the hallway, but she isn't here. Nor is Eli's dad, who looks ridiculously young and handsome considering he has very grown children. Sophie is busy talking to Charlie and Ava is chatting with Eli.

So I lift Francie up and smile. She touches my face. "You pretty."

"So are you."

"Charlie says me naughty."

My throat tightens. "He doesn't mean it. He's just unhappy."

"He's naughty too," she says, her brows knitting.

I begin to laugh then try to hide it. This is way above my pay grade. Disputes between companies I can do, but between toddlers?

I'd need to call in the UN.

Luckily, Eli joins us and Francie immediately reaches for him. He hitches her onto his hip, looking so at home holding her tiny body it makes me want to do things to him.

What is it with men holding kids? I'm a feminist, I really am, yet I'm melting at the sight of him holding his sister. Like full blown ovary-exploding heat going on inside me.

"Here you go," Sophie says, handing me a glass of wine. "Sometimes alcohol is necessary to put up with the Salingers."

I take it gratefully.

"You're a Salinger now," Eli points out to her, looking amused.

"I'm a West-Salinger," she says. "It's different."

"She and Liam hyphenated their names," Eli says.

I nod approvingly. I'm liking this family more and more.

"Anyway, marrying into the family is very different than being a natural born Salinger," Sophie continues.

"You make us sound like serial killers." Eli frowns.

"Nope. Just overwhelming." She takes my hand. "Eli tells me you're from New York," she says. Francie tugs on Eli's face and says something to him. He nods and looks over at me. "Francie wants me to give Charlie his gift. I left it in the car. You okay here?"

"I'm good." I smile at him. He walks out of the kitchen with Francie slung over his shoulder like he's a firefighter. She giggles loudly.

"I've lived in New York for the last sixteen years," I tell Sophie, returning to our conversation. "Before that I was all over the place but I managed all four years in LA for high school.

"Was your dad in the military?" she asks. And I realize Eli hasn't told them who I really am.

It touches me.

"He's a hockey player, too." My heart is racing, but it feels good to tell the truth. To stop hiding.

"How long have you been seeing Eli?" Sophie asks.

"A little while." I think back to that first time we touched. When they lost the game and he dropped to his knees in front of me. Breathed me in.

It feels like a lifetime ago.

"Will you go back to New York?" Sophie asks.

"That's where my work is," I tell her. "So yeah, when this project is over I guess I will." And there's that twinge again. I don't like thinking about endings. Especially this one.

She looks over at Myles and Liam, who've walked into the

kitchen to join us. "Liam and Myles both worked in New York until recently."

"You're from New York?" Liam asks. "Where about?"

We descend into a conversation about different companies in Manhattan. It turns out that Liam and I have some mutual acquaintances. He still travels to New York regularly, but his home is now in Charleston.

"I don't miss it at all," he says, when I ask about his move here. "Whenever I have to travel for work all I think about is coming home." He looks over at his wife. Their gazes connect and she smiles softly.

"Sophie, on the other hand, can't wait for him to leave," Myles says dryly. "Because he's a sap."

"Only for her," Liam says, good-naturedly. "And you're the king of saps, man. So don't start with me."

They banter again. Myles goading Liam about chasing after Sophie at five in the morning when he thought he'd lost her.

Liam teases Myles about having to drive him from New York to Charleston because he needed to see Ava.

It's sweet. But it also makes me feel wistful. They're all so at ease with each other. When I'm with my family they find it hard to know how to talk to me. I'm just so different from them and they don't understand what I do.

Maybe they don't try to understand it.

Sophie rolls her eyes at her husband and brother-in-law trying to one-up each other, and tops up my wine glass. "Boys," she mutters. "Don't even get me started on the subject of the Salinger Olympics."

"The Salinger Olympics?" I repeat. "What's that?"

Ava groans. "You don't want to know."

"But I do. What is it?"

"It's my brothers' way of trying to prove who has the biggest dick," Eli says, kissing my neck. He's holding a gift in one hand and Francie's tiny hand in the other. He passes the gift to Francie. "Give this to Charlie," he says. "And ask him if you can be friends again."

She nods, her face serious, then walks over to where her – I guess Charlie must be her nephew – is sitting. She passes him the gift and he leans forward to kiss her cheek.

"Oh. Those two." Ava shakes her head. "They're giving me whiplash." She looks at me. "Myles made up the Salinger Olympics to keep his brothers out of mischief every summer. They'd compete against each other to see who'd win Gold."

"What would they compete at?" I ask.

"Swimming. Tree climbing. Fighting." Ava shrugs. "Seriously, they're such boys."

"I usually won," Myles says pointedly.

Eli lifts a brow. "No you didn't."

"Exactly. I'm the overall winner. I have the most gold medals," Liam says proudly.

They get into another spat, and Ava opens up the photo app on her phone, passing it to me. "This is from the year Myles and I got together," she says. "I got to experience the Olympics first hand. Start at that one and scroll down."

So I do. And with each passing picture I get more and more amused. Six grown men, looking stupidly handsome in their shorts and sports tops, battling for victory. In one of them Eli is raising his hands in victory, his top off, his skin glistening with perspiration. In another he's standing by the side looking furious.

My man hates to lose. My face flushes at the memories of how single minded he can be.

"What are you showing her?" Eli asks, sounding suspicious.

"Just some photos," Ava says.

"Not baby ones, right?" He glances awkwardly at the kitchen door, where his mom has just walked in. "Tell me they're not the baby ones," he begs.

"Eli was a beautiful baby," Linda says, smiling at me. "But he wouldn't wear clothes."

I can't help it, I laugh. "I need to see those photos, too." His family is a hoot. I can't remember the last time I had this much fun.

Linda's face lights up. "I have some on my phone."

"No." Eli walks up to his mom, holding out his hand. "Those need to be deleted. And we need to talk about you carrying around naked photos of me."

"You were a baby," she says, rolling her eyes. "And you were adorable."

"You're not looking at them," Eli tells me.

I shrug. I'll let them battle it out. And then I'll look because I'm way too nosy not to.

Linda grumbles and slides her thumb on her phone, taking forever before she holds it out to Eli, as though she's admitting defeat.

But then Ava's phone pings in my hand.

"Mom," Eli says, his voice low. "Did you just send them to Mackenzie?"

"Technically, she sent them to Ava," I say. "I'm holding her phone."

Eli lunges for it. I raise my hand up, trying to get the phone out of his way because I need to see baby Eli in all his glory. He reaches again and I back away.

"Give it to me." His voice is cajoling. "You don't want to see them."

"I really do," I breathe. My heart is pounding as he takes another step toward me. He's like a lion, eyes on his prey. I love the way he's looking at me.

"Remember how big his little peter was?" Linda says.

"Mom!" Eli growls. "Stop it."

I'm shaking with laughter. I look over his shoulder, assessing my chances of getting past him long enough to look at these pictures. They're not good.

He's big and he's fast and I'm me. But I have one advantage. Determination. I'm going to see those photos, even if it kills me.

"Come on," Eli murmurs, taking another step forward.

I take one more back. My ass hits a tabletop. Damn.

"There's no escape," Eli tells me. "Give me the phone, Mackenzie."

"But you had a big peter," I tell him. "Your mom says so."

Myles coughs out a laugh and it distracts Eli long enough for me to duck around him, making a sprint for victory. But then his arm curls around my waist and I'm lifted through the air until my back thuds against his hard chest.

"Got you," he whispers in my ear. He takes the phone and slides his finger over it. "If you want to see how big my peter is, you only have to ask nicely."

I wrinkle my nose at him. "Spoilsport."

"It's okay," Sophie shouts out. "Linda sent a whole bunch of their baby photos to our group chat. Just tell me your phone number, Mackenzie."

Eli groans. And I smile because I like to win, too.

CHAPTER
TWENTY-ONE

MACKENZIE

The next two weeks pass in the blink of an eye. With the advanced sales for the exhibition game looking so good, it's clear we're going to be able to pay off the IRS debt. I hate to admit it, but Dad was right. The game is a great idea.

The production team has been calling every day, and their scout has been down to check out all of the arrangements. They explain they'll be in the background but they'll be here every moment dad is. He's going to love it but I already hate it.

Eli has been stoic about all the changes. Three days ago the rink was swarmed with cameras, as they recorded practice, followed by candid interviews with Eli and the team which they're planning to use as teasers for the big game.

I could see him getting impatient when they asked if Eli could dumb down a little.

"We want to create a narrative for you. It would be so good to paint you as the Ted Lasso of the hockey game."

Seriously. The man has the patience of a saint.

I showed him how appreciative I was when we got back to my place that night. He's a professional, but I also think he's only tolerating this for me. And for Gramps.

It's Friday night, which means it's game night. This week the Mavericks are at home playing against the Wolf Pack, managed by one of Eli's old teammates.

And I want to make tonight good for him. No matter what happens to the score.

Because he's special. I've realized that much over the past few weeks. So as the spectators pour into the arena and the seats fill up, I grab the bag I've stashed in my desk drawer. I went to the mall last week to get this, while the Mavericks were playing in North Carolina, and I smiled the whole way home.

Either he's going to love this or he's going to hate it.

It's amazing how busy the arena has gotten since news of the All-star game and my parent's reality TV show have gotten out. Our season ticket sales have gone up three hundred percent, and we're attracting students from the local schools and colleges, too. It all helps to create a buzzing atmosphere, as Carter wins the face off and gains control of the puck.

"You're wearing a Mavericks jersey," Brian says, when I take the chair next to him.

"Yeah. I thought I'd better show some team spirit." I smile and touch the big M embroidered on the front.

"I could have gotten you one. We have spares," he tells me. He's kind of sweet when you get to know him.

"It's okay. I wanted this one."

At half time I don't head down for my usual hot dog. Instead, I head for the executive bathroom and grab my phone, turning around so I can take a photo of the back of my jersey in the mirror.

Salinger. 8.

It's such a cliché, but dammit I want to wear his number on my back. I want *him* to know I'm wearing it.

I made a huge mistake the last time I watched a home game by not showing him I cared and this time I'll do whatever it takes for him to know.

He won't check his messages. He never does during a game. But afterward maybe he'll come find me.

I'm all hyped up during the rest of the game. Eli comes on for the last fifteen minutes, but he works up a sweat, slamming the puck across the ice, and I manage to work up a sweat watching him.

And when the game ends and we win, the sound of cheering is deafening. We all jump up and the rest of the box can see exactly whose name is on the back of my shirt, if they hadn't noticed before.

I can't bring myself to care.

I'm still grinning as I head back to my office and send the photo I took earlier to Eli, along with a message.

I'm completely naked under your jersey. – Mackenzie x

Locking the door, I shimmy off my jeans, along with my panties, bra, and socks. For good measure I find a pair of high, high heels with straps that criss cross my ankles. Then I reapply my make up and wait for a reply.

Where are you? – Eli

Come find me. – Mackenzie

. . .

There's a pause, then I see the dots appear on the screen as he types.

Mac, I've got a boner the size of the Empire State building here. If I prowl the hallways I'm gonna end up getting arrested. Where the fuck are you? – Eli

I can't help but grin. I send him another photo. This time of my legs and my shoes, my ankles crossed as I sit on my desk. To get the right angle, I have to contort my body into a completely unnatural shape, but my legs look good so it's worth it.

Guess. – Mackenzie

In less than two minutes, he's banging on my door, and I remember I locked it. Trying not to laugh at the way he jiggles the handle impatiently, I walk over and unlatch it, stepping back as he barrels inside.

"Lock it again," he says, his voice thick.

His gaze sweeps down over my body. A little thrill rushes through me at the unashamed way he's ogling me.

"Turn around," he says when the door is secured.

So I do, the stiletto heels of my shoes hitting the tiled floor.

"Walk over to the desk."

He doesn't say please. It's weird how I like that when usually I hate it. I want him to order me around. I want him to show me who's boss.

We're equals in every way, but sometimes a girl likes to play.

I stroll to the desk, my back toward Eli. I glance over my

shoulder and he hasn't moved. He's looking at my legs, his eyes dark.

Placing my hands flat on the desk I lean forward, pushing my ass out and letting my back arch.

The jersey gathers around my hips, exposing me to him.

"Do you know how beautiful you look?" he rasps. "Did you wear that for me?"

"Yes."

"Did people see you wear it?" he asks.

"Everybody," I breathe.

There's a shuffle. I want to look back but I also want to keep playing this game. The one where I'm his to do with as he pleases. Then I hear footsteps. Unhurried and steady.

Two warm palms press against my hips. I'm so turned on it isn't funny. All he'd have to do is push his finger between my legs to find out. But he doesn't. Instead, he pushes himself against me, the thick ridge of him digging into my ass.

"You made me search for you," he whispers.

"I know."

"You like playing games?" His breath is warm against my ear. "Is that what it is?"

"Yes."

"I bet you fucking do." He slaps my behind, once. It's unexpectedly hard. I let out a yelp.

And then I get wetter still.

My breath is ragged as he traces the curve of my hips, the outside of my thigh, the inner part of my knee where the skin is sensitive.

Another slap. Just as hard. I get even wetter.

"You like that?" he asks after I let out a soft groan.

"Yes." I'm not sure I can form any other words right now.

"So do I." He kisses my neck. It's such a sweet contrast to the surprising sting of his palm.

There's another shuffle, then I feel something different. His mouth, kissing the skin where it's still sensitive from his slap. His lips trail down the curve of my behind, to the fold of skin where my ass meets my thighs,

And then his tongue darts out and licks me.

I have to muffle my mouth with my hands not to scream.

"Are you going to be good?" he asks me.

"I'm trying."

"If you make any noise I won't let you come." He slides his palms up my thighs and pulls them apart, placing my feet wider apart.

And then he feasts on me.

I've never met a man who enjoys a woman the way Eli Salinger does. It's like I'm his favorite meal and he hasn't eaten in a month. I press my mouth against the back of my hand, trying not to cry out as my body goes into overdrive. My legs shake hard enough for him to have to steady me with his strong palms.

And then he goes in for the kill.

His tongue is incessant and talented, coaxing the pleasure out of me with teasing licks. He pushes a finger inside of me, then two, curling them until I'm on a cliff edge of desire.

Another lick and I careen down into oblivion.

My body convulses around his fingers, my legs shiver, and those stupidly high heels I'm wearing give way. He reaches for my hips again, holding me against him, before turning me around and sliding me back onto the desk until I'm sitting on the surface, my legs spread, the glow of my orgasm still suffusing me.

The smile on his face is so big I can't help but smile, too. He leans forward to kiss me and I curl my hands around his neck, so happy that this man is here.

That he's mine.

I press my cheek to his, and whisper in his ear. "Fuck me, Salinger."

And he does.

Twice.

The second time with me bent over the desk again, so he can come inside of me while he sees his name written across my back. And when he does, letting out a long, low groan that's so sweet it makes me ache, it feels perfect.

Like everything.

"Wear this jersey next week," he says once he's cleaned me off. I'm still wearing nothing else, but I'll have to put my jeans on before we leave. Even if everybody else has left the building, it's way too cold outside to have bare legs.

Plus, there are security cameras. And I might not mind having his name on my back, but I do mind exposing myself to the staff.

"Okay." I nod.

"And the week after."

I smile. "Am I allowed to launder it between wears?"

"Nope."

I laugh again. I'll definitely wash it. But he doesn't need to know that.

"And the week after that."

"That's Bye Week," I remind him.

"I know." His eyes catch mine.

Bye Week is when the exhibition game will be played. When the Mavericks face the team captained by my dad.

He's not only asking me to show him support. He's asking me to show more. To show I care. To show I'm his.

My heart slams against my chest.

"Okay." I nod.

He kisses me again. This time it's sweet. I lean into his kiss, every part of me on fire.

"Did it hurt when I slapped you?" he asks, his brows pinched.

"No." I swallow hard. "I liked it."

"You did?"

"Yeah. I don't think I want to be slapped every time. But tonight it was hot." I liked the little game we played. Sure it was mild, but it was sexy. My cheeks pink up when I think about it.

"We should go home now," he says. "Before I take you against this desk again."

"Not even you can do a hat trick that quickly," I tell him.

"Don't try me." Gently he lifts me off the table, then he drops to his knees and unfastens the straps of my heels. They left little red welts and he presses his lips against the tender skin.

I ruffle his hair and he looks up at me, his eyes are so open and honest it makes my heart hurt. "Where are your clothes?" he asks.

"In the desk drawer. I can get them."

But he won't let me. Taking them out of the drawer, he slowly dresses me. Starting with my panties, followed by my jeans and socks. We don't bother with my bra because that's too much effort. He stuffs it into his pocket and I slide my shoes on.

When I'm almost decent, he holds his hand out and I take it. He pulls me close to him, using his free hand to smooth down my hair.

"Thank you," he whispers. His own hair is messed up from the way I mauled it during our first romp on my desk. He looks sated and boyish, and it touches me.

And I don't think he's thanking me for the sex. Or maybe he is. But there's more. I think he's thanking me for the jersey. For putting myself out there.

For trying not to be afraid.

There's a lump the size of Manhattan in my throat as I stare back at him.

"Any time," I tell him. And then I let him take me home.

CHAPTER
TWENTY-TWO

ELI

"What are you doing?" Mackenzie grumbles. If there's one thing I've learned about this woman, it's that she hates waking up. Unless my mouth is doing the waking. Then she's as sweet as a damn cookie.

But we don't have time for that today.

"I'm getting up," I tell her, pulling on my shorts. "And so are you."

"It's Saturday." She frowns. "I want to sleep."

"We need to head to the arena early. Before we head to Misty Lakes."

"What? Where?" She rubs her eyes with bunched hands. Damn, this woman is adorable.

My lip curls. "You're going to skate on your own today. Then I'm going to reward you by taking you to my cabin for the weekend."

She looks more awake now. "What kind of cabin?"

I pull a t-shirt over my head. "It's pretty. By a lake. I built it myself. Now are you getting up or do I have to drag you out of bed?"

I'm kind of excited. We have a few days off before next

week's exhibition game. Some of the team headed home to see their families, a few of the others are headed to Vegas to play the tables.

As for Mackenzie and I, we'll be spending it naked by a roaring fire if I have anything to do with it.

And lucky for me, I *do* have something to do with it. Misty Lakes is a vast estate owned by my dad. As kids, we'd spend every summer there with him, messing around in the lake, and getting up to no good.

As we became adults, we got to choose a piece of land around the biggest lake and build our own cabins. We got some help, but mostly we built them with our own hands. By the time I got to build mine, both Myles and Liam had already constructed theirs and they gave me a hand.

But mine is definitely the best. It has two bedrooms and a hot tub I had installed last year. It's my favorite place to chill out.

Now I get to do it with Mackenzie. If she'd get out of bed.

"I'll put some coffee on," I tell her.

"Good idea," she mumbles, turning over and slamming her face into the pillow. I head out to her kitchen and switch on the machine. It's more of a wet bar than a kitchen, like you often get in these serviced apartments. After the machine warms up, I slide a pod inside and grab a cup from the cupboard.

She's still face down in her pillow when I get back. I put her cup on the table and lift her hair up to kiss the back of her neck.

"How about we skip the skating lesson and just head to Misty Lakes," she mumbles into her pillow.

"Nope. We haven't come this far to stop now." It pisses me off that her family let her think she couldn't skate. Okay, so she's never gonna win a medal, but that doesn't mean she can't feel comfortable on the ice.

It's like they saw she wasn't going to be a winner and ignored her.

She groans again and twists in the bed to sit up. Her hair tumbles down over her shoulders, though a few strands are sticking in weird directions.

I hand her the cup, and she gulps it, probably scalding her tongue. And then something miraculous happens.

You know that part of *Beauty and the Beast* where the beast turns back into a prince? It's like that, but with Mackenzie. Though she isn't a beast but a grumpy-ass caffeine addict.

A really beautiful, grumpy ass.

"Oh." She closes her eyes. "I needed that. Thank you."

"Now get in the shower. We need to pack quickly. Don't forget your swimsuit."

Her brows scrunch down. "It's freezing outside."

"I have a hot tub."

The corner of her lip quirks up. "You do? Why didn't you say so?" The woman practically jumps out of bed, her hips swinging as she walks naked to the bathroom. I watch and admire.

And try to ignore the persistent pulse of my need.

I've gotta be honest, it's an act of supreme discipline that allows us to get out of her apartment within an hour, without me ravaging her. She's wearing a pair of tight yoga pants and a gray hoodie that stops mid waist, and all I want to do is drag her back to bed.

The rink is empty when we get there. Still grumbling, she slides her skates on then looks up at me.

"Are you putting your skates on or what?" she asks.

"Or what. You're on your own."

There had been a ghost of a smile on her lips. It disappears completely, though, replaced by a frown. She looks at the rink and back at me.

"No. I need you with me."

I cup her face, then lean down to brush my mouth against

hers. "You don't. You can skate, you've done it a few times now."

"When you've been there to catch me."

"All I want to do is see you skate across the ice and back," I tell her. "That's it. Then we hit the road for hot tub time."

A soft sigh escapes her lips. I know how hard this is for her. The fear that's built up over the years. The embarrassment from her viral video. The feeling of being less than because her family ignored her.

"What if I fall?" she asks.

"Then you'll get up, skate over to me, and we'll head out."

"Do I still get the hot tub?" There's a quiver to her voice. This woman who's so confident about everything.

Except this.

"You still get the hot tub and me in it," I tell her.

Her lips part as she lets out another ragged breath. A look of determination comes over her face as she stands on her blades. She reaches for the handrail and puts one skate onto the ice, and I've never been more proud of anybody in my damned life.

"At least I'm wearing panties," she jokes.

"More's the pity."

She puts the other blade on the ice, still holding onto the rail. Her back is to me, and I watch as her shoulders straighten, her back tightens.

And then she pushes away and glides on the ice. Okay, glide isn't quite the right word. Wobbles maybe. Whatever it is, she's doing it. All alone on the rink, with nobody to hold her or race to catch her.

Just Mackenzie and her biggest fear.

I hold my breath until she reaches the other side, stopping dead as her fingers cling to the wooden boards. She doesn't move for a minute, and I start to worry she's having a panic attack.

"You okay, Hunter?" I call out.

She's facing the other way but I still hear her. "Just catching my breath."

No, she isn't. But it's fine. "Did I tell you I've got a chef coming to cook us dinner tonight?"

She looks over her shoulder. "What kind of chef?"

"One who cooks the best steak you'll eat outside of Manhattan."

"In your cabin?" She doesn't sound so sure.

"He's good," I tell her. "I promise."

She turns. It's not pretty, mostly involving her slapping her ass against the barrier and clinging on to it behind her. But at least she's facing me.

"One minute," I tell her. "That's all it'll take for you to skate back over here."

She nods. Then looks down at her skates. I mentally will her to look back up again, because if she looks at her feet she's done for.

"Look at me," I tell her.

"Only if you take your hoodie off."

I laugh. But I do it anyway, pulling my hoodie and t-shirt off, leaving myself bare chested and fucking freezing next to the ice.

"Come get me," I tell her, my nipples shrivelling into tiny points.

And she does. This time it's less unsteady. She glides toward me, a huge ass smile on her face that matches the grin on mine.

"You're beautiful," I tell her. "You look amazing." And as she reaches the edge of the ice, I scoop her up in my arms and she flails her legs in an attempt not to cut me with her blades.

"You stripped for me," she says, grinning like an idiot.

"I would have taken my pants off, too." I gently put her down, wiping the hair from her face as I lean in to kiss her.

Her hands are like ice on my bare shoulders as she kisses me back, that big smile never leaving her lips. A shiver snakes down my spine and I quickly grab my t-shirt, because seriously, my nipples are like rocks.

"Come on. Let's go have some fun."

————

MACKENZIE

Eli's cabin is just over the border into Virginia. It takes us a few hours to drive there, but it passes in the blink of an eye as we listen to loud music pumping out of his stereo system, the two of us singing along. Eli has a surprisingly mellow singing voice, and it makes me feel kind of needy. Luckily, he must realize because he spends most of the trip holding my thigh.

His dad's estate is vast. A graveled road winds through the trees which form a canopy above us, blocking out most of the sunlight. Eli slides his sunglasses over his head and looks at me from the corner of his eye.

And then I realize why. He's waiting for my reaction as we escape the forest and I see the green rolling hills ahead of us.

"Is this all your dad's?" I ask.

"Yeah. As far as you can see. My cabin's on the other side of the hill. You'll see the big lake in a minute."

We turn a corner and there it is, sparkling like diamonds. Trees surround the lake, and I can't see the cabin at all. I can see a huge sprawling house, though, at the summit of the hill.

"My dad and his wife are away with Francie," he says as we reach the house. "We've got the place to ourselves."

"Who owns all these cars?" There are five of them. One is a Jaguar, another is a Tesla. I can't work out the other three.

"My dad."

Oh. He pulls in next to one of them and turns off the engine. "If you prefer we can stay in the house."

Hell no. I want to stay in the cabin this man built with his own hands. "You promised me a hot tub," I tell him. "And cabin sex."

He grins. "And I always keep my promises."

Climbing out of the car, Eli helps me out from the other side before grabbing our bags. Well, mine is more of a case, but I had no idea what to bring to a cabin by a lake, so I've over-packed. Eli bears the brunt of my indecision, having to carry it down the pathway that leads to the sparkling water. "That's Myles' cabin," he says, pointing at a pretty wooden building with a wraparound veranda at the far end of the lake. "He's planning on rebuilding next summer, to make more room for the family."

He points out all of his brothers' cabins, before we finally make it to his. And I'm biased, but I really do think it's the nicest. He's painted it a soft green, and like his brother's, he has a porch all around. At the front a huge wooden hot tub overlooks the lake.

"I love it," I tell him and he beams.

I'm kind of impatient to get inside, not only because it's freezing but because I haven't spent a lot of time at Eli's place. I think I've been afraid of being seen going in and out of there, which seems silly now.

"So this is…" He stops dead in the center of the doorway and I almost barrel into him. Then he groans. "Those mother-fuckers. I'm gonna kill them."

"What's the matter?"

"Seriously. I'm gonna make it painful. Chop one ball off at a time."

"Let me see," I say, trying to look past him and into the cabin. I'm trying not to laugh because he never gets riled up like this. "Get out of the way."

He steps away and my attempts not to laugh completely fail me. The front door leads into a cozy living room. And every wall in it is plastered with that photo of Eli as a baby. Naked. Blown up so you can see everything.

His mom was right. He was impressive from the start.

"Oh my God. Your dick is everywhere." Tears sting at my eyes.

"I can't believe they did this," Eli mutters, grabbing his phone. He punches his finger against the screen and lifts it to his ear. His call connects and I hear the buzz of a voice before Eli replies.

"Sleep with one eye open, you asshole," he says. "I'm gonna get you."

The conversation continues but it's freezing so I step past him, trying to look beyond the Eli homage on every wall. It's hard though, because he *was* a cute baby.

The living room has a fireplace on one side, with logs stacked up from the floor to the ceiling beside it. There are trophies and photographs on the long mantlepiece – whoever did the redecoration put them back when they were finished. If I couldn't see Eli's irate face, I'd think he did the wallpapering himself.

He walks inside, his phone glued to his ear as he tries to tug one of the photos off. It refuses to budge. "What did you stick it to the wall with?" he asks the person at the other end. I don't hear the reply but I can see the look of horror on his face.

"I'm gonna have to steam them off." He shakes his head. "No, *you're* gonna have to steam it off. You did this."

I walk in front of him and take the phone from his hand. His brow dips as I lift it to my ear.

"Hi," I say.

"Hey, Mackenzie. Do you like Eli's new look?"

It sounds like Liam. "I love it. I want it to stay."

Liam coughs out a laugh.

"Seriously. It's going to be the next new trend. Anyway, Eli and I have to go now. We have a hot tub to use."

Liam lowers his voice. "Is he really pissed? We thought it would be funny."

"We?"

"Holden and I. Though we had to pay Brooks to do it last weekend when he was at the house."

I look up at Eli. His jaw is so tight you could cut your fingers on it. "He's fine," I say. "He'll get used to it."

"Have a good weekend," Liam says. "We'll see you at the game."

"You're coming?"

"Yep," Liam says. "All of us. Gotta support Eli's team."

"You should probably wear a cup," I tell him, trying not to laugh again.

"Good advice," Liam says, sounding like he means it.

I hand Eli back his phone and he growls something unintelligible into it then turns it off and shoves it in his pocket. He looks at the walls again and grimaces.

"They love you," I tell him.

He wrinkles his nose.

"They're going to your game next week," I tell him. "That's love."

"Your family is going, too," he points out.

I open my mouth to tell him it's different. That for them it's a promotional opportunity. I'm so nervous about seeing them, especially Isabella.

But then I close it again. This weekend is about us. Especially about him, from all the photos on the wall.

And honestly, I'm here for that.

CHAPTER
TWENTY-THREE

MACKENZIE

There's never been a doubt in my mind that Eli Salinger is a gorgeous specimen of a man. But apart from the night we went to the club – when he was barely speaking to me – I've rarely seen him dress up.

But tonight he's made an effort. There are no sweats or hoodies to be seen. He's in a pair of charcoal gray dress pants and a white shirt, the sleeves rolled up to his elbows, revealing his strong forearms. He's leaning on the kitchen door, chatting to the chef, a bottle of beer in his hand.

We spent most of the afternoon in the hot tub, looking out at the lake, making out like teenagers, and then I got to experience the mist fall down over the tree canopy.

It was magical and beautiful.

Then Eli insisted I got full use of the bathroom to get ready. It was actually lovely. I can't remember the last time I put so much effort into looking pretty, and I've missed it.

I showered, shaved, painted my nails, and curled my hair. Then I carefully put on my makeup before putting on the dress I packed after Eli told me we'd be dressing up for dinner.

He's pulled a table into the center of the living room, two sturdy wooden chairs on either side, set with a white linen tablecloth and fine china. The fire is blazing – I should have known Eli was a fiend for the flames. Most guys are. My brothers turn into little boys whenever somebody brings firewood near them.

The walls are still papered with photos of naked baby Eli. But I ignore them and head for the kitchen.

"Hi." I trail my fingers along the back of the sofa as I walk. "Something smells good."

Eli looks me up and down. Then he swallows hard. Good, exactly the reaction I wanted.

He's made a lot of effort tonight. I want to do the same.

When I reach him he kisses my cheek and whispers in my ear. "You look beautiful."

I press my palm against his chest. "You don't look so bad yourself."

"Come meet Saul," he says, taking my hand in his. "Saul, this is Mackenzie Hunter."

Saul looks like he's in his early fifties. He's wearing a white chef's coat and a black bandana tied on his head. Putting down the spoon he was holding, he reaches out his hand.

"It's a pleasure to meet you." His handshake is firm. It's pretty hot in the kitchen but he's not sweaty at all. "First course should be ready in about twenty minutes."

"Is there anything I can do to help?" I ask, because it feels weird to stand around when he's cooking in Eli's kitchen.

"Nope. Just relax and enjoy." He opens the refrigerator door. "You like white wine, right?"

"I do," I tell him.

"I'll pour it." Eli takes the bottle from Saul and pours it into a crystal wine glass. I lift it to my nose and inhale.

"That's good," I tell him.

"It's from Australia. I go once a year to check out the harvests." Saul leans over the pot he's stirring and frowns. "More pepper."

"You can tell that by looking?" I ask him.

"Nope. By smelling." He grins at me. "And I know Eli loves pepper."

Eli shrugs. "I like all spices."

"Except that time you ate a whole chilli," Saul says. "In your daddy's kitchen. I've never seen a kid turn so red."

"You've known Eli since he was a child?" I ask, interested.

Saul gestures at the living room. "Not since he was *that* little." He lifts a brow and Eli looks suitably embarrassed. "I started working here in the summers when Eli was around seven or eight. I was at catering college and needed the money."

"That must have been interesting," I say, sipping the wine. It really is amazing. Saul has excellent taste.

"You could say that." He grabs a carrot and chops it so fast my eyes can't register the movements. "None of them liked the same thing. This guy wanted steak, Liam wanted chicken, Holden decided he was a vegetarian for a year." He shakes his head. "In the end, I had to tell them I wasn't a short order chef. They'd eat what they got and they wouldn't throw a fit."

"A good lesson for life," I say.

"Right? Six pampered boys and me. I had to win." Saul grins this time. "Anyway, let's stop talking about this boring asshole. Tell me about you. Eli says you're from New York."

"That's right." I nod, feeling a tiny pang of homesickness. "I've been living there since college."

"It's a great place to be. But crazy, too. I ran a restaurant there for a few years. But I decided I actually liked to sleep occasionally."

"What do you do now?" I ask him. "Apart from cooking for Eli?"

Saul laughs. It's deep and low. "This is a favor. I owed Eli one."

"What for?"

Eli and Saul exchange glances. "My daughter got into a little trouble," Saul says. "Eli and Holden sorted it."

"It was nothing." Eli shakes his head. "Just some asshole who needed a talking to. I was in Boston at the time and Saul's daughter is in college there."

It's clear Saul doesn't want to talk about that, so I change the subject. "Do you work in a restaurant around here?"

"I have a couple of places in Northern Virginia," he says. "I flit between them. And then do some occasional private work."

"He's being modest," Eli says. "He cooked for Obama when he was in the White House."

"You did? What was that like?" I lean forward, fascinated. "Do you just walk up to the front door with all the food and ask them to let you in? Does he have a taster to make sure you're not poisoning him?"

Saul laughs again, good naturedly answering my questions as he cooks. Eli turns on some music – something low and slow – and refills my glass.

And by the time I stop asking stupid things like whether they have a normal dishwasher and what Barack and Michelle are really like, the food is ready and we sit down at the table Saul and Eli laid earlier.

"Won't you be joining us?" I ask Saul.

He shakes his head. "I'm gonna head out. Got places to be." He looks at Eli. "Remember the instructions for the next courses?"

Eli taps his head. "I got them in here." He and Saul hug. "Thanks, man," Eli tells him.

Saul kisses my cheek and I hug him, too. I wish he'd stay, he's fun. "It's a pleasure to meet you," I tell him.

"And you," he says. Then he lowers his voice. "This is the first time Eli's introduced me to a woman."

I blink, surprised.

"Don't tell him I told you," Saul says, with a throaty chuckle. Then he leaves and it's just the two of us.

"I'll have to get his address from you," I tell Eli. "So I can send him a thank you gift."

"I'm sure you'll see him again," Eli says, and a weird thrill rushes through me. He pulls out my chair and I sit down, then he walks around the table to sit opposite me.

Our first course is amazing. A mushroom, noodle, and chili broth that tastes so much better than it should. I finish before Eli and try to steal some of his, and he covers his bowl like an annoyed boy.

"That's mine."

I laugh because I like it when he gets riled. He's usually so calm and unruffled.

Except for when I'm around. I file that thought away to think about later.

Our main is beef wellington – a huge fillet wrapped with a home made pastry that is so good it should be illegal. By the time we get to dessert, I'm way too full but Saul must have anticipated that and made us the lightest chocolate soufflé with passionfruit sauce you could imagine.

"I'm going to have to marry Saul," I say, putting my hand on my too-full stomach. "There's no way another man could make me this happy."

Eli lifts a brow. "I beg to differ."

"I'm serious," I tease. "I'm pretty much pregnant with his beef wellington babies right now."

Pushing his chair back, Eli stalks around the table and it feels like it's game on. He reaches for me but I squeal and scramble out of my chair, running away from him.

But there's not much running away to do in his tiny cabin. It doesn't mean I don't love it when he chases me – because I do. But I'm too full and too lazy to run out of his front door and into the cold.

Maybe tomorrow. Tonight I'm ready to be caught.

Eli wraps his arm around my distended waist, and then scoops me up.

"Ugh, I weigh a ton," I tell him. "And I'm liable to vomit if you don't put me down."

"Okay." He nods.

"I'm serious, Salinger. Put me down."

So he does. And then he kisses me. Sweet little ones that make my toes curl. He wraps his hands around my neck and pulls me against him.

The man's stomach is as flat as a pancake. This isn't fair. Where did he put all that food he's just eaten?

He kisses my jaw. "I'm still hungry," he murmurs, sliding his hand down my back.

Something distracts me. Or someone. About a hundred of them, little Eli's with his apparently big peter. I pull back from him, wrinkling my nose.

"I can't," I tell him. "Not in here. I feel like I'm being watched."

He frowns. "By who?"

"You. *Baby you*. And your peter."

He rolls his eyes. "Jesus, woman. You could just close your eyes."

"I can't," I tell him seriously. "It feels wrong."

With a groan, he scoops me up again. This time I don't complain. I let him carry me into the bedroom and throw me on the bed, food baby and all.

And then he closes the door, blocking out all views of the interesting wallpaper, and advances toward me with dark eyes. I scoot up the bed, my pretty dress wrapping around my hips, revealing the black lingerie I wore to entice him with.

He glances at it, looking pretty enticed.

"Take them off," he says. So I do.

And from the way he devours me, he really is still hungry.

————

"Wake up."

I groan and turn onto my side. "Not again," I tell him. "It's Sunday. Let me sleep." Dragging somebody out of bed two days in a row should be illegal. But Eli ignores my protests and opens the curtains, light streaming into his bedroom.

"Are you getting up, or do I have to drag you out?" he asks.

"You're gonna have to drag me," I tell him, completely serious. Nothing is going to part me from this bed and comforter right now. Next week is going to be a shitshow and I need sleep so I'm prepared.

A hand wraps around my ankle and tugs. I sit up, but that only helps him drag my ass out of bed. I try to pull away but the man has a grip of steel.

"Okay, okay, stop, I'll get up."

I focus on him. He's wearing shorts and nothing else. And yeah, I ogle his broad, muscled chest because seriously, if I'm opening my eyes this early I need some kind of compensation.

"Come over here," he says, his voice sweet as honey. He walks to the window and the light bounces off his tan skin.

"Why are you so awake?" I ask him, putting my bare feet on the floor. Ooh, he has underfloor heating. Maybe I'm not so mad after all. "Don't you sleep? Are you some kind of vampire?"

He ignores me and holds out his hand. I wrinkle my nose and take it. He pulls me in front of him, so I'm sandwiched between his chest and the window. His arms wrap around me as I finally look out.

"It's snowing."

"Yep."

It's a Hollywood kind of snow. Soft flakes that drift down, coating the trees and grass. Just a blanketing, but enough to make everything look like a Winter Wonderland.

"Are we going to get snowed in?" I ask him. A mixture of hope and dread pull at my chest. Hope because if we do, I won't be there for my family's arrival into town. Dread, because I have no idea who will rein them in if I'm not there.

"Sadly not," he says, kissing the top of my head. The man is hard again. I can feel him pressing against my behind.

I wiggle and he chuckles.

"It's going to warm up after ten," he says. "The snow will be gone by the time we leave."

"At least we'll have our memories," I say, feeling a little sad that our time at his cabin will be over soon. "Can we go out in it?"

"I was going to suggest we get in the hot tub," he says. "But we can go for a walk if you prefer?"

I tap my finger against my lip. "A hot naked guy in a hot tub or a cold walk around a freezing lake. Let me think about that."

He smirks.

"I'm gonna go for the walk," I say, reconciled to the fact that I can't get back to bed. I grab some clothes from my case and head for the bathroom.

"You'd choose a walk over a naked hot guy?" he asks as I open the bathroom door.

"It was a close second," I tell him.

His phone rings, and he groans. I take the opportunity to jump in the shower, because last night we made a mess of ourselves and the bed.

Again.

I'm under the steaming hot spray when Eli puts his head around the door. "What are we doing on Tuesday?" he asks me.

"I'm going to be trying to not murder my sister," I remind him. She messaged me last week to tell me she and her partner in the ice skating show are flying in early. The show wants to record them practicing on the ice in front of the team.

And she's decided that rather than stay at Gramps' house with the rest of the family, and a lot of the production crew, she'll stay with me.

I can't wait.

"Ah right." Eli looks disappointed. "Liam and Sophie will be in town. Wanted to know if we're free for dinner. I'll tell them no."

"You can go," I point out. "I'll be with Isabella."

"She could come, too?" he suggests. His face is kind. Understanding. And it makes me feel worse.

It's so lovely in this little cocoon of the two of us. With nobody else to talk about us or judge us. Or film us.

But I know he's going slow because of me. My fears. Yes, I wore his number on my back, but we still haven't gone out in public together and it's not because of him, it's because of me.

I've been kidding myself that if I pretend it's just for now, I can walk away and not be hurt. But I care too much about him for that.

"She doesn't know about us." I pause and then get strong. "Yet."

"Yet?"

My throat tightens. I feel exposed standing naked in the shower as he watches me. I have to do this. Show him how I feel. It's not fair to him that I'm holding back because I'm scarred by something that happened all those years ago.

"I can't tell her until I tell my parents," I say. "And knowing my dad he'll want to catch it all on camera." There's no way I'm having my love life exposed to millions of reality TV watchers. "So I thought I'd tell them after the game. Once the filming is over and he can't make a thing out of it for ratings."

The softest expression washes over his face. "You're okay with telling them about us?"

I take a deep breath. "Yes. I want to. I just need to time it right." I wait for him to say something but he doesn't.

"You want me to, right?" I ask, not understanding his silence.

He walks into the shower, still wearing his shorts and scoops me into his arms.

"Your phone," I tell him.

"Oh shit." He looks at his cell still in his hands. "Ah well." He puts it outside the shower and comes back to hold me again. Water is pouring down his hair, his face, his body. And he's got a smile as wide as the ocean.

"Are you okay with me telling them?" I ask again, needing the reassurance.

"Hell, yes I'm okay. I'm fucking ecstatic," Eli says, still grinning.

The weird thing is, so am I.

CHAPTER
TWENTY-FOUR

MACKENZIE

My sister stares at me, her perfectly formed brows pulled together. "I don't get it. Why don't you want them to know I'm your sister?"

Isabella arrived this morning with a camera team. For the last hour she's been sitting in my office getting her makeup and hair done. It's been kind of distracting trying to write a letter to the IRS while listening to discussions on what lip color will contrast best with the ice.

And now it's just the two of us in here, and I'm finally able to talk to her about this stupid situation I've gotten myself into. If I'm being honest, I'm regretting the whole thing. Just goes to show that little lies never stay little.

"They just don't know. I didn't want them to." I pinch the top of my nose because I caused this mess. "It's complicated." And I'm already wishing I didn't start this conversation. "Can you just do this for me?"

"So what's our backstory?" she asks. "Have we met before? Are we complete strangers?"

She's wearing a pink skating dress that skims her perfect curves. It's amazing how much she and mom look alike. I take after my dad with dark hair instead of blonde, and hazel eyes not green.

"Do we need a backstory?" I ask. "It's just for a couple of days."

"But I'm staying with you."

"I know." She isn't going to stop until I've made up an entire story for her. It reminds me of when we were little, and even though she was the oldest, it was always my job to read us both to sleep. "Okay, we've met before. And we've been talking a lot on the phone, so we've kind of bonded and are going to spend more time together."

"So we're like best friends?" she asks. "I love that."

There's a weird lump in my throat. "Yes, friends."

She takes my hand. "I won't betray you," she says, and it makes my chest feel strange. "I'll make them believe me. I'll give the best performance of my life."

"You don't need to do that. Just don't let the cat out of the bag. Not now."

"Will you ever tell them?" she asks. And now I'm feeling bad again. I like the guys on the team. It seemed like a good idea to be professional when I first arrived, but now I wish I'd been honest.

Even if I had to pay the price.

"I'll tell them after this weekend." When my whole family – entourage and all – have left.

"Isabella?" Somebody knocks on the door. "The cameras are set up and Justin is ready." They want to record their practice to air clips of on *Ice Stars*, before they do their live performance later in the week.

"Are you coming down to watch?" she asks. "As a friend?"

"Okay. Yes." I nod. "You go ahead and I'll be there in a minute."

She beams at me. "Thank you. I'll feel much better knowing you're there." She grabs her skate bag and checks herself in the mirror the makeup artist brought with her. "Wish me luck."

"Good luck. You've got this." I go to hug her, but she turns away at the last minute, leaving me holding out my arms like a zombie. Pulling them back to my side, I watch as she leaves, before I grab the filming schedule the production person gave me, looking over it.

The morning is starting off with Isabella and Justin doing their dance practice. Then they'll get the team on the ice for her to teach them some dance moves – I guess that's the comic relief that will contrast nicely with the testosterone of the hockey game.

Eli's been a complete sport about moving things around to accommodate Isabella and the cameras. I apologized profusely – *again* – and he just laughed it off.

It's only been two days since we left Misty Lakes and I already miss it. I miss the ease of our time together. The way we bared our souls to each other. I miss being real with him, because I now realize I haven't been real in a long, long time.

Yes, I've been successful at work, and that's been great. But my love life and family life have been a mess.

It's time to change all that.

By the time I get to the rink, Isabella and Justin have already started practicing. I take a seat halfway up the bleachers, far enough away not to be caught on camera, and watch my sister tame the ice.

She's so graceful it makes my heart hurt. There's nothing more beautiful than seeing Isabella execute a perfect triple axel before she lands as soft as a snowflake back on the firm surface of the ice.

I try not to think about my stupid efforts to get across the rink and back without falling over. But then I remember Eli taking his top off for me and I can't help but smile. It's okay that I'm not good at this. I'm good at other things.

And my life is better because Eli is in it.

The whole team is watching her from the tunnel. Goran is grinning and saying something to Carter. Then I see Eli watching her and that tightness in my chest increases.

Is he comparing her performance on the ice to mine? I know he would never say it, but maybe he's wondering how we came from the same parents. I sometimes wonder that myself.

After an hour of them performing the same routine, they finally call it a day. Isabella and Justin grab a drink and talk rapidly to each other, while the director walks over to talk to the team.

They all nudge each other, then Eli leans forward to say something to Goran whose face immediately turns serious.

And then the director says something to Eli, and he shakes his head.

Isabella joins them, pulling her skates off as she shakes each of their hands. I can't see her face, but I can see her talking to Eli and dammit, I'm jealous.

Stupidly so.

And also annoyed because this situation is down to me. I asked her not to tell the team we're related. I also asked Eli not to tell them about our relationship.

Every time the team laughs at something Isabella says I feel like I'm poking at an open wound. All those years of therapy and success at work, yet I'm still jealous of my sister.

I hate that.

But it also tells me something I think I've known for a while.

I'm falling for Eli Salinger. And I don't want to lose him because I'm an idiot and make stupid decisions about my personal life.

Goran is the first to take to the ice with Isabella. He's

wearing his full hockey gear, save for his helmet, which I assume wouldn't look so good for the promos. He looks huge next to Isabella, like he's Shrek and she's Fiona. Somebody puts on some music and they skate around the ice.

Slowly Goran warms up. She shows him a move, and he replicates it perfectly. Then she takes his hands and puts them on her waist and they skate around together.

After he does an impressive toe jump, the rest of the team gets competitive. One by one, they dance with Isabella, some of them more effectively than others. Then they call Eli's name, and he shakes his head again. Isabella beckons to him so Goran and Carter drag him onto the ice.

My phone rings. I grab it too late, and I know I've ruined whatever take they're doing with the cameras, because everybody looks up at me, including Eli.

I smile apologetically and stand, whispering to the caller – Rachel – to wait, and I'll talk to her in a second.

Then I leave and the music starts up again. Somebody cheers and I don't look back because I can only imagine that Eli is dancing with Isabella.

I trust him. I know he wouldn't do anything. But I still hate it.

"Sorry about that. What's up?" I say.

"I don't know. I just got a weird feeling and wanted to check that you're okay."

My sister's dancing on the ice like a princess with my boyfriend that nobody knows about. My family is about to descend on the town and nobody knows I'm related to them. Oh, and I'm getting stupidly jealous when I should know better.

"I'm fine," I tell her. "Really. Catch me up on what's going on in New York."

———

ELI

It's getting late and I haven't seen Mackenzie all day. Practice was nonstop – the team's completely energized about the game on Saturday, and they pushed themselves harder and faster than I've ever seen them during a match week.

They're making me proud. Even Goran and Carter calmed down after having fun on the ice this morning. And yeah, it was funny watching them try to dance with Mac's sister, who by the way looks nothing like her.

But this afternoon was all business. They're determined to give the All-star team a run for their money.

Once they've left for the evening I check my watch. I have an hour before I'm due to meet my brother and his wife for dinner and I want nothing more than to see Mackenzie for five minutes because it's been a long damn day.

"Eli." The voice that calls my name isn't the one I want to hear. But Isabella is Mac's sister so I smile anyway.

Even if she doesn't know I know.

"Hi," I say, stopping a few feet short of where she's standing outside the locker room. "I thought you finished practice a while ago."

"I did, but I had a few retakes to do." Her smile is wide. "Thank you for all your support today. I'm sure the last thing you want to do is give up your practice time for some stupid show."

"It's fine. We got practice in this afternoon." She knows this. "And the guys enjoyed themselves." I scan her face for any resemblance to my girl but I can't see it. I guess it's like me and Holden. We couldn't be more different.

"How about you?" she asks.

"What?" I blink my thoughts away.

"Did you enjoy watching me?" She pulls her bottom lip

between her teeth. Red lights flash in my eyes. Shit, did she think I was flirting when I was watching her?

Danger, Will Robinson. This is not good.

"You're a good dancer," I say, checking my watch again, exaggeratedly so she gets the message. "I need to go, I'm late."

"Oh, I was wondering if you'd like to come to dinner with me."

"I'm busy," I tell her. "That's what I'm late for. I need to meet my brother." As soon as the words leave my mouth, I realize I didn't say no.

Fuck. I start to tell her that's what I meant but she beats me to it.

"Oh I didn't mean tonight. I'm busy too." She smiles widely. "We could do tomorrow though, if I can get out of a family meal."

"I'm sorry," I say, trying to think of a good excuse that doesn't involve telling her I'm in a relationship with her sister. Mac would hate that. She looked so happy in my cabin shower when she told me she was going to tell her family about us after the game.

I don't want to take that away from her.

"It's not a good idea," I say, shifting my feet. But I don't want to alienate her either. She's Mac's sister, after all. "But good luck with the show."

She doesn't blink an eyelid. In fact, she smiles. "No problem," she says. "It was just a thought."

"Have a good night," I tell her.

"You too." She turns and walks away, her hips swinging. And there's a tugging at my gut, because I need to tell Mac about this. Her sister hitting on me is not a good thing, even if I've nipped it in the bud.

I wanted to tell her I was taken. I wanted to tell her I'm falling for Mac. But I couldn't and I don't like that.

Letting out a sigh, I head up to see my girl, thinking that if we'd been open about everything from the start we wouldn't have this problem.

I don't do lies and I don't do secrets. And yet here I am, doing both.

———

It takes me ten minutes and a text to find her. I'm skulking around the hallways of the office block like a teenage boy sneaking into his girlfriend's house. Eventually she meets me in the staff room, which is thankfully empty. There's a big ass smile on her face when she walks in and closes the door behind her, flipping the lock for privacy.

Then she walks over and curls her body around mine and I feel like I've come home.

Leaning down, I kiss her hard. She's mine. I'm hers. We just need to stop fucking around and do this.

"I missed you," she says breathlessly when we stop. "How was your day?"

"Long. Yours?" I stroke the hair out of her face. She wears it down more often now and I like it.

"Weird. I had a bit of an epiphany," she says. "I was watching Isabella on the ice and got stupidly jealous. I don't know if it was because she looked so amazing, or how the team seemed to melt to goo when they were with her, but whatever it was," she waves her hand. "I realized I'm being stupid."

"There's no way you should be jealous of her," I say.

"I know, but I was. I even felt sick when I saw her talking to you."

I frown. "When did you see that?" I'm going to have to do this. Tell her and get it over with.

She puts her hand on my chest. "This morning, but it doesn't matter. I realized that I've been letting old history come between us. She was so sweet to me this morning, and I kept thinking about that. How many times has she tried to be my friend and I've pushed her away? I'm tired of hiding because I'm scared of being vulnerable around her."

I swallow but there's no moisture in my mouth.

"She even agreed to not tell anybody she's my sister. And it's only afterward I realized it must hurt her. It's like I'm rejecting her, and I shouldn't do that." She tips her head to the side, looking so earnest it hurts. "We're going to have a girls' night tonight," she says. "The kind of night we should have had years ago. Just us and some face masks and cocktails. We'll watch a stupid romcom and giggle and I can't tell you how excited I am about that."

"That's good," I mutter.

"Yeah. We're picking up the stuff on the way home." She looks so excited.

And I realize I can't tell her about the way Isabella came onto me. Because she's so damn excited that she's getting her sister back.

And I want that for her. My family is pretty much everything to me. She deserves to have the same experience with her sister and brothers. I'm not going to be the one to mess that up. Especially since her sister doesn't know we're together.

If she did, that would be different. But she made an innocent mistake.

She'll probably laugh about this once everything's out in the open.

"I'm glad you're reconnecting," I say, deciding to keep the details about her sister to myself for a few more days. "Family is important."

"Yeah." She nods. "I'm starting to see that." She loops her arms around my neck, her warm eyes catching mine. "Thank you for helping me understand how important they are."

"How did I do that?" I'm genuinely confused.

"Just watching you with your brothers. Seeing how they

plastered your cabin with that photo. It's just…" She shakes her head. "It just means something. Having people who are always on your side."

"Yeah," I say, my voice thick. "It does."

She brushes her soft lips against mine. "I'm going to miss you tonight."

"I'll miss you more," I tell her.

"Can I call you later?" she asks. "When you get back from dinner?"

I curl my hand around her neck and kiss her hard. "You'd better."

CHAPTER
TWENTY-FIVE

MACKENZIE

"There," Isabella says, lifting the mirror to show me her handiwork. "You look perfect."

I blink at the reflection staring back at me. I look like me but... almost beautiful. Not as gorgeous as Isabella, because I'll never have a nose that straight or lips that full, not without surgery anyway, but I look good.

And I feel good. Not just because we've shared a bottle of champagne tonight.

"Thank you," I tell her.

She beams at me. "I wish we'd done this years ago," she says. "I don't know why we didn't."

"Because you were busy practicing and competing, and I was either looking after the boys or at college."

And then there was the other stuff. The things we don't talk about. Danny and the way he pulled us apart.

The stupid guy we both fell for and let come between us and neither of us had the guts to talk it out.

"You'll have to show me how you applied this eyeliner," I say. "Every time I do it I look like I'm Koko the Clown."

"It's all about a steady hand," she tells me. "You can have all this." She waves her hand at the bag full of high end cosmetics. "I'm given so much I can't use it all."

"Are you sure?"

She grins. "Yep. It's yours."

It's weird how nice it is to have her here. I can't believe I was dreading it so much. "Thank you," I say again, taking her hand and squeezing it.

"Thank you," she says. "For letting me stay with you."

It would have been churlish not to. My serviced apartment has a spare room, and I know Isabella hates to be alone. She always has, even when she was small.

And yes, I'm missing Eli. He'd normally be here by now, helping me cook dinner, or taking a shower after practice. But it's only a few days until we can be together again.

I'm an adult. I can deal with that.

"So what happens after this?" she asks me, topping up our champagne glasses.

"I guess I take it all off and go to bed."

She laughs. "Not your face. I mean after you finish here. Get Gramps' baby up and running again. Will you go back to New York?"

I swallow. "Yeah, I guess." I haven't worked that bit out. Neither Eli nor I have. And we should probably talk about it, but I have no idea how to make this thing work if we're hundreds of miles apart.

"No need to look so sad," she says. "I know how much you didn't want to come here."

"I like the team," I say quietly.

She gives me a strange look. "They're lovely guys. They had a ball trying to dance. Goran, is that his name? I swear he was flirting with me."

And there it is. The jealousy again. Which is stupid because the only thing I feel for Goran is friendship.

"Eli Salinger, on the other hand," she says, her eyes lighting up. "Now he's my kind of hockey player."

The thought of Isabella flirting with Eli is like a smack to my gut. I feel sick at the thought of it. I don't think I can listen to her talking about him like that.

"There's something I need to tell you," I say.

Her phone rings. "Hold that thought. I need to take this." She slides her finger across the screen. "Issy Gauthier," she says, her voice light. "Oh, hi. That's what you heard, huh? I can neither confirm nor deny." She's silent for a minute then gives a little laugh. "Okay, yes. He had a minor issue with his Achilles, but he's seen the physio today and he'll be back at practice again in the morning." Another pause. "Yes, that's right. In West Virginia. Damn, you know everything." She catches me looking at her and rolls her eyes as though this is the most boring conversation she's ever had. "Uhuh. Yeah. Damn, you really do know. I can't confirm that, no. But when I can, you'll be the first to know."

It carries on like that for another few minutes until she finally hangs up. "I'm sorry, the damn gossip sites are getting worse. They found out about Justin's ankle injury. I've no idea how. It only happened this afternoon." She sighs. "I'm telling you, nothing is secret anymore."

I don't point out that nothing is secret because she just confirmed everything to the person she was talking to. But it reminds me that when I come clean about Eli, I need to do it on my terms. Yes, it's lovely being close to my sister again, but I still don't trust her completely.

So as much as I'd like to confide in her about Eli, I'll pass for now.

"I think I'm going to head to bed," I tell her, feeling suddenly exhausted. "There are a few emails I need to write before tomorrow."

"Oh." She sounds disappointed. "Sure. I guess I should head to bed, too. Though I don't have to be up so early tomorrow. We're not practicing until the afternoon."

The team will be practicing in the morning. And probably in the evening, too. "You can sleep in then," I say.

"Oh, I'm going to see Gramps," she says. "With the camera guys. And then I'll probably head to the rink and wait for practice."

"I'll see you there."

She smiles. "Yep."

"Good night," I tell her. "Sleep tight."

"You, too. And don't work too hard."

I head straight for my bathroom and take off the makeup Isabella so meticulously applied. Then I step into the shower and let the hot spray rain down on me for way too long. When I get out, I twist my wet hair into a towel and pull on a pair of pajamas before heading to bed, grabbing my laptop and my phone along the way.

I wasn't lying to Isabella. I have emails to write. But instead of tapping away at the keyboard, I stare absentmindedly at the screen and do some controlled breathing to get my heart rate under control.

It's not Isabella's fault I'm feeling so jealous right now. Yes, she did me dirty big time, but it was years ago.

I'm over Danny and so is she. Yes, it hurt when they got together, but we were over long before they ever started dating. And we weren't exactly close then.

I trust Eli completely. He's a straight down the line kind of guy. Not at all like Danny. Where Danny abandoned me completely the day I went viral, Eli's spent the last six weeks teaching me how to skate without falling over.

He's shown me what it's like to be taken care of. Again and again.

I pick my phone up and quickly tap out a message.

• • •

I'm in bed. Let me know when you've finished your dinner and I'll call. – Mackenzie xx

Just leaving now. Can you wait for ten minutes until I get home? Or I can call you from the car. – Eli xx

I can wait. – Mackenzie xx

I force myself to reply to some emails while I wait, but every minute that ticks by feels like an eternity. When my phone finally rings I snatch it up and answer so fast it makes my head spin.

"Hi," I breathe.

"That was quick." He laughs. "You okay?"

"No."

"What's up?"

"I missed you tonight. And I know that makes me sound weirdly clingy and I hate it, but it's true."

"If it makes you feel any better, I like it."

I wrinkle my nose. "I guess it does a bit."

"And I missed you, too. Liam and Sophie were sad you couldn't join us."

"Maybe next time?" I say, feeling sad.

"Yeah. I'd like that. So how was your evening with your sister?" There's a banging sound, like he's closing the door.

"It was good. We ate pizza and drank champagne and she did my makeup. I think we're trying to make up for the last twenty years."

"Good," he says. "I'm glad."

"I think I should tell her about us. Or maybe not. I don't know. I should probably talk to my bosses first. Out of professional courtesy." And because I'd quite like to keep my job. "What do you think?" I ask him, looking for reassurance.

"I think it's up to you," he says. "Of course I want to stop hiding this. But you need to do it at your own pace. Sophie said something tonight that got me thinking."

"What did she say?" I ask, curious.

"She said it's always the women who suffer when gossip comes out. And I don't want you to suffer. So you tell people when you're ready, and if you need to make sure your job is safe first, then that's what we'll do. We have all the time in the world."

The ache in my chest loosens a little. "Okay. But after the exhibition game, I'm going to ask to talk to him. Is that okay?"

"Yes, that's more than okay."

"And I'll tell my family."

"Good."

"And then…" I frown. "What do we do then?"

"Then we get on with living."

A smile pulls at my lips. "I like the sound of that. But what about the commute between here and New York?"

"We'll work it out," he says, sounding sure of himself. "It's five hundred miles. That's nothing."

"Eli?" I say.

"Yes, beautiful?"

"I need to tell you something else."

"You can tell me anything. You know that."

I want to tell him I love him. That I trust him. That I've never felt like this for anybody before.

But fear pushes the words down. I start to garble. "The guy I kind of dated. The one I wore no panties for…"

"Yeah?" His voice sounds tight.

"Isabella got with him afterward."

"What?"

I swallow hard. "Just for a little while, they lived together.

It ended up a complete mess." I don't tell him I was the one to get her packed and back home. "But yeah, after everything that happened we didn't really keep in touch."

"Mac, I..." He trails off. "I'm sorry."

"Not your fault," I tell him. "Anyway, it's old history. And I'm so glad it is. I think Isabella and I might finally fix our relationship. I'm so glad she came here. And I'm glad my family will be here, too. It's time for me to stop hiding who I am."

There's silence for a moment.

"Did I say too much?" I ask him.

"No, not at all. I'm glad you told me. I'm just sorry you had to go through all of that."

"It was a long time ago," I tell him, really feeling it this time.

"Yeah, it was."

I put my laptop to the side of the bed – the side where Eli usually sleeps, and snuggle down, my phone still in my hand. "Where are you now?" I ask him.

"I'm in my bedroom. Just took off my shoes."

"Will you keep talking to me while you get ready for bed?" I ask him.

"Of course."

And he does, his voice low as he tells me about his night with his brother and sister-in-law, about the steak he ate, and the chocolate dessert Sophie had but Liam stole. I snuggle against his pillow – it still smells of him and it makes me feel all warm inside, as I listen to his low voice, my eyes getting heavy.

When I wake up in the morning, the phone is still on the pillow beside me, completely out of battery. He must have talked me to sleep, and I like that too much.

I love it.

I love him.

And after this stupid game, I'm going to tell him that.

CHAPTER
TWENTY-SIX

ELI

With two days to go, every member of the team is feeling it. The laughter and teasing of a few days ago are gone, replaced by determination and concentration as we practice penalty corners. I've already reminded them we have one advantage – we're already a team. Greg's side is good. Each man as an individual is absolutely better than us.

But together? I'm pretty certain we can run circles around them.

I've spent the past few weeks watching each one of them play. Trying to anticipate how they'll mesh as a team. Assessing their weaknesses and working out how we can profit from them.

As we come to the last minute of practice, I glance up to see Mackenzie sitting in the bleachers. She catches me looking and smiles, and damn, I can't help but grin back.

I tap my watch so she knows I'm keeping time. Ten minutes and I'll go up to her office to see her. Her smile widens and I'm about to wink when I hear voices echoing from the tunnel.

The rest of the team does, too, and they stop passing the puck momentarily. Then the cause of the commotion appears rink side, his every move being recorded by two camera men who follow him like sheep.

"Hey, that's him," Carter says, nudging Goran in the chest.

"Who?"

"Greg Gauthier," he says.

"Is it?" Goran asks, taking off his helmet and squinting. "He looks old."

"He *is* old, doofus."

"You see that big stick with the furry end?" I say, pointing at the boom one of the camera team is carrying.

"Yeah?" Goran replies.

"That's a microphone," I tell him. "It picks up everything."

"Ohhh." Goran nods. "Oops."

Next to Greg is a beautiful woman. Mac's mom, I assume. And behind him are some faces I recognize.

His team of All Stars. They're all talking and the cameras are still rolling and I'm keeping an even expression even though I'm feeling slightly annoyed that they're recording this without clearing it with me first.

And also annoyed because this isn't the way I wanted to meet Mac's parents. I glance up at the bleachers to see her reaction, but she's gone.

"Eli Salinger," Greg says, his voice full of bonhomie. "I hope you don't mind me coming to spy on the opposition."

I push a smile onto my face and skate over to where he's standing. He reaches his hand out and I shake it.

Maybe a bit too hard.

He winces a little as I release his palm, and I'm left with the smallest sense of satisfaction.

"We're just finishing up," I say, glancing over his shoulder. "Did you want me to get the ice cleaned up so you can get on here?"

"Oh no," he says. "We start practicing tomorrow."

Between his team, our team, and Isabella's ice dancing, that's three sets of practice taking place on the ice. It's annoying because we still need more time but there it is.

"We just wanted to say hi."

"Hi," I say deadpan.

"And cut…" a voice calls out. A man pushes his way through, holding a clipboard. The director, maybe? Do reality shows even have directors? Maybe he's a producer, I've no idea. "Eric, is it?" he asks, looking at me.

"Eli," I tell him.

"Sure. Can we do that again? Could you ask your team to play for a minute and we'll walk in?" he asks. "It won't take long."

"Seriously?" Isn't Reality TV meant to be… reality?

"Sorry," Greg says. "We won't take much of your time." He smiles widely at the rest of the Mavericks. "Then when we're done that I'd love for you guys to introduce yourselves. I've been looking forward to meeting you all."

The team talks excitedly to each other because Greg is the Olympic hero they all grew up with. So I nod and we do it all over again, except this time Goran doesn't mention Greg's age and the producer / director / whatever he is looks pleased and nods.

"That's a wrap for today, gentlemen." He shakes my hand. "Eric, good to meet you."

I don't bother to correct him this time. I'm too intent on getting into the locker room and reminding the guys that we have a game in two days so they need to get rid of the stars in their eyes. It's going to be aired on the network – nationally. And yes, there's no real skin in the game, at least not when it comes to the league.

But for these players the skin is about exposure. Their future careers. I don't want them to be known as part of the team that failed.

Once again, I wait until they've all left before I call the cleaning crew and let them know we're done. When I walk out of the door, I see Mac and her sister in some kind of intense conversation by the exit into the parking lot.

Mac looks up and sees me watching them. Does she want me to pretend I haven't seen her?

I can't. I just can't.

"Is everything okay?" I ask, walking toward them. Isabella's wearing a pair of yoga pants and a cropped hoodie, her skate bag in her hand. She turns to look at me, and her furrowed brow immediately smooths.

So much for sisterly love.

"I'm trying to persuade Mackenzie to come to dinner." She winks at me. "Since I don't have an excuse I have to go. But she's not having any of it."

"Not hungry?" I ask Mackenzie.

"I… ah…" She blows out a mouthful of air. "No."

"It's been a long day," I say. Oh well done, Salinger. Great repartee.

"It has," Mac agrees. "I just want to go home."

I shift my feet. "Actually, there was an issue I needed to discuss with you," I say to Mackenzie. "Boring team stuff."

"Okay," Isabella says, shrugging as she looks at Mac. "I'll meet you at the car."

Then she looks at me and gives me a beaming smile. "You were good on the ice today," she says. "You're gonna give my dad's team a run for their money."

She turns around before I can say anything and pushes through the door, the cool air rushing in and making Mac shiver. I wait until it closes before I walk over to her.

"Are you okay?"

She nods. "I'm fine. Just tired, that's all."

I reach out to cup her face. Damn, I want to kiss her. She looks so vulnerable and it tugs at something inside of me.

My inner knight in fucking armor.

Instead, I incline my head and we walk up to her office. There are still a few people around because there's so much to do before game night, and I know she doesn't want me to show affection in public.

"Just a couple of days and this will be over," I tell her. She smiles at that, and I do, too.

I miss taking her home every night. I miss waking up with her in the mornings.

"I can't wait," she tells me. "I know this is for Gramps, but it's all too much. The people, the cameras. My family."

I reach for her waist, pulling her against me. It takes a second or two, but finally she relaxes and I hear her breathing start to even.

"Just tell them," I say. "If that's easier. Tell them who I am, tell them what I know. I'll tell the team who you are."

"It's okay," she says. "It can wait. I'll be fine."

"Okay then." I tighten my hold on her. "You want me to come over while your sister's out?"

She shakes her head against me. "You need an early night. You're rostered at six tomorrow morning for practice."

The joys of sharing the ice with another team, plus Isabella and her partner. But Mac is right. If I'm telling the team they can't go out and need to be in bed by ten, I can't exactly go over to hers and spend the night buried inside of her.

As much as that's what I need right now.

"Okay," I say softly. "I'm gonna kiss you now, and then I'm going to leave."

She looks up, her eyes sparkling. "I'm good with the kissing part."

Yeah, me too. I cup her face with my hands, my mouth hungry against hers as I show her exactly how good I am with it.

———

MACKENZIE

The rest of my dad's team – including my brothers – arrive the next morning as the Mavericks are practicing on the ice. This time they don't disturb them with cameras, but I still hang back as Brad and Johnny throw their arms around Dad and Mom.

Brad grins when he sees me, holding his hands out wide. And I'm ashamed to say I check for cameras before I walk into his arms and let him envelop me in a bear hug.

"Sis," he says. "Missed you."

"I missed you, too," I manage to say, even though my face is squashed against his stupidly hard chest. Like my dad, Brad and Johnny have this natural ease with life. Nothing phases them. Not even me reminding them that when the cameras roll I'm not related to them at all.

"Where is the rest of the team?" I ask Dad.

"Sent them to get some breakfast. We start practicing at noon." He pulls Mom against him and gives me a smile. "We missed you at dinner last night."

"I had some work to do."

"All work and no play makes Mackenzie a dull girl," Brad says, earning him a punch in the arm from Johnny. "What?" he asks. "I was just kidding."

"She wasn't so dull when she bailed your ass out of jail," Johnny reminds him. "*Twice.*"

"Speaking of work," Dad says, ignoring their squabbles, "I need to talk to your security guy. I've had to change a couple of players around because we have some injuries and they'll need passes."

"Who?" Brad asks.

"Stanton tore his achilles playing football with his kid," Dad says. "And Ryker is sick."

"So who's playing instead of them?" Brad looks unhappy.

Dad ruffles his hair, even though Brad is taller than him. And probably has twenty pounds on him, too. "Don't worry, I got it covered. I think you'll be happy."

"Brad's just scared he'll let in too many goals," Johnny says. "He can't cope without a decent defenseman."

"Good thing he has you then," Dad says lightly. I call our security guy and explain the situation. He tells me to send Dad over with the details.

And then finally they all leave. Except Mom, who lingers as my two hulking brothers bump into each other as they walk out of the door.

"Is everything okay?" Mom asks. "You look anxious."

I let out a mouthful of air. "I'm just worried about everything going smoothly tomorrow night. It's a big night for the team. And for Gramps."

She nods. "I know. But you're doing a wonderful job." She reaches out to touch my cheek. "Thank you for letting Isabella stay with you. She hates hotel rooms."

"It's fine. I'm happy to have her."

"She said you two had reconnected."

"It's been good to talk with her," I say. I know Mom hated the fact that we barely spoke to each other for years.

"Sisters are important," she says. "There's nobody like a sister to give you some support." She looks at me carefully, as though she's trying to weigh what to say. "She was so upset when you told her you didn't want anybody to know you were related."

Mom's not only talking about Isabella. And she's not just talking about this week either. I know it hurt her when I changed my name. It must have felt like I was rejecting our family.

But it was the only way I knew how to protect myself at

the time. Looking back maybe I should have brazened it out, been stronger. But when you're in the eye of the storm the only thing you can think about is how to get out.

"I know," I say, patting Mom's arm. "I'm sorry."

"I'd like us to all get along. It's been lovely working with Isabella," she continues. "And your dad loves watching the boys. But I want my other daughter, too." She slides her hand into mine. "I'm proud of you, sweetheart. I wish you'd let me show that."

"I know," I say, my voice thick as she pulls me in for a hug. She's so tiny it feels like hugging a twig. But she smells just like I remember. It makes me feel like I'm fourteen again. Desperate for her love. But maybe it was there all along.

"Okay, the security is all done." Dad walks back into the room. "I'm gonna head down to the guest locker room. You coming?" he asks Mom.

"I'll pass," she says, wrinkling her nose. "I've done my fair share of locker rooms."

Dad winks. "I know that, baby."

Ugh. Gag alert. But the way mom smiles at him is kind of sweet. There's still chemistry between my parents after all this time.

And it makes me yearn for Eli more than I can say.

CHAPTER TWENTY-SEVEN

ELI

It's the next day and the two teams are actually bonding with each other. Greg's older and wiser team take the Mavericks under their wing. Goran has a long, deep discussion with Greg about the next steps he should take in his career. Mackenzie's brother, Brad is exchanging goalkeeping stories with Max, the two of them agreeing that the rest of their teams are assholes.

And I'm talking to Johnny, Mackenzie's other brother, who's a fucking hoot, just like I thought he'd be. He reminds me of my youngest brother, Brooks, except he's not such an asshole.

I find myself wanting to ask him about Mac. About how she had to give up so much to take care of him and his brother when they were growing up. But instead I laugh as he recounts a story of how he and Brad swapped positions in college for one whole semester and nobody noticed.

Greg keeps looking at his watch, because his two new recruits haven't arrived yet and they start practice in five minutes. I've promised him we won't stay and watch – it's only fair that the All Stars get a chance to learn how to play together without their opponents taking notes.

In a weird way it feels good to finally meet Mackenzie's family. Sure, I'm pretty much avoiding Isabella, but once Mackenzie tells her the truth about us she'll hopefully see the funny side.

And Brad and Johnny are completely chilled. I'm hoping they'll stay that way when they realize I've been spending most of my time with their big sister.

Greg is interesting. I heard him telling Goran about how hard it was to get out from his father's shadow when he was a kid. Every team would target him when they played because he was Wayne Gauthier's son and they wanted to show him who was boss.

I guess being a celebrity in his own right has made him feel better about himself. So I'm giving him a partial pass for being so camera hungry.

"Here they are," Greg calls out, standing and walking over to the two new guys who've walked in. He's in my line of sight so I can't see past him.

But then he steps to the side and my blood runs fucking cold as my gaze rests on a pair of ice-blue eyes I know all too well.

It's fucking Hart. Center for the Toronto Maple Leafs. The asshole who caused the injury that sent me right out of the NHL and over here to the Mavericks. I haven't seen him since that day, but he's grinning at me now, and I'm trying to keep my cool.

Greg says something to him and he turns his head, not bothering to acknowledge me.

Good. That's good. Because I'll probably punch his face in. The guy didn't apologize even though my injury was his fault. And even though I had to retire from top class hockey before I was ready to.

With a tight jaw I bring my attention back to my team,

calling out their names. They look up at me and I nod at them.

"Time to go, team."

For once they do as instructed, without me having to yell at them three times. We head to the locker room and I tell them to sit down, annoyed at how much I'm affected by Hart's arrival.

I pinch my nose and take a deep breath, trying to get my head straight.

"Okay," I say. "The fun's over. Thank you for being so gracious to our guests, but now it's time to focus on our game."

They nod, wisely keeping quiet.

"And it's time to think like a winning team."

———

ELI

"Hart's here," I tell Holden, because he's the only one I can call right now.

"What do you mean he's *here*?" Holden says. "Where?"

"At the arena. Practicing. He's been recruited to the All Stars."

"What? Who invited that asshole? Don't they know what he did to you?" Holden can keep a grudge better than anybody I know.

"I guess not." Or they don't care. I think it's likely the first though. I can't see Greg inviting Hart to play just to piss me off. He's not that kind of guy. He wants this game to be fun, to be a spectacle people will enjoy.

Otherwise, it'll reflect badly on him.

"So what are you going to do?" Holden asks. A voice echoes – an overhead announcement in the hospital I think.

He's supposed to be off work for the next few days, taking some long-unused vacation time to come watch this game with our family.

I guess he couldn't quite drag himself away from his patients until the last minute.

"I'm not going to do anything," I say. "I just wanted to warn you. And ask you to warn the others that he's here."

My whole family will be at the game. I don't want them being surprised by Hart coming on and playing.

"You're still going to play though?" Holden says.

"Yeah, that's the plan." I have clearance from the team doctor. It's an exhibition match and I can't see myself being on the ice for more than thirty minutes. I want to give the whole team a chance to play. "Don't worry, I'm not going to try to get revenge."

Holden chuckles. "Good. You already ruined one knee, let's try to keep the other one working, okay?"

"That's the plan," I tell him. It's good to hear his voice.

"So I talked to Liam and Sophie last night," Holden tells me. "They told me you and Mackenzie are getting serious."

"Yeah we are," I say softly, because I'm still in the arena.

"They also told me what he got Brooks and Linc to do to your cabin."

I roll my eyes as he laughs again. But it's good to hear him happy. He works so hard with kids that need all the help he can offer. It's rare that he turns off from being a doctor.

"That was fun," I say, deadpan. "I'm still working out how to get them back."

"I'm looking forward to that."

There's another voice echoing through the other line. "Listen, man, I gotta go," Holden says. "But I'll see you after the game tomorrow night." He clears his throat. "Don't do anything stupid."

"I won't." I already feel better. "Thanks for listening."

"Any time."

———

MACKENZIE

I'm in my office when I hear the soft tap at the door.

"Come in," I call out and my Mom walks in, giving me a soft smile when she sees me at my desk.

"Am I interrupting?" she asks.

I shake my head. "Just answering a few emails," I tell her. "Is everything okay?"

She pulls the door shut behind her and sits down at the chair opposite me, the desk between us. There's a strange look on her face that I can't quite place.

"Danny's here," she says.

For a minute I say nothing. Maybe I didn't hear right.

"What?" I ask. "Why?"

"Your father had two drop outs. He called in two new players. One of them's Danny." She twists her hands together. "He didn't talk to me about it because I would have told him he's an idiot. He just doesn't think sometimes." She looks up at me, and I realize the expression on her face is fear. "I'm so sorry. Please don't let this come between us again."

"Does Isabella know he's here?" I ask. Because yes, Danny hurt me, but he hurt her too.

And she hurt me. It's a mess. And I have no idea why Dad wouldn't have anticipated this.

Because he's an idiot. And he doesn't hold a grudge so he doesn't think anybody else does either.

She shakes her head. "She's going to throw a fit when she finds out," Mom says. "And she has the semi final dance off on Sunday night."

I know this. She has to fly directly to L.A. after the exhibition match so she can be in L.A. on Sunday. Justin has already flown back. "Can you talk to Dad?" I ask. "See if he can find somebody else?"

"I have and it's too late. Even if he finds somebody they won't get to practice with the team." She grimaces. "I'm so sorry, honey. I know Danny hurt you more than anybody."

"I was a kid then. It feels like old history."

"Really?" There's hope in Mom's voice. "Because I feel like we're just getting you back. I don't want to lose you again."

"You won't," I tell her. "I promise."

And it's not a lie. I'm over what happened. All I want to do is think about the future. With Eli. I'm pretty much avoiding the ice so it won't be hard to avoid Danny.

Isabella, on the other hand, won't be able to.

"Are you going to tell her he's here?"

She nods, looking resigned. "I'll tell her tomorrow morning."

"Good luck."

"Thanks. I think I'm going to need it." She reaches for my hand. "Thank you," she says. "For being so calm. For being you."

I squeeze her hand. "It's okay. Everything's going to be fine." And tomorrow night it will all be over. The game will be played, the cameras will go, and I can come clean about everything with Eli.

I'm not going to let a piece of slime like Danny ruin anything. The future is too bright for that.

"I love you," Mom says. "So much."

CHAPTER
TWENTY-EIGHT

MACKENZIE

The next morning dawns and I arrive early to the arena. The staff areas are buzzing – Brian is throwing a fit trying to make sure that we're ready for the influx of spectators and cameras – and the rink is also full, with Dad's team having first practice.

Mom grabbed Isabella as soon as we arrived, pulling her off to a side room, presumably to tell her about Danny. I left them to it, not only because I don't want to be anywhere in the vicinity when Issy finds out that our ex is playing for Dad's team, but also because I have a billion things to do before tonight.

I'm also missing Eli like crazy. He's way too busy for me to talk to right now. I haven't even told him my ex is here. I don't want to do anything to cause problems with the team. Not after the towel incident.

Brian's talking me through the profit and loss sheet for the game when the door to the staff area opens and Pam from accounts walks in.

"Have you heard what's going on down on the rink?" she asks, inclining her head at the door.

Brian looks panicked. "What?" he asks. "Is there something wrong with it?"

Pam shakes her head. "There's a huge fight. Screaming and everything. That pretty girl from the ice show and one of the players are going at it."

My stomach sinks. I guess Isabella knows about Danny being here. I look at Brian. "I'll go see what's happening."

He nods, looking relieved that he gets to stay in the relative safety of the staff area. "I'll keep working on this."

As soon as I walk down to the rink area I can hear the shouting. When I push open the door, Dad's players are standing by the boards, watching Isabella and Danny going up against each other.

Even worse, the cameras are there, too.

I spot Dad and widen my eyes at him, trying to send him a mental message to get between them, but he doesn't get it.

And then I see Mom and rush over to her. "Somebody needs to stop them," I whisper.

"I'm on it," she says. "I just wanted to give her a minute to let it out. Better now than during the game."

She's right. "Bring her up to my office," I say. "She can let it all out there."

Mom nods, her face stormy, and walks over to where Isabella and Danny are facing off against each other.

"Well maybe you should have kept your diseased riddled dick locked up where it belongs," Isabella screams. There's laughter from the team. Thank God the Mavericks aren't here yet. They will be soon, though.

Mom calls out Isabella's name and she turns around, blinking. "Honey, you have a phone call," Mom shouts out, lying through her teeth.

"Just keep away from me," Isabella says, jabbing her

finger at Danny's chest. He's wearing his full kit so I doubt he can feel it.

"Whatever." He skates away and Dad finally seems to wake up. "Let's get on with this, shall we?" he says. "Before the Mavericks arrive."

Mom finally pulls Isabella off the ice. There are tears on her face, ruining her makeup. Her skin is blotchy and her eyes are ringed with red.

"You okay?" I ask.

She shakes her head. The three of us walk back to my office, past the staff who are watching with wide eyes.

Brian opens his mouth to say something but I shake my head, and he wisely looks back at his spreadsheet.

None of us says a word until we're all inside and the door is closed.

I lead Isabella over to my chair and make her sit down, while I pour her a glass of water.

She takes it with shaking hands and sips at the cool liquid, tears still flowing down her face.

"Do you want to talk about it?" I ask her.

"Not really," she says, her lip wobbling. "Unless it's about how we cut Danny's balls off with a pair of rusty scissors."

"Ouch." I wince. "But sure, we can do that." I touch my lip. "Maybe shears would be better. Or a plastic knife."

"You hold him down and I'll do the rest," she says, her voice stronger. "I hate him."

"He's not worth hating," I tell her. And it's true. I'm over him. Over all of it. The thought makes me feel light.

Isabella, on the other hand, doesn't seem over anything. "I can't believe I ever let myself fall for him." She gives me a sad look. "Or that I lost you over him."

"Well, let's not let him ruin our day," Mom says.

"I can't believe Dad recruited him after everything that happened," Issy continues, ignoring her. "Did he do it on purpose? To get more publicity?"

"Your dad is stupid," Mom says. "But not that stupid." She looks at her phone. "I've asked the makeup team to meet us at Gramps' house," she says to Isabella. "I figure the longer we can stay away from here the better."

It's a good idea to keep them separated. I smile at Mom and she smiles back.

"Will you come, too?" she asks.

"Me?"

She smiles. "Yes, you. I'd like to spend time with both my girls. We'll get our hair done, eat some bad food, have some fun."

"I can't," I say. "I've got too much to do." There's not enough staff to cover everything we need to finish before the game. If I leave them I'd feel terrible.

"Are you sure?"

I nod. "I'm sure. But I'd like to do that... another time."

She beams. "I'd like that, too." She looks at Isabella. "Go ahead, honey, I'll be right behind you."

Isabella nods and stands, looking more like her normal self. She puts her arms around me and hugs me tight. "Thank you for not hating me anymore."

"Likewise." My voice is muffled by her shoulder.

She walks out, closing the door behind her and it's just me and my mom.

"I'm sorry," she says. "That you're all caught up in this. You shouldn't have to deal with the cameras or the drama. And you certainly shouldn't have to deal with Danny. I've told your father he owes you big time for this."

"It doesn't matter," I tell her. "It'll all be over after tonight."

"When you agreed to come here and help Gramps, I was so excited. After all these years, it felt like you might finally want to be part of our family again." Her face crumples. "And now we've made you unhappy."

For the first time, I see things from her view. How hard it

must have been for her two daughters to be fighting. And then rather than talk to her, I turned away. Changed my name, moved to New York, refused to have anything to do with being a Gauthier.

I pushed her away because I was scared she'd choose Isabella over me.

I think of all those times she tried to call and I was too busy with work. All those times she messaged and I didn't reply for days. Or at all. I made a choice to isolate myself so I didn't have the pain of them doing it to me.

"I'm not unhappy," I tell her. "I've never been more happy."

"Really?" Her eyes light up. "Is that true?"

"It is," I tell her. "It really is."

"Oh honey." She pulls me into her arms. "That's all I want. To know you're happy."

For a second I tense. I'm not used to so much physical affection from my family. But again, that's because I'm the one who's run away from it. I will my body to relax and I hug her back as she sobs into my shoulder.

"I'd like to talk to you and Dad after the game," I tell her. "With no cameras."

"Of course there'll be no cameras," she says. "I'm putting my foot down. I've had enough of living my life on screen."

"You're not doing the reality show?"

She shakes her head. "No. And I'm hoping that once I talk to him, your father will see sense. They can use what they have, but I'm not doing this anymore." She pats my cheek. "What is it that you want to talk to us about later?"

I take a deep breath. "I've met somebody." There, I've said it. Now I can't go back on it.

Not that I was planning to. But it's good to have insurance.

"You have?" She looks genuinely excited. "Who is he? Somebody from New York?"

"Can I tell you later?" I ask her. "It's just there's so much to do, and Isabella's waiting for you."

She nods. "I hate waiting, but I'll do it for you." She pats my cheek. "I'm so happy for you."

"Thank you." I open the door and she goes to walk out.

"Oh, Mackenzie?"

"Yes?"

"Would you like me to send my hair and makeup people to you when we're done? They'd be happy to work in here."

"That's really sweet of you but I'll be fine." I don't have the time but also I won't be on camera. I'll be hiding in the staff box, away from it all. "I appreciate the offer though."

"Anytime, honey." She goes to walk away but can't resist giving me one last hug. "Thank you for coming back to us. You don't know how much it means to me."

CHAPTER
TWENTY-NINE

ELI

I make it til four o'clock before I finally cave and walk upstairs to the staff offices. It's mayhem up there. Staff are everywhere, running with pieces of paper in their hands, shouting out for help. They see me and their eyes widen and they slow down just enough to wish me luck.

And I realize how important this game is to all of them. Not just because Wayne needs the money but because they love the team as much as I do. It's David versus Goliath but we have sticks and pucks instead of slingshots and stones.

I knock on Mac's door. She calls out to come in and when I push it open I see Wayne sitting in front of her.

He grins, looking genuinely happy to see me. I walk over and shake his hand then look at Mac, waiting to see the anxious expression she always gets when her family is around.

But it isn't there. And I'm so pleased to see Wayne. It's the first time he's been to the arena since his surgery.

"How are you?" I ask.

"I'm good." He lifts his brows at the walker next to him.

"Ready to not be using this thing, but the nurse insisted." He shrugs. "She's around somewhere."

"She's gone to check out your seating arrangements for this evening," Mac says. "Remember?"

"I remember. I got a bad hip, I'm not senile," he grumbles.

"Okay," the nurse says, walking back in. "We're good. There's easy access to the rink side seats."

"I told you there was," Wayne says.

"I know. But you also lie a lot," she says, taking no shit from him.

"How's the team?" Wayne asks me. "They holding up okay?"

"They're nervous but they've worked as hard as they could. It all comes down to what happens on the night," I say. "They'll be pleased to know you're here."

"Can I come see them?" Wayne asks. "I'd like to give them a talk before the game."

"It's your team," I remind him. "And they'd love that. They're sick of hearing my voice." I smile at him. "You can do the press conference afterward if you'd like."

He laughs because he knows how much I hate those things. Journalists get a kick out of seeing a hockey player go down. "Oh no, that's all yours." He looks at the nurse. "How long we got?"

"An hour before you need to be in your seat. I want you comfortable before the rest of the spectators come in."

"You want me sitting down for two hours before puck drop?" he asks. "Damn."

"It's either that or we go home and you have an early night," she tells him.

Wayne sighs. "Okay then. Let me go talk to the staff then we can head for the locker room." He looks at me. "Meet you there?"

"I'll be there," I tell him.

He nods. "Then let's go."

Mackenzie watches them leave, a smile playing at her face. When we're finally alone she focuses on me and I'm mesmerized by her eyes.

"Hey stranger," she says softly. My heart does this weird flip. I don't care about the game, I just want to take her home and into bed.

Instead, I walk over to her and pull her into my arms until her face is resting against my chest. I stroke her glossy hair and can smell her shampoo.

It's all I need.

Running my finger along her jaw, I tip her face up until our lips meet. Her mouth is soft, pliant and I kiss her like I haven't seen her in a month. She wraps her arms around my neck, her breasts pushing against me, and I immediately go hard.

Reluctantly, I step back. Because I'm not here for that. "Are you okay?" I ask her.

She looks up at me. "I'm good."

"Really?" Because it's been a weird few days. And I know how much her family messes up her mind.

"Honestly," she says, nodding. "I think I might be the only one who is okay in this building, but I am."

"What was happening with your sister and Hart?" I ask her. "I didn't know they had a past."

She runs her tongue along her bottom lip. My eyes follow it like it's the holy grail. "I'll tell you later." She breathes out softly. "I've told my mom I've met somebody."

"You did?" I ask. "Who?"

She starts to laugh and it's music to my ears. "I'd like to introduce you to them later. As my boyfriend."

I swallow. "You sure?"

"Yes." The smile wavers. "Are you sure? I mean, I assumed... we talked..."

"Of course I'm fucking sure." I pull her against me again. "I'm ready for this. I told you that."

"Then let's meet after the game." She reaches up and softly strokes my cheek. It feels so good I struggle not to groan. "And if you change your mind..."

"I won't change my mind. Let's do it."

"Okay." She nods. "Good."

"I have to do the press conference right after the game," I tell her. "And then I'll need to say hi to my family. But after that I'm yours. Where do you want to do it?"

"I thought we'd do it at Gramps' place. There won't be any cameras there. Plus if my dad decides to beat you up we can make a run for it."

"Where would we go?" I ask her, not wanting our conversation to end. Because then I'll have to leave and I've missed her so goddamned much.

"I'm not sure," she says, wrinkling her nose.

"Vegas. We'll have a shotgun wedding. That way he can't pull us apart."

"He wouldn't pull us apart anyway," she says. "He'll probably think it's good publicity."

There's a knock at the door. I step back again and she takes a deep breath. "Come in."

This time it's Brian. He has the latest printout for her and wants to talk it over. He's so caught up in the numbers he barely notices me standing there.

"I'll leave you to it," I tell her, giving her a crooked smile.

"Good luck," she says, her eyes meeting mine. "Not that you need it. You guys are going to win."

"I hope so." The smile on my face doesn't waver.

"I'll be cheering you on," she says. "And wearing my jersey."

I want to hold her again. I want to tell Brian – the poor guy – to fuck off and leave us alone. I want to drop to my knees and worship at her until her breath does that catching thing that always makes me hard.

I want to love her. Forever. I should have told her that. Before Brian walked in.

"Go," Mackenzie whispers. And I realize I'm standing there, staring at her, my breath coming way too fast for its own good.

"Later," I tell her.

"Yes."

Brian's making some notes on his papers, leaning over her desk. Thank God the man loves numbers more than life.

I love you. I want to mouth it to her. I want to do it again tonight, when I'm on the ice.

But instead I push those words down. Because I'm not saying it in front of Brian. And I'm definitely not sending it in a message to her phone.

"Oh, good luck," Brian says, finally looking up from his printout.

"Thanks, man," I say. And then I leave.

———

MACKENZIE

I pull on my jersey and check my phone. It's a few minutes until game time and I need to get out there and sit with the staff, but a message from my mom grabs my attention.

Hey sweetie. We're sitting with Gramps, rinkside. Want to come join us? – Mom x

Hi Mom. Thanks for the invite but I promised I'd sit with the staff. I'll come find you when it's over, okay? – Mackenzie x

. . .

Sure. Probably for the best. Isabella's not exactly in a good mood. She's spent most of the afternoon planning her revenge.
– Mom x

That sounds like Isabella. Danny should be worried.

I feel kind of sorry for Mom, because I've seen Isabella when she wants revenge. The day I picked her up from Danny Hart's apartment, when everything between them imploded, she poked a hole in all of his condoms and soaked them in chili juice for an hour, before drying them all off and sliding them back into the box in the bathroom cabinet.

I have no idea if he used them or not, but the thought of it makes me wince.

I slide into my seat next to Brian just as the teams skate onto the ice. The arena is completely full and everybody is screaming as Dad leads his team out. Then the Mavericks follow to another roaring cheer. Kids are waving flags, adults are jumping up and down, as the teams take their places ready to face off.

I look down trying to see Mom and Isabella. But then Gramps appears on the big screen and if the arena was loud before, now the cheers are deafening.

Everybody loves Gramps. It's been a long time since they've seen his face. He smiles and waves a hand and the screams get louder.

Mom is smiling next to him. And next to her is Isabella and… wow.

Yep, she's definitely in vengeance mode. She looks absolutely amazing. Her hair is glossy and tied back casually, though it probably took her hairdresser hours to create that effect. And her face is perfectly made up to highlight her high cheekbones and wide eyes.

She wears vengeance well. I hope Danny realizes what a dick he is.

Then the game begins. I know I'm supposed to have torn loyalty, with my dad being on one side and the Mavericks on the other, but like the rest of the staff I'm cheering for our team. Five minutes later, when Carter hits the puck into the net and our team takes the first goal, all of us are on our feet screaming.

Then I see Brian has Eli's name on the back of his jersey, too. I can't help but smile.

The big screen shows Gramps' reaction. He's fighting with his nurse because he's trying to get on his feet and she's stopping him. Everybody starts chanting his name as he grins.

Next to him, Isabella is on her feet, too. I guess she's decided which team she's supporting.

Of course, it could be something to do with the fact that the goal was mostly Danny's fault for losing possession. He body checks Carter and the two of them look close to fighting.

Then he deliberately skates close to where Mom and Isabella are sitting. It looks like he says something to her, but I don't know what.

"That number three's an asshole," Brian says.

"Yup." I nod.

The game gets more scrappy as time goes on. From a skill and experience point of view, Dad's team should be on top by miles, but the Mavericks have the home advantage, and they're also young and hungry. When the second intermission arrives it's almost a relief, because the sin bin keeps getting filled up thanks to stupid fights that break out across the ice. Dad and Eli both look grim as they lead their teams into the tunnel.

The Mavericks are winning three goals to two, and everybody around me is beaming. I head down to grab my usual hotdog, too superstitious not to. And as I bite down, mustard and ketchup oozing all over my lips, I see my beautiful, glamorous sister walking toward me.

"Oh hey," I say, trying to swallow down the oversize

mouthful I've bitten off. Then I dab my mouth with the white napkin the vendor gave me, though I'm sure I'm just smearing red and yellow around my face.

"Hi." She smiles at me. "Still loving those hotdogs, huh?"

"Best part of the game." I lift a brow and take in her black dress. It's skater style, clinging to all her perfect curves. "You look great."

"Thank you. So do you." She lifts a brow at my jersey. "No hiding which team you're supporting."

I shrug. "I saw you cheering them, too."

"Yep. I'm on team anybody but Danny."

"I saw him say something to you." I'm curious now. Especially when she frowns. "What was it?"

"Oh he's a delight." She sighs. "He told me that my vagina was as wizened as my neck."

"He said the word wizened?" I ask her.

She grins. "No, he's not smart enough for that. I think he said arid. Or dry. I'm not sure."

"You're looking remarkably cool," I say, because she really is. "Mom said you were vengeful."

"I'm not vengeful," she tells me, grabbing my dog and taking a bite. It's weird but I like that. I like that we're sisters again. That she doesn't think to ask.

I also like that she's got mustard on the tip of her nose.

"Good." I check my watch. There's only a few minutes left in the intermission. "Are you going back to Gramps' house with Mom and Dad after the game?" I ask her.

"Yeah. But I have to catch a flight to L.A. first thing. I thought I'd stay there tonight so I went and picked my things up from your place earlier." She looks almost sad about that.

"That's fine." I nod.

"Good." She nods, too. And for a moment we say nothing.

"I'm going to miss you…"

"It's been so nice to see you…"

We both talk at once, then start laughing. She wrinkles her nose – still with the mustard on it – and I grin back at her.

Through the crowd I can see the Zamboni drive off the ice, and everybody starts to cheer again.

"I should head upstairs," I say. Isabella nods, and then she leans forward and hugs me, pressing her lips against my cheek.

It's only when I'm sitting next to Brian again, and he starts pointing at my cheek that I realize she rubbed mustard all over it.

Dammit.

———

ELI

"Everybody needs to keep their cool," I say, my voice a low warning as the game is about to restart after a commercial break.

"Yeah, well if that asshole would stop trying to fight me, everything would be fine," Carter grumbles.

"Shut up," Goran hisses. "The kids are listening."

We arranged for the students we've been coaching all year to be here watching. They're sitting next to the tunnel, and when Goran waves at them they wave excitedly back.

I know exactly who Carter's moaning about. Hart has decided to be asshole-in-chief for the All Stars. Every time any of my team goes up against him he tries to start a scrap.

Each time he does, he looks over at me. I've been sitting on the bench for most of the game. I think that's what's annoyed him the most. He can't get to me, so he's getting to my boys instead.

So this time I'm calling his bluff. I'm going to play whenever he does. Bring it on.

And he does. Literally. As soon as I have the puck he makes a beeline for me, cross checking me with his stick, earning him a two minute stint in the sin bin.

When he's back on the ice, he's really pissed. Greg skates over and grabs his shoulders, whispering something I can't hear. Hart nods, but then he looks over at me, his eyes narrowed.

I smile sweetly back at him.

Carter scores again, putting us ahead by two, and I'm grinning like a loon when I look up at the staff box. I can't see my girl, but I know she's there, wearing my shirt like she promised.

And I know she's looking right down at me. That makes everything better. It also makes me distracted, and Hart takes advantage of it, skating behind me and jabbing his stick against my legs.

Of course I fall onto the ice, air escaping my lungs in a rush. Luckily, my knee is fine and I'm straight back up, but I taste blood in my mouth. My tooth must have pierced the inside of my bottom lip as I fell. There's a small spot of blood on the ice which means I have to head for the bench to get my mouth cleaned. Simons jumps onto the ice to replace me as I skid into the break in the boards and make my way to the bench.

"You're bleeding." It takes me a moment to realize it's Isabella talking. She's sitting with her family and Wayne on the bench next to the team. Or at least she was. Now she's standing, leaning over, holding something out to me. A tissue.

I take it and rub my mouth because there's seriously hardly any blood and I want to keep on playing. She smiles and shakes her head. "Come here," she says. So I lean forward and she grabs another tissue, wiping the corner of my lip, her fingers curled around my arm to steady herself.

"No fucking way." Hart frowns, watching us. "You two?"

Isabella smiles then pulls me closer. Before I can say

anything her mouth is on mine, kissing me like I'm the oxygen she needs. It's only when I hear the huge roar of the crowd that I realize we're on the big screen.

And everybody is watching.

I wrench away from her, but she doesn't seem to notice. She's too busy looking over my shoulder.

"He's much better than you in bed, too," she shouts at Hart. "He actually knows how to make a girl feel good."

"What the hell?" I frown. Is this really happening? People are on their feet, shouting and jeering. Phones are being held up, recording our every move. My heart hammers against my fucking chest because this is Mackenzie's sister.

The one she's only just forgiven. The one who broke her heart.

I want to shake some sense into Isabella but she doesn't even know what she's done. She doesn't know about me and Mackenzie.

I'm just some guy she's using to rile up Hart.

"You're good to go," the medic tells me, not that he did much for me anyway. And I'm still reeling, putting my helmet back on as I ready myself to get back on the ice.

"Are you and her a thing now?" Simons asks as he skates toward the bench, allowing me to replace him.

"No." I shake my head as I vault onto the ice. I look up at the staff box but I can't see Mac. Can't see anybody. There are too many people, there's too much noise.

"I need to get out of here," I tell him, yelling above the cheers. I need to see her, explain. I can't believe it was on the damn screen. Before I can say anything else I get body slammed by Hart. I don't fall down this time, but I'm fucking winded and annoyed and about to erupt.

"Enjoy my leftovers, fuckface," he tells me. "And by the way, her sister was much better."

Blood rushes through my ears, almost matching the roar of the crowd.

And then I realize. He's *the guy*. The one who broke the two of them apart. The one who abandoned Mac when she went viral.

Danny Hart.

I'm a fucking idiot. If I hadn't been so distracted by the game I would have realized earlier. No wonder he and Isabella were fighting it out.

He's the one that tore the family apart. And now my girl, the woman I fucking love, had to see this happen again. Watch her sister kiss her boyfriend.

Red mist descends. I throw my gloves to the ice and he does the same, before I launch myself at him. "Fuck you, asshole," I tell him, grabbing his chin because he needs to hear what I have to say.

In the part of my brain that's still working I hazily register that play has stopped. The referees are surrounding us, monitoring the fight.

Hart grabs my jersey, pulling me toward him and I push him hard. His face is screwed up and angry, but I'm angrier. I'm fucking furious at him. He hurt Mac. He hurt me. I'm so ready for this game to be over.

And then he spits in my face. I feel it hit my cheek and it makes me want to heave. Through the ringing in my ears I hear the screaming crowd.

They think I'm defending Isabella. *Damn*. This needs to be finished.

This time I mean business. I push him until he's down and I'm on top of him, my fist back and ready for impact. But then a hand grabs my arm. Two referees pull me backward, putting five feet of air between me and the asshole who hurt my girl.

"I'm stopping," I mutter. "Let me go."

So they do and I wipe the spittle from my cheek and slowly heave myself up, skating backward as Hart does the same.

I don't need to look at the referee to know what I need to do next. I'm heading to the penalty box. Even worse, we'll be a man down because I instigated the damn fight. This time I can't even look up at the box to see if Mac is there. Or at the team because the kids I've been working with all year have watched me lose it on the ice.

I'm completely ashamed. But also annoyed. I should have punched that asshole.

My ass hits the bench as the referee whistles and the game plays on.

CHAPTER
THIRTY

MACKENZIE

It's only when something like this happens that you realize how quickly word spreads nowadays. Once upon a time gossip was spread through letters, taking days or months to land on people's doormats.

Even when I went viral it wasn't until the next day that the video was uploaded onto a gossip website and people started clicking.

But in today's world of Tiktok and Snapchat and instant gratification it only takes a few seconds for everybody to share the video of Eli and Isabella kissing. Within ten minutes it's a Romeo and Juliet-worthy meme, with Eli and Danny scrapping on the ice as they fight over my sister.

A romance for the ages. Beautiful to look at but completely fake.

It still hurts, though. Mostly because I only have myself to blame. I sit in my chair and listen as the staff gushes about how beautiful that kiss was, how unfair it was that Eli had to pay a penalty.

Whether that means that Isabella will be spending more time in Morgantown now that she and Eli are in love.

My phone starts to blow up. Rachel messages, asking me what the hell is going on. Followed by Sophie, Eli's sister-in-law, who is somewhere in the arena. I turn my phone off, because my heart is racing so hard I think it might explode out of my chest.

I know Eli isn't having an affair with my sister. I know this was her vengeance for Danny Hart winding her up.

I know this. And still, it hurts.

The game continues for another fifteen minutes. I watch vacantly, not taking anything in. Eli comes back on eventually, and Danny is nowhere to be seen.

When the final whistle blows, everybody roars, and I have to look at the screen to see that we've won. Goran and Carter are doing some kind of ice dance together on the rink.

"Are you coming down with us?"

I blink, realizing that Brian is talking to me.

"What?"

"To the press conference," Brian says slowly, giving me a strange look. "I just asked you twice. Are you okay?"

All of the staff are invited to the press conference. My dad thought it was a good idea, he wanted to thank everybody for their efforts. We're supposed to line up at the back while he and Eli take questions, then he'll make a speech at the end.

"Yes, I'm coming," I say, standing. I'm still wearing Eli's jersey. One of his actual ones that he gave me after the last game. It smells of him.

"Are you sure you're okay?" Brian asks.

"I'm fine." I nod, feeling anything but. "Let's go."

The press room is heaving by the time we get there. A long trestle table has been set up at the front for the team members to sit at, and in the main body of the room are rows of chairs, all of which are full. Cameras are aimed, people are talking at each other rapidly.

Everybody is staring at the door where the players will come in. Brian reaches down and squeezes my hand and that stupid, simple gesture brings tears to my eyes.

I think I'm going to be sick.

Then the door opens. The players are freshly showered, most of them still with wet hair, and their hockey gear has disappeared, replaced by tailored suits. Goran is grinning widely, Carter is striding in like he's king of the hill, Max just looks bored.

And Eli? Where is he?

The other team walks in. My stomach drops when I see Danny. I look around the room and realize that Mom and Isabella aren't here. Hopefully Mom's taken her home, because we don't need any more dramatics.

And then I see *him*. Eli and my dad walk in together. My dad takes the first seat in the center of the table and Eli follows. His hair is damp, brushed back from his face. His lip is swollen and split. It's a strange contrast to his perfectly knotted gray tie and crisp white shirt.

His face is absolutely expressionless as his eyes scan the room. I swallow hard as his gaze lands on me.

And doesn't leave.

My lips part and I exhale softly. There are about forty journalists between him and me. I know he's not going to make a scene, because he knows how much I'd hate that.

I just want this all to be over.

My dad puts on his trademark smile and leans forward into the microphone. "Well, folks, don't ever tell me I don't put on a show for you."

And of course the journalists laugh.

"I'm going to ask you one thing," he continues, still grinning. "Just pretend to be interested in the game, okay? The first ten questions need to be about that." He glances over at Eli, then at Danny. "And after that, we'll take a personal question for each member of the teams. Just one." He lifts a brow. "Including me."

The first few questions go smoothly. Dad answers one, Eli another, then they ask Carter about his goal and he basks in the limelight. And I realize why Eli is here. Not because he wants to answer any questions but because he loves his team.

They deserve this kind of exposure. He's going to make sure they get it.

And when the technical questions are done, thirty hands shoot up. My dad picks a journalist in the center and everybody else groans at not being chosen.

"This question is for Eli Salinger," she says. "Are you and Greg's daughter in a relationship?"

Eli's lips are tight. He glances at my dad and then over at me. And I realize that if he says no he's lying.

We are in a relationship. I nod at him and he frowns, not understanding.

You can tell them. It's okay. I love you.

"I, ah…"

"He's just taking my sloppy seconds," Danny says, leaning into his mic. "I told him he needs to aim for the Gauthier double. Both sisters. I can highly recommend it."

Eli's on his feet before Danny can finish speaking. His eyes are narrow, his jaw tight, as he stalks toward the man who once broke me.

Goran and Carter stand, too. They don't know why Eli's so mad but they're on his side no matter what. But then the last person I expect to back him up is behind him.

My dad.

"Son," he says, putting a hand on Eli's shoulder. "I'll take this one."

And then my dad reaches for Danny's collar, yanking him out of his chair. Danny tries to push Dad off him, but there's still a lot of strength in my old man. He releases Danny's collar and shoves him hard, until Danny falls backward, landing ass first on the floor.

"If I ever hear you disrespect my daughters again, I'll hit you so hard you won't know what fucking year it is," Dad says, his voice gritty. Danny frowns and starts to open his mouth. Cameras are clicking and phones are being held up. My face flames even though only three people in the room know I'm one of the daughters he's referring to.

"Shut the fuck up," Carter tells Danny. "Seriously, man. I used to fucking worship you, but if you say a single word I'm going to slam my fist against your teeth."

Eli's eyes connect with mine again. He leans in to whisper at Carter, who reluctantly nods and goes to sit down. Danny stalks over to the door with as much dignity as he can muster, which isn't a lot.

And then he sees me.

He frowns and looks back at Dad, then at me again, before dramatically turning to the waiting journalists.

"I hope you enjoyed me landing on my ass," he says. "But if you want to see something better, just Google Mackenzie Gauthier. She's standing right there." He points at me, and everybody turns to stare. "There's a hilarious video of her baring everything on the ice. Check it out, I think you'll love it."

CHAPTER
THIRTY-ONE

ELI

Mackenzie's face falls. The journalists start doing exactly what Hart told them to, googling her name.

Brian turns to look at her with a frown and she nods. There are tears in her eyes and I'm going to kill Danny Hart.

If I can find him.

Just as soon as I know my girl is okay.

Okay I'm not going to kill him but the urge is strong. Luckily, I'm stronger.

Greg looks horrified. I'm not going to tell him that half of this is his fault. There's no way he should have brought Hart here to play. And he's also the one who asked Mac to come here in the first place – if he hadn't she wouldn't be going through this right now.

But then I would never have met her.

And I'm so damn glad I did.

"Mr. Gauthier," I say.

He turns to me, blinking at the proper use of his name.

"I'm in love with your daughter," I tell him. "And we'll talk later about how you've treated her."

"You're in love with Isabella?" he says, looking confused.

"No. Mackenzie. I'm so in love with her it hurts."

And then I walk past my team mates, around the table, and toward the only person in this room that really matters. She's frozen to the spot, her eyes on the dozens of phone screens being watched by journalists.

Of that day she skated onto the ice and her life changed.

Be strong, I think. *Baby, please be strong.*

I stop a foot short of where she's standing. Brian is holding her hand. I remind myself to send him a crate of beers for looking after her.

"I got this," I tell him.

"Didn't you just kiss her sister?" Brian asks. Then wisely shuts up when he sees my expression.

I reach out and cup her face. "Mac…"

She nods her eyes watering.

"Listen to me. We're going to walk out of here, okay? And then we're going to get through this. Together."

She nods again. She's trembling. Brian's still holding her hand, the trooper. Fuck the beer, he's getting a barrel of whiskey.

"It's going to be okay," I say to her. "I'm not letting you go. Come on, let's go home."

Her eyes meet mine as she shakes her head. I frown, wondering if I'm going to have to carry her out of here.

"No," she says, her voice hoarse. "I'm not running away from this. I'm going to answer their questions."

"What?"

She blows out a mouthful of air. "I'm not going to hide any more," she tells me, and pride heats my body.

This woman. She's killing me. In the best damn way.

"Are you coming?" she asks, letting go of Brian's hand. She rolls her shoulders and looks at me.

"Where?"

"To the table. Let's answer the peoples' questions."

"You sure about this?" I ask her.

"Certain." She lifts a brow. "You?"

"I've never been more sure of anything in my life," I say. And for the first time she smiles.

I take her hand and we walk back to the table. Her dad is looking at us but saying nothing. I'll talk to him later, we both will. But now I'm taking Mac's lead.

"You and Mackenzie?" Goran asks, glancing down at our hands. She's holding on so tight her knuckles have gone white, but you wouldn't know it from her face.

She looks serene.

"Yep." I nod. "Can I explain later?"

He shrugs. "Sure. Hey, can I still bring her coffee in the mornings?"

"If you like."

We take the center two seats. Mackenzie taps the mic and laughs when a loud bang fills the air. She clears her throat and somehow her hold on my hand gets even tighter.

I squeeze back.

"Well, I think you've all had the chance to watch my highlight reel," she says. And damn if they don't all laugh the way they laughed for Greg. "I'd like to tell you a little story. About a girl who made a mistake and embarrassed herself all because she fell for the wrong guy. Then who hid away because she was embarrassed." She smiles, and though I can tell it's fake, nobody else can. Lifting her arm, she glances at her watch then looks at the journalists again. "Buckle up and get comfortable, because this could take some time."

———

ELI

. . .

"I'm mortified," Isabella says, running toward us as we leave the press conference. I'm still holding Mac's hand. She's still trembling, but it's getting softer.

I don't think I'm ever going to let her go.

"I'm so sorry," her sister continues. "I didn't know about you two." She looks at Mac, her eyes wide. "If I did, I never would have touched him. Not after everything."

"It's okay," Mac says. "I know you wouldn't have."

Isabella's lip wobbles. "But I should have known. I should have guessed." She shakes her head. "If I'd been the sister to you I was supposed to be, you would've confided in me ages ago. Instead I was so busy plotting revenge I didn't think..." she trails off and looks at me. "I'm sorry I kissed you. I shouldn't have done that."

"No, you shouldn't." I'm not quite as forgiving. She's hurt Mac before and I'm wary that she'll do it again. But she's also Mac's sister and I intend to be around this woman for the rest of our lives. "But I'll get over it." Just not today. Maybe not even this month.

Her parents join the three of us and Mac apologizes for not telling them before. Wayne is leaning on his walker and it's my turn to apologize for falling in love with his granddaughter when I was supposed to be working for him.

He waves me off. "Don't sweat it. My wife was my coach's daughter. He beat me up enough for the two of us."

"She was?" Mac asks. "I didn't know that."

"There's a lot you don't know about me," Wayne says. "Maybe we can change that."

"I'd like that," Mac says softly. "Very much." She leans down to kiss his cheek and the nurse leads him back to the van he arrived in. I'll go see him at the nursing home tomorrow to apologize for my conduct on the ice.

But now I just want to go home with Mac.

Her lips curl up and I realize she's looking at somebody

over my shoulder. I glance in the direction of her gaze and realize it's more than just one person.

It's my entire family.

Myles and Ava are at the front, with Liam and Sophie behind them. Then there's Holden, Brooks, and Linc, along with my mom, my step-mom, and Dad with his wife.

I try not to groan. "Shall we run?" I ask Mac. Because two huge families are about to meet.

I don't think either of us are ready for it.

"Who's going to eat who for breakfast?" she asks me.

"I have no idea." That's the scary thing. My family is huge and disordered and hers... well, is exactly the same.

Maybe that's why we're so compatible. We know the pain of being the only normal people in our family groups. Though I'm sure my brothers would beg to differ.

"Imagine our wedding," she says, then slaps her hand across her mouth. "Ugh, ignore that."

But I can't ignore it. I'm too fucking happy thinking about it. Thinking about marrying this woman.

Thinking about how lucky I am.

"It's going to be a blast," I tell her.

"If it happens," she mutters.

"Oh, it'll happen. It's a matter of time," I tell her.

CHAPTER
THIRTY-TWO

MACKENZIE

Going viral isn't what it used to be, thank God. Within a couple of days Eli and Isabella's kiss – and his subsequent fight with Danny Hart – is just an already-stale TikTok, replaced by the latest gossip du jour. We don't get a call from Jimmy Kimmel. No hashtags trend.

My name is barely mentioned anywhere.

Isabella also makes it clear there's nothing between her and Eli when she does a *Dirty Dancing* routine with Justin and the two of them kiss heavily afterward. I have a feeling she did it on purpose to take the heat off of me, which is kind of sweet.

And so life goes on and our own lives return to normal within a matter of days.

And I have to fly back to New York to face the music. Or rather *we* do, because Eli is sitting by my side on the airplane, holding my hand, telling me it'll be okay. That I'll keep my job.

I feel strangely calm as we walk through the arrivals

terminal, where his brother Holden, is waiting for us. I already like him a lot. He's the quiet one of the family. Last week when they all came back to Gramps' place after we left the arena – don't ask – I got to spend more time with all of Eli's family and I think I'm in love with them.

My younger brothers and his had a blast trash talking us all. And Myles and Liam gave me some good advice for when I talk to my boss about having a relationship with a client.

They even offered me a job if I end up getting fired.

But Holden, he's different. He watches and listens. When he talks, it's because he has something important to say. Maybe that's what makes him a good doctor.

"You sure you want to head straight for the office?" Holden asks as he drives us into the city. I'm impressed by his patience when a car honks loudly because he's stopped at a red light. I hate driving in Manhattan. I rarely do it.

But he doesn't seem to give a damn.

"Yes, please. I have to meet my boss at twelve."

Eli squeezes my hand. "I can come in with you."

I shake my head. "You two go ahead and do… whatever it is you've got to do. I'll call you once I'm done." And by then I'll either be packing my desk up or… I don't know. What will I be doing? I'm not sure.

It's been months since I've walked into Warner Power's lobby, and everything feels completely alien. It's too clean, too bright. People don't shout at each other. It's like the place has no soul.

Or maybe it was sold to the devil.

I press my security pass onto the electronic reader, waiting for the metal waist-high gate to swing open, but instead a red light appears. My stomach twists, because if they're firing me this is a hell of a way to find out.

The security guard walks over and checks my pass. "When were you last here?" he asks.

"A few months ago."

"That explains it. We had a reset last month. Been catching all the consultants by surprise. You guys barely come in here, do you?"

"If we're not with a client we're not earning," I say, repeating the mantra that's been beaten into me since day one of working for Warner Power.

"Billable hours." He nods. "Saw all about that on a TV series. *Suits* was it?" He takes my pass and walks over to the little waist heigh desk with a computer on it, next to the gate. "People working all the hours God sends and still panicking that they're not earning enough. When does it stop?" He presses my card against a reader and types something into the laptop. "Nobody gets to stand and smell the roses anymore, do they?"

"What are roses?" I ask and he laughs, passing me back the card.

"It should work now. Have a nice day."

Carmine is at the front desk when I walk out of the elevator and into our offices. "Miss Hunter," he says, smiling.

"Hi Carmine. How's it going?"

"Good as always." He glances down at his laptop. "Mr. Power has asked that you go straight to his office."

I take a deep breath. "Okay." If they fire me it'll be Carmine who has to escort me out of the building. I've seen him do it before, his thick muscled arms carrying boxes of personal belongings as the poor person who's just lost their job trails behind him in tears.

I can't even remember what's in my desk anymore. Probably a change of pantyhose because those damn things always run. And a few cereal bars for the days when I don't have time to eat lunch. I think there might be a pair of sneakers under my desk, put there years ago when I had the great idea of going for a walk every lunchtime to get some exercise.

I used them exactly once.

When I reach Mr. Power's office his assistant nods me in, and I take a deep breath before I knock at his door.

"Come in."

I do as I'm told, pushing it open to find Kenneth Power and my boss, Mark, sitting at his desk. They both look up at me as I walk inside.

"Um, hi." I attempt a smile. I just want this over with. I know I messed up, and could have caused so many problems.

But really, I didn't. I just didn't.

"Mackenzie," Mr. Power says. "Take a seat."

I slide into the empty chair next to Mark. He lifts his brows at me but says nothing. Some things don't change. He's still talking with his eyebrows.

"So," Mr. Power says, steepling his fingers as he leans his elbows on his desk. "I guess we have some things to talk about."

I shift in my seat. "I guess we do. And I'm extremely sorry if I brought the company into disrepute."

Mark's brows knit. "Disrepute?"

I swallow. "By having a relationship with a client. I'm sorry. I know it's unprofessional." A firing offense. "I didn't mean to cause any issues."

"What are you talking about?" Mr. Power asks.

"The press conference."

He and Mark exchange glances. "Where you talked about what happened years ago?"

I nod. "And that I'm in a relationship with Eli Salinger. The head coach of the Mavericks."

"But he's not our client," Mark says, glancing at Kenneth Power again. "Your grandfather is."

"I told Mark about your relationship to the team," Mr. Power says. "I figured since it's open knowledge now that would be okay."

"Of course." I nod. "So I completely understand if you need me to leave. All I'd ask is that you let me resign instead of firing me. It'll look better on my résumé." And that really isn't a lot to ask. I've worked my ass off for this company. Yes, I broke their rules and made them look bad, but surely they could do this one thing.

I need to work to survive, after all.

"I'm sorry, what?" Mark shakes his head. For once his brows stay still. "You think we're firing you?"

Mr. Power starts to laugh. "What is this, the dark ages? Why would we fire you for being in a relationship?"

"Um, isn't it in my contract? No fraternizing with clients?"

"Well, yes," Mr. Power concedes. "But that's to protect us. And it's good etiquette for the most part. But we're not inflexible. If staff members become involved with somebody who works in a client's location and they come and talk to us about it, we're amenable to talking about it."

"The hours we all work, if you don't date somebody in the same office, you're never going to date," Mark adds. "My wife used to work here."

"I was going to talk to you about it," I tell Mr. Power. "Once the exhibition game was over. Things just went a bit awry."

Mark smiles at me. "I know you would have. You're a professional. That's not why we've asked you to come here."

"It isn't?" I'm still so confused. Thinking about how I won't have to pack up those barely used sneakers.

"We want to give you a promotion," Mr. Power says. "The one you worked so hard for."

"A promotion?"

"The one we talked about when we last spoke," he says, giving me a strange look. "Remember?"

"I remember."

"I know we said it would be after the end of the project, and you're not quite there yet, but I've spoken to Wayne and he's amenable to releasing you early. We can send another consultant down to finish things off, while we put you at the head of your new team."

"You're going to be a partner, Mackenzie," Mark says. "Congratulations." He shakes my hand and I shake it back, but my head is spinning with thoughts.

I've always dreamed of a promotion. Becoming a partner at a firm like Warner Power means you've pretty much made it in life. Yes, I'll be working harder than ever because now half my job would be schmoozing clients and finding new ones, but the rewards are huge.

And more than anything it's the kudos that matters. It's the equivalent of winning the Stanley Cup.

So why do I want to cry?

"When would I come back?"

"Next week. We have a big project we want you to bid on. You'll need to build your team," Mark says. "I'll be sorry to lose you as part of mine."

There's ringing in my ears. *Next week.* I won't even get to stay and see the Mavericks to the end of the season. I won't have Goran bringing me coffee every morning. I won't be eating hot dogs at intermission.

My stupid heart is aching.

"I…"

"Speak to Rina on the way out," Mr. Power continues. "She'll organize the concierge service to bring all your things home. She'll also arrange for your new office." He lifts a brow. "With a corner view."

"They're the best." Mark grins.

I open my mouth to say something, but no words come out. I need to talk to Eli. I need to think about if this is really what I want to do.

And I can't get my thoughts straight in here.

"Can I think about it?" I ask Mr. Power.

He exchanges glances with Mark. "Um, yes?"

"Thank you," I say, pushing my chair away from the desk and standing.

I need to call Eli, but not from the office. There are too many ears, too many gossips. I rush for the elevator and punch the button, grabbing my phone as I step inside.

But of course there's no signal. Stupid metal cages. And though there's only one floor to go, it takes forever.

Long enough for me to envision a thousand scenarios. How is it that you can get everything you want and it still feels like you're missing something?

The elevator pings and I step out into the lobby. I finally have cell service, so I punch at the call icon, and immediately I hear the ring.

But not on my phone. In the lobby. I look over at the bank of seats where visitors wait to be taken up for meetings and he's there.

Eli's legs are so long that his knees are hitting the coffee table in front of him. He's staring at his phone, his hair mussed up, his Mavericks hoodie looking way too good on him.

He lifts the phone to his ear. "Hello?"

"I'm here." I walk through the security gates and Eli looks around until his eyes alight on me.

And I crumple.

———

ELI

As soon as I see her face I want to hit somebody. Probably myself for getting her into this situation. She told me she loved her job, that she didn't want to lose it. And I pushed and pushed because I wanted us to go public.

Then we did. Spectacularly.

I practically leap over the arm of the sofa to get to her, folding her in my arms.

"What are you doing here?" she asks, looking up at me. Her eyes look like a stormy afternoon.

"I told Holden to turn around. I couldn't sit at his place while you were facing the music alone." I stroke her hair with my palm. "I'm so sorry they fired you."

She shakes her head. "No, that's not it. Not why I'm upset."

What could be worse than losing her job? I open my mouth to ask her exactly that and she continues.

"They offered me a promotion."

My fingers curl into her hair. "What?" I don't get it. Why's she on the edge of tears about a promotion?

Hockey players have been known to spend weeks celebrating a win like that.

"They want me to be a partner," she whispers.

A grin pulls at my lips. "That's amazing, Mac. I'm so proud of you." I tip her chin with my finger. "You deserve that."

"But…" She inhales softly. "What about us?"

I'm still flailing around in the dark here. "What about us? We'll go celebrate tonight. But don't you want to see your friends right now? Tell them the good news? You couldn't have been up in the offices for more than ten minutes."

"I needed to see you."

A little bit of my heart explodes. This woman never needs anything.

But she needs me now. And I'm here for her. Always.

"Go up and see them. I'll stay here and wait. I've found this Instagram account with cats."

"What?"

I wink at her. "They do tricks. I got a full day of entertainment if I need it." I pat my ass. "I've even brought my charger."

"But we need to talk," she says.

"Okay…" I tip my head to the side. "What about?"

"Us. If I take the promotion, I have to move back to New York. Next week." Her eyes catch mine again and for a minute I'm lost in them. I still can't work out why she's so freaked out. "We've only just found each other."

And then it dawns on me. She's scared. The woman who insisted that we were just for now is scared that her words will come true.

"*If* you take the promotion?" I repeat. "Don't you mean when?"

She swallows. "Not if it means losing you."

Fireworks go off inside of me. And I start to laugh. It's partly relief and partly disbelief because she needs to get to know me better. She needs to understand that I've waited my whole life for her.

A few hundred miles aren't going to be a problem.

I cup her face with my hands, still grinning.

"What's so funny?" she asks.

"You, mostly." I shake my head. "You think you can scare me off with a promotion and a move?"

"I…"

"You can't," I tell her. "There are planes. There are cars. There's a whole summer when I get a break and I'm sure you have PTO, too. There are weekends and holidays and there's the rest of our damn lives to work this out." I brush my lips against hers. "Because we will work it out. I'll give up hockey if I have to, become your sex slave."

Her lips twitch. "What does that involve, exactly?"

"I'll show you later," I promise. "We'll call it an audition. But I'm serious, Mac. This is good news."

"I heard you were in the building," a female voice calls out. I look over at a woman wearing a severe black dress and even more severe lipstick. "Oh," she says, seeing my arms around Mackenzie. "Oooooohhhhhhh." This one has at least five syllables.

Mac smiles. "Rachel." She beckons her over. "This is Eli. Eli, this is Rachel. My best friend."

"You're the hockey player," Rachel says, eyeing my hoodie. "The second best looking Maverick."

"Second?" I ask, because at heart I'm a competitive motherfucker.

"The Swede is my first," she says. "I have a thing for cheekbones and coffee." She folds her arms in front of her chest. "So what's going on? Everybody's saying you got fired."

"She got a promotion," Eli says.

"Of course she did." Rachel sighs. "It explains everything."

"It does?" Mackenzie asks.

"Yep. You hate happily ever afters. Remember when we went to see that reshowing of *Titanic*." She looks at me, and I smile because we have something in common. We both love this woman.

"You got into a mood because Leo died," Mackenzie says. "You wanted to hunt down James Cameron and egg his house, despite the fact we're both grown women, the movie was made thirty years ago, and we both know they wouldn't have fit on that damn door."

"They would have," I interject helpfully.

"See." Rachel throws up her hands. "There was a perfect way to get an HEA, but no. Miss Pessimistic here decided to pee in my cornflakes about it."

"We're not doing this again," Mackenzie warns her friend. "Last time we discussed this you didn't talk to me for two days."

"I'm just saying that art needs to have happiness," Rachel counters. "Or at least the hope of happiness. But you don't like that. You're more comfortable when everything goes wrong. Maybe you even like it. Happily ever afters are scary for you."

"Maybe I just know that they're not possible," Mac says, but her heart isn't in it. Her brows knit and she looks at me. I'm trying not to smile back at her because I'm enjoying their conversation too much.

"You're going to be our maid of honor, right?" I ask Rachel.

"Absofuckinglutely." She nods. "I want to be standing right next to her when she realizes how wrong she was."

"Me, too."

"I like him," she tells Mac. "A lot."

"Wait, what?" Mac says. "Maid of honor? We're not getting married."

"Not yet," I say. "I'd kind of like us to be living in the same state first. But it'll happen." Weird thing, but I've never been more sure of anything. Maybe it's getting older. Seeing one career finish and another one start. Or maybe it's just her.

All I know is that I'm ready for this. And if she isn't, I'll wait patiently.

For as long as it takes. Forever.

"He loves you," Rachel whispers.

"I do." I nod.

"I love him, too," Mackenzie tells her. "So much."

Our eyes meet and we're both grinning. It's the first time we've said it and it wasn't to each other.

We'll sort that out later.

"Can you two kiss and get this happily ever after over with?" Rachel asks. "Then we can go up and tell everybody about your promotion, then we'll all go down to the bar and get drunk." She looks at me. "You're invited."

"I'm honored."

"Don't be. I just want you to introduce me to some of your hot hockey friends." She waves her hand. "I'm going back to the office now, because your kiss is bound to be hot and I haven't gotten laid in a year. I'm about half a second away from asking if I can join in."

"You can't," Mackenzie and I say at the same time.

Rachel laughs and turns on her heel, leaving us alone. Save for the security guard, the people sitting at a table having coffee, and the steady stream of workers coming in and out of the lobby.

"Who'd be your best man?" Mackenzie asks, and I try not to laugh at the change of subject. "At our imaginary wedding where Rachel's the maid of honor."

"Holden," I say, without a doubt in my mind.

"Why Holden? You have six brothers. Won't the rest of them be upset?"

"I don't think so. Holden's my guy, that's all."

"That's so sweet." Mac smiles.

"You okay with him coming out tonight to join in your promotion celebrations?" I ask her.

"More than okay. I like him. Though he might find it intensely boring. Unless he's a masochist."

I cough out a laugh. She has no idea how close she is to being right. So close and yet so far away.

But that's all for another day. Right now she's smiling up at me and I'm grinning down at her, wondering how I got so lucky.

"Can I kiss you at work?" I ask her. "Or is that the kind of thing that gets you fired?"

Her nose wrinkles as she considers my question. "Actually, I have no idea," she says. "Why don't we find out."

So we do.

EPILOGUE

MACKENZIE

I sneak into the arena just as everybody is leaving. I should have been here earlier – to watch the game itself – but my flight was canceled and I had to scramble to get on the next one. I know the result though – I was following the game the whole way on my phone. Even if I hadn't, it's clear we won from the smiles on the faces of our supporters as they leave the building.

I still have my security pass and I flash it at the guard who knows me and nods me in. "You missed a good one," he tells me.

"I know." I grimace because I'm sad I wasn't here to see the Mavericks make it through to the Calder Cup.

It's a big moment for Eli. At the beginning of the season, nobody thought the Mavericks would finish anywhere but in the bottom two. But the team is coming into their own. With each game they play they're getting stronger.

I'm so proud of them all I could burst.

In the past few months I've managed to get to a few games, sitting with Gramps in the staff box now that he's more mobile and able to walk around. He comes into the arena a few hours a week to make sure things are ticking over, but Brian has stepped up and become General Manager.

He's doing great. I'm proud of him, too.

Heading toward the staff area, I use my pass to unlock the door, stepping into the hallway that leads to the locker room.

"Mac!" I look around to see Goran walking toward me, his hair damp and a fresh pair of dress pants and shirt on.

"Hey." I hug him. "Congratulations."

"Thanks. We're just heading to the press conference. You coming?"

"I'll be at the back," I tell him. "But we'll catch up tonight, right?"

Eli is hosting a party at a club in town for all the players. We probably won't stay long, because he wants them to let their hair down, and that's difficult with the coach around.

Before the playoffs begin and things get serious again.

The press conference has already begun by the time I sneak into the room. Eli is in the center, next to Gramps. The team surrounds them on either side.

But I only have eyes for him.

The best thing about having a long-distance relationship is how happy you are to see each other. How you make the most of each moment you're together. Whether it's Eli flying into New York or me flying here, when we're together we're focused on each other.

We have an app that we use to schedule our weekends, depending on whether they're playing at home or away and whether I need to be in New York for meetings. Over the past few months I think we've only missed two weekends together.

So yeah, it's working out well.

And I know over the next few months we'll need to talk about the future. Because we both want to be together for good. And I'm not scared of that at all. I want it.

I want him.

Forever.

As he answers a question about a power play, his eyes flicker up and meet mine. He finishes his answer in a low voice, as a smile slowly curls his lips.

For a moment it's like we're the only two people in the room. That smile holds a promise I know he intends to keep. One that'll involve him carrying me into his bedroom later and showing me just how much he's missed me.

And then hopefully he'll make me breakfast in bed the way he usually does, because he's an early bird and I hate waking up.

Except to him.

"This question is for Eli," a reporter says. "Have you spoken with Danny Hart since the exhibition match took place?"

Eli shakes his head. "No. And I don't intend to."

None of us have heard from Danny, thank God, but Dad tells me his contract hasn't been renewed after this season. He messed with hockey royalty one too many times. Dad knows people and so does Gramps and I assume they have something to do with his career coming to a screaming halt.

The truth is, I don't care. I have no interest in Danny Hart.

My family, though, is another matter. Since the exhibition match we've gotten together a few times. I went to L.A. to watch Isabella in the skate-off in the *Ice Stars* final, where she and Justin came in second.

And they all came to New York to see me last month. Eli and I took them out to dinner. There's talk of us visiting them in L.A. over the summer.

Things are getting better. I have a family now and it feels good.

"What are your plans for when the season is over?" a reporter asks Eli.

A smile lingers on his lips. "Well first of all we're going to win the Calder Cup," he says, and the reporters laugh.

"And then I'm going to be spending some time in New York. With my girl."

A blush steals across my face. A couple of reporters turn to look at me. But then they turn back, because they're more interested in Eli than me.

And that's how I like it. Because I feel exactly the same way.

"Will you be coming back to coach next year?" another reporter asks.

Eli leans into the microphone. "I will. I've signed a one year extension to my contract."

"And then?"

His gaze locks on mine again. I'm smiling because we've talked about this. We've talked about everything.

About how we're both willing to compromise our careers to be together. About how we don't want kids of our own but want to adopt.

About how wherever we end up, as long as it's together, we'll be happy.

"And then," he says, his voice thick, his eyes never leaving mine. "I'm going to live happily ever after with the woman I love."

I press my hands to my chest and mouth "I love you," to him.

"I love you, too," he says, deliberately talking into the microphone, his voice echoing through the press room.

The team and the reporters laugh, and I'm smiling big.

Because I'm a born-again convert. A happily-ever-after believer.

And ours has already begun.

THE END

DEAR READER

Thank you so much for reading STRICTLY FOR NOW. If you enjoyed it and you get a chance, I'd be so grateful if you can leave a review. And don't forget to check out my free bonus epilogue which you can download by typing this address into your web browser: https://dl.bookfunnel.com/d1avbocfhy

The next book in the series is Holden's story - find out what happens when he clashes with Blair Walker in STRICTLY NOT YOURS

WANT TO KEEP UP TO DATE ON ALL MY NEWS?

Join me on my exclusive mailing list, where you'll be the first to hear about new releases, sales, and other book-related news.

To sign up put this address into your web browser.
https://www.subscribepage.com/carrieelksas

I can't wait to share more stories with you.

Yours,

Carrie xx

ALSO BY CARRIE ELKS

Chasing The Sun

Heart And Soul

Lost In Him

THE HEARTBREAK BROTHERS SERIES

A gorgeous small town series about four brothers and the women who capture their hearts.

Take Me Home

Still The One

A Better Man

Somebody Like You

When We Touch

THE SHAKESPEARE SISTERS SERIES

An epic series about four strong yet vulnerable sisters, and the alpha men who steal their hearts.

Summer's Lease

A Winter's Tale

Absent in the Spring

By Virtue Fall

THE LOVE IN LONDON SERIES

Three books about strong and sassy women finding love in the big city.

Coming Down

Broken Chords

Canada Square

STANDALONE

Fix You

An epic romance that spans the decades. Breathtaking and angsty and all the things in between.

If you'd like to get an email when I release a new book, please sign up here:

CARRIE ELKS' NEWSLETTER

ABOUT THE AUTHOR

Carrie Elks writes contemporary romance with a sizzling edge. Her first book, *Fix You*, has been translated into eight languages and made a surprise appearance on *Big Brother* in Brazil. Luckily for her, it wasn't voted out.

Carrie lives with her husband, two lovely children and a larger-than-life black pug called Plato. When she isn't writing or reading, she can be found baking, drinking an occasional (!) glass of wine, or chatting on social media.

You can find Carrie in all these places
www.carrieelks.com
carrie.elks@mail.com